VIRGINIA PRIMITIVE

VIRGINIA PRIMITIVE

A TALE OF JIM CROW

SALLIE REYNOLDS

REDHAWK INK

Library of Congress Catalog-in-Publication Data Available

Reynolds, Sallie

Virginia Primitive / Sallie Reynolds —2nd United States edition

I. Fiction 2. Woman Authors

p. cm.

ISBN-13: 979-8-9873288-0-4 c. (paperback)

Printed in the United States of America 10 9 8 7 6 5 4 3 2

To Lila Neal Doggett

1

1944

HOW I CAME INTO THE WORLD AS A FISH

"Li-lulie?"

She's frowning at her fishing line in the river.

"*Li*-la."

"Lila, what happened when—"

"Hysh a minute."

I hysh.

Slow swirly river, mud red as blood. *This water may have a few fish in it, but it's lazy. Lazy and thick just like the Nigras.* Daddy always wears his starched white doctor coat, so you almost have to believe him.

But he doesn't know about the underwater current that can suck you deep and drag you all the way to the ocean. Lila says you won't even be bones at the end. And he doesn't know about black folks either. I'm supposed to say *Nigras* or *colored people.* But Lila snorts when a white person says that. *Might as well go on say nigger.* So I say *black folks,* which she mostly does. They are not lazy. Lila and her friends crackle with life just the way your hair does on a cold day.

Plus she knows everything. *What you don't know, Lila, isn't worth knowing.* That's Mother.

And then it's Daddy who snorts.

I jiggle my feet. If I jiggle 'em fast enough, the shoe straps'll slip and they'll fly off into the river. *Ploop! Ploop!* And I can jump in to the rescue.

Then Lila will pay me some mind.

I can swim. Daddy taught me, threw me in right here where Lila and me are fishing. I swallowed a hundred buckets of water and I couldn't breathe. If I hadn't of moved my arms and legs like a dog, I'd of drowned.

Thick lace of oak leaves over me, dry ones under me. I blow on a grass blade—*screeeee*.

Something happened when I was born. The grown-ups never say it plain. Daddy won't even say it in doctor talk. Grandmother, who usually doesn't care *what* she says to you, pretends she didn't hear. But Mother hints, when she's mad at me, that I did something bad to her, just getting into the world.

"Li, yesterday—

"Honey, you know I know what you want and you know I aint go tell you." She means my parents'll skin her if she does. I already know that my parents have a secret grown-up language to hide things from me. Li doesn't use it with me most of the time. She doesn't hide things, except when they make her.

"But why can't I know? I *need* to know, really, really. What happened when I was *born?*" Sometimes if I say *really really*, or *I need*, she'll give in. "I swear I won't tattle." I won't, either. Only when I was little, long time ago, I'd get upset and things would leak out of me. "How'll I ever know *any*thing, if you don't tell me?"

Blow on my grass blade, hard as I can. *Screeeeeee!* Till my cheeks crack. "It's not *fair.*"

"Well, it aint. Be quiet a minute." Will I! No jiggling and screeing. Just sit like a mouse. Snakes hypnotize mice, you know, and the mice stop moving entirely. Let themselves get eaten. My Li-lulie won't eat me!

Lila's not a snake, of course. She's a grown-up person, but if she *was* an animal, she'd be something that's strong in the night and calm and steady, making everybody safe. Like Dance. Dance is big and strong and when he's not gardening or driving Grandmother's car, he plays the guitar. Nothing bad would dare come around Dance. He'd scare away a bear. He's like a bear himself. Only a good bear, like the one in the fairy tale, except he chose namby-pamby Snow White over sassy Rose Red. Ugh. But Li says "That's life."

Me, I'd be a bird, but which one? A pretty one would be nice, even if it is namby-pamby. But I'd end up a smart-aleck jaybird, sure as sugar.

Lila sits straight, straw hat way back on her head, bobbing the fishing rod in her fingers. "This the way to *tease* the fish on the hook," she says. "Keep your hands light, honey. Keep 'em moving."

"When I was *born*—" I whisper.

She laughs. "You too good at fishing, child."

Ugh. She knows I actually hate fishing. Take one off the hook? Double ugh.

"Well then—that was a *time*, though."

Oh, she's going to tell the *old* story. I know every word and I love it, but it's not the story I want right now. She knows I want the secret story.

"Your gramama so excited she mistook and left the phone off the hook, and your daddy couldn't get ahold of her to tell her you'd got here. So he had to drive all the way from the city hospital to tell her. But you know Miz Roberts, she lock up tight as a tick every night of her life, and he couldn't get in the house. So he climb the rose trellis under her window. She hear him and snap up the blinds, waving that little two-dollar pistol she got. *'I will shoot you, sir! I will shoot you!'*"

Lila makes her voice quaver like Grandmother's and heaves up and down laughing. That always makes me want to laugh too. You lift your shoulders up to your ears and pook your stomach out.

"Your daddy so scared he fell off that trellis and bust his ankle."

"*Mother* got hurt too. The day I was born. I did something bad and they cut her open without any an-es-thees-ya. They sewed her with a wire."

She shoots me a look. "Who you been talking to?"

I zip my mouth. She frowns, but really she likes that. Lila Rule Number 3: *"Don't ever tell. Don't matter who."* Rules Number 1 and 2 change all the time, but Number 3 is steady as stone.

Well, her sister Haddy told me just yesterday. But Haddy's so mean I'd be scared to tell on her even if I didn't know it was wrong to tattle. Haddy pinches when nobody's looking. Besides, she'd just get Lila in trouble.

"I *hate* secrets! Secrets cut you up like knives."

Lila has her lips pursed tight. "Some things none of your bidness."

"If my getting born aint my bidness, what is?" I hold my breath and put on my serious face.

After a minute she sighs. "That thing happen, honey, you had *nothin'* to do with it. They cut her 'cause your daddy and the other doctors aint want her lungs to give out. She had the pneumonia." Lila's voice goes high. New-*mon*-ya. A sign she's telling the truth. Then she stops. Mouth turns to a line.

I wait. My face is going red—I can feel it—my throat is closing up. "They cut her open, to save me and she *felt* it! It was a pain so bad she wanted to die!" I'm yelling, can't help myself.

It wasn't Haddy told the part about the pain and wanting to die, either. It was Mother. Last time she was really mad at me. And Lila hyshed her.

Lila hyshing Mother! I can almost breathe again, thinking about that. But then both of 'em played like nothing happened atall, so I thought it just was something Mother put on. Till Haddy spilled the beans.

"Hysh now!" Li hyshes me *all* the time. "You got to believe me, honey, that won't because of you. If she'd broke her leg, sick as she was, they would of hurt her just the same."

I broke my leg last year when I was still five, and Lila, who nursed me after Daddy put on my cast, knows every detail. How at the hospital I was put to sleep with a stink-box over my nose and mouth, and how I had dreams of witches with long sharp fingernails. How when I woke up, I threw up a hundred times, and she put a cool cloth on my head and said, *Shhh! You'll get well before you get married!*

Lila's watching me now, frowning. She puts her finger on her lips. *Secret?* Well, ours are *important* secrets, not the kinds that cut you up. I put my finger on my lips too. That's our sign.

I start to ask why Mother blames *me*, if it was like a broken leg. But I know why. And Lila would die before she said it.

I touch the scar on my left leg where Daddy cut the cast off, only he went too deep and cut me too. It's my good luck scar. And I use it to tell my left from my right.

My mother's pain, like a broken leg. I can feel that. And I'm sorry. Really. A broken leg hurts. But *I* didn't do it to her.

The choking is going away some. "Promise?" My voice sounds croaky. "Cross your heart it wasn't my fault?"

Lila crosses her heart. And the choking feeling slides completely away. You can always believe Lila, even when it's something sad or bad. Even when everybody else says the opposite. When she crosses her heart, you *know*.

She pulls up her fishing rod till the bobber and bait hang in the air. "You done?"

I nod.

"Go get some acorns then. I make us some dolls."

Lila has a little bitty knife, a shiny blade folded into the dearest little pearl handle you ever saw. Beautiful Fairy Knife. I can touch it, but I'm not allowed to open it. Li takes acorns and twigs and makes people and horses and even cows with horns. She digs holes with the knife to put in the legs and all. Uses her own hair for tails and manes. Snap! She'll pull out a few strands and dab 'em on at the right spot with a little mud and spit. Only spit's not really glue so they fall off after a while. One time she made a farmer with a little straw hat. Wove it out of grass, slick as—I'm not supposed to say "snot." "Mucus, Willis," Daddy says. "Mucus."

The worm's wiggling on the hook. I turn my back and go for the acorns. I hear the hook plop back into the water, so I turn to watch Li fix the rod on a forked stick, jam the end of it into the dirt, and put one rock under it and one rock on top of it. Then she settles her knees wide so her skirt makes a basket. I throw in the acorns. She gets her little knife out of her apron pocket.

"Before you was born," she starts again, back to the old story, and I settle in to listen this time. "Your daddy so excited you were comin'." Her dark, shiny head—she puts Vaseline on her springy hair to make it lie flat. I like it better springy. It's like a crown. She tilts to one side, eyes like sea-glass marbles. *Where'd you get green eyes, Li? From the gittin' place!* Her fingers twirl the acorns and she chooses two without even looking. Her hands turn and turn.

"Every day he listen to you."

"Listen to me? How can you listen to a baby inside?" I always ask that.

"Every day he bring a contraption from his office—that thing like a horn he put on his fore-head—and lean down to your mama's belly. *'Lemme hear my one and only in there!'*"

She holds up a big acorn with a stick neck, four stick legs, and a small acorn head. "Cow? Or horse?"

"Cow." I like the long twig horns.

Ploop! The red-and-white bobber goes under the water—a bite! She frowns, puts down the cow and yanks up the rod. A

6

fish! A catfish, big and slimy, with a mustache. She swings it out of the water. He's near big around as her arm and slippery, you can tell by the shine. Catfish doesn't have scales, but skin like satin. She holds him over the rim of the tin bucket and goes after the hook with a pair of pliers. He opens his mouth, doesn't make a sound. He looks like he's breathing, but he's not. He acts like he's hurt. Daddy says animals don't feel things the way we do and I'm not supposed to worry about them. But I do.

"See these whiskers? Catfeesh got real sharp spines in there, go right through your finger, you don't look out." She pulls out the hook and a string of blood. I want to watch, but I don't want to. "Well, let 'im have 'is satisfaction." He splashes into the bucket.

"How do you satisfy a fish? Doesn't he know he's got to die?"

She wags her head. Not "no." More like "don't know."

"And get *eaten*? Lila, how do fish breathe, down in the water all the time?"

"Better ask your daddy."

"He'll just say 'All you need to know is they aren't like people.' Why is it nobody will talk to me about what animals feel? Was Daddy's satisfaction listening to me inside Mother?"

"One time he call me, *'Lila, come here.'* " She can imitate Daddy's voice to a T. "He put that contraption on my forehead and make me press it into your mama. And I heard you, honey. You were in there swimming around."

"Swimming! What did I sound like?" I always ask and I always forget what the answer *feels* like so I don't remember what the answer *is*.

"Like a little fish, swimmin' round, bumpin' into the sides."

"I sounded like a *fish*?" That's the part I never get right. Everybody knows fish don't make any sounds. And if they don't feel anything, how come they want to get away?

"Put your ear to that bucket."

The fish is swimming around. We never had this part of the

7

story before. We never had a fish. I *think* I can hear a sort of swishing. No, I'm just hoping.

"Go on. Git your ear right up side the bucket."

I stretch out, stomach to the ground, and get my ear right on the bucket.

Do I hear anything?

Pound pound in my throat. The metal creaking with the river water behind it—cold. Sucking me under, wanting to drag me to the ocean. My hair makes scratch-scratch sounds if I move my head. Dirt and stones bite into my legs.

If I was like a fish, how did I breathe inside Mother? There's water in her where I was, I know that. So I couldn't breathe like a person.

Then I *hear* it. I do! A little, little sound. A swish. The fish. A baby! A baby in its sac, swimming, brushing its mother's nest with its fins . . .

2

1979

MATTER

"Nothing much the matter with this one but age," Dr. Brackson says to me. He himself is older than Lila, and shorter and fatter. Standing there with his battered old stethoscope pressed to her life sounds: heart, lungs, bowel. Peers with a light close into those eyes, pale green and misty from cataracts. "Little diabetes (*di-ah-beet-ees,* he says), but she controls that with half a pill a day, don't you, Lila."

Little brown elf under a white paper sheet, Vaselined hair making a grease spot on the mat. Where is the crisp silent cotton of my father's time? Now everything's disposable. Even people. Which is not new.

Lila closes her eyes, tucks out of sight the safety pin that holds her slip strap together, embarrassment and fury in the turned-down mouth, the knotted fists. Her forehead is deliberately smooth. She says nothing.

"Complains about her heart." Lila always greets me with her middle finger pressed to the center of her chest. *I been sick, gal,* rub-rubbing with that finger, *sick as a dawg. But your mama come to me right often, you know how she do—big sad eyes! Say you on your way here, so I get myself up out of the bed.*

I always phone her, but my dead mother's message speaks louder. For every one of the ten years I didn't come to see Lila—wrote, called, sent birthday and Christmas presents, of course—I owe her a certain number of these scenes. I owe her, owe both of us, for the sins of my parents, who moved away and died, first Mother, then Daddy. They left her poor, didn't take care of her the way they'd promised. *Don't you worry, Lila. We'll look after you!* The Great White Lie. And they left me without Lila.

"I just want to be sure," I say to Dr. Brackson.

Lila shoots me the Look. *Whatever you doin', stop this minute!* Comes down the years, that Look. Now it's telling me that while she comes to Brackson, she doesn't want me telling him anything real about her. *He old, don't know much any more, poor old thing. I just go to 'im so he won't feel bad.*

Whenever I bring her in, he guides me back into the examining room, Lila in tow, as if she were the child and I the worried parent. He even talks to me, as if Lila can't understand plain English. She takes off her glasses so she can't see a thing, squinches her eyes up, and moves a million miles away.

Snap! Brackson is cutting her thick diabetic's toenails. They stick up like little gray lumps of dried chewing gum. He strains and grunts. His hand shakes. Brackson is fat and bald, false teeth click in his head. A doctor, for god's sake, with ill-fitting teeth. Skin pale, splotches on his face and hands. I can't to save me picture Daddy like this. Diminished.

"Bracks!" Daddy would snort. A Yankee, newly arrived from Maryland, trying to woo his patients away. Oh, that snort! That "Bracks!" His rival wasn't even worth the full weight of his name. Bet he never cut a patient's leg taking off a cast, though, the way Daddy cut mine.

Familiar odors here. Ether, acetone, Lysol. But the old graces—real sheets, polished green linoleum floors scored by the wheels of the examining table, steamy smell of the auto-clave, and solid, serious glass bottles, vials, syringes. Gone.

Every time we get near Brackson's office, Lila says, *I'd go to Doc So and So,* naming someone long dead. *Now* that *was a doctor. Most good as your daddy.*

"All the good ones dead," she says now.

Brackson looks startled. Lila and I were cruising on our private wavelength, leaving him behind. Oh, I pray silently, please please don't launch into the dead docs. Daddy, Dr. Philips, Dr. Childress. And don't, oh don't get started on your sister Haddy. Or Eddie.

Her dear Eddie, her boy, her one and only.

"Why don't I learn how to cut those toenails?" I say hurriedly—catch myself—I'm *embarrassed.* And that shames me even more. What do I care what she says? She's reacting to way he's treating her. The way he and all white people treat "poor ignorant Nigras." Brackson, free, white, and 21, as they say around here, has given out plenty such stuff, even if he once was a Yankee. Why can't I just let him take his knocks?

Southern manners, that's why. Southern *poison.* You probably have to be from the South to understand this: Down here, "manners" is a Code, a set of behavior that oozes like snail slime over the truth. It paints a picture that is a lie, and you can't call it. What would happen? The world would crash down, that's what. Folks would have to see the truth behind their lives and they will die first. I loathe it, but it's as much a part of me as breath, even though I've been up "Nawth" for more than twenty years. I fight giving in to it when I catch myself. But my automatic first response is to soothe and smooth —rub away the knots of truth. Maybe it isn't always helpful to use the truth as a sledgehammer, but at least we could be honest enough to acknowledge that we're hiding gall under all this molasses.

When I walk down the street here with my arm through

Lila's, I can feel the white people around us thinking "nigger." Not the affectionate black-to-black "nigga," which is sort of like "buddy," but the cruel "nigger" that cracks like a whip. And it's not aimed at hurting Lila, or me, individually. It's aimed at the insult that we represent. We aren't two people walking down the street. We are a white woman and a black woman breaking the Code.

I can't feel what the black people we meet are thinking. For all my love of Lila, I don't really know the life. And while I'd love to ask her, I haven't worked up the nerve.

Nowadays it's rare for anybody white to say "nigger" aloud. Not saying that has now become part of the Code for "good people." My family even back in the day never let the word pass their lips, and I'd have been whupped raw if I had. But the word is still burned into the air. As we walk along, if we meet a white person, my grip on Lila's arm will tighten, just as if I'd seen a snake on the sidewalk. I said to her once, "You are all the white people here think about."

"*Me?*"

"Black people are stuck in white people's minds down here."

"I aint stuck in *nobody's* mind!"

But we all are stuck in somebody's mind. I want to ask who's stuck in hers, or her friends' and neighbors'. But I still don't have the nerve.

Quicksand—walking on quicksand. Even when I was little, I was terrified of that word "nigger!" At any moment it might break open the world and the burning truth would bubble out of the dark, bringing with it the sound of shattering glass and the smell of sulfur.

One time, I was ten I think, I asked Lila about "nigger"— who could say it and why couldn't I? I'd hardly got the question out, when up goes the chin! *Just because I and Eddie say it, don't make it right for you.*

And at that very moment, "nigger" froze in my head. Solidified into what separated us. That word, and her son Eddie, who without meaning to, she placed in the same circle, became the symbols of our flesh. Lila and me, forever divided.

So privately I say it again and again, in hopes to tame it. But that hasn't happened. Lila used to say my face would freeze if I stuck my tongue out, and then of course I couldn't stop wanting to for the rest of the day. After that moment, the word was just like that. And Eddie was shoe-horned in.

A further truth: in those days down here, children and blacks didn't count. We were ordered around, considered less than human, insulted, abused. Often with affection, but never with respect. Grandmother or Mother would say, right in front of me, *Willis has some of her father's worst characteristics."* Then list them. "Know-it-all, stubborn, disobliging, willful." No descriptions, which I might have protested, just those labels. Or *Eddie in his little white serving coat looks cute as a button.* Or *Lila tells the wildest tales, she probably doesn't even know what she's saying!* How can you respond to that? My mother used to say, *Willis tells little lies.* I didn't know how to handle that either. I couldn't say I'd been dreaming or making up a story. Or, God forbid, that I didn't want to discuss the issue. Child or black, we didn't count.

Do we count today? Is Brackson really taking Lila seriously, the way he would a white patient? The only doctor I ever had who saw me, a woman, as competent and human, was a Persian, and I insulted him by asking if Persian meant Iranian. His face closed with a snap. But he always told me what I needed to know to make an informed medical decision. To him, I was simply another intelligent human being.

"Risky," Brackson says now. What? Ah yes, my cutting Lila's toenails. "These things are hard as a mule's foot, and if you nick her skin, with her di-a-beet-ees—" If *I* nick her? He looks like he's shaking dice. And there he goes again—would he have said "mule's foot" if it were *my* toe?

Why won't Lila tell me the name of the local black doctor? That's not the only thing she doesn't tell me of course. Sometimes she just closes up. A book with some of the pages stuck together. I left her alone too long, and she finds little ways of twisting that till I'm reduced sometimes to the mental age of three, shouting, *But you're the one who left me!* As if she had a choice. Then up goes the chin. Sniff! And I am overwhelmed with guilt.

All this, says my friend who's a New York psychoanalyst, is the matter Lila and I have to work out. The Matter of Us, like the Matter of Britain. And those things we aren't able to sit down and talk about will have to be *lived*.

It occurs to me now, thinking about this for the umpteenth time, that something worse is happening here. Flinching away from Brackson's response to Lila, I see now, is part of a pattern in me that's just as prejudiced as my parents' reactions. I absorbed something—the thought of Lila, whom I love truly, as somehow lesser. Less aware, less capable, less something. We treat old people like that, too, but Lila, while she's old, is not impaired in any way. The very opposite is the truth.

We are the ones missing everything. Missing our mental hands and thumbs. Our humanity. Because we live a thousand lies.

Here's the truth: Lila, all her life, has had to be a perfectly functioning human being in order to live through the day. One slip and she'd be the limping antelope on the savannah. I see her, in my mind's eye, as the epitome of intention. The Gazelle of Perfect Deflection.

How can I ever say to her, *I see what I've done. I am*—oceans *beyond sorry!*

My New York friends ask me, from time to time, what I'm doing, coming here now. Am I playing Lady Bountiful, "helping this poor old woman." My answer is, "Are you being *gracious* when you balance your mother's checkbook or take her to the doctor?" Though the real question of course is not what I am doing but how Lila perceives me.

During our long separation, she wrote me a remarkable letter. Not the "how are you I'm fine" kind of letter, or one that hides everything under the blanket of food. A real one. I'd been hospitalized and the insurance company refused to pay: "Dear Willis," she wrote, "I was sorry to hear about your troubles. I think of what you and I have been thru. They took you to the cleaners but they didn't take your life. Just think what you can do with that, like I ust to tell you. You can do whatever you set your mind to, so do what you do. Some is mistakes but correct them and go on. With love from your as ever Lila."

That understanding, that cool assessment of the possibilities from a general on the battlefield, took my breath away. The letter brought me down here. For myself that first time, because I felt alone and embattled and it held out a lifeline. But I keep coming back now for Lila, as well, she is not only alone but old and poor. If she were a white man, she'd be Governor. But she is who she is, and she needs a daughter.

That first visit, the letter was in my pocket as I drove into town. It was a Sunday morning, I'd been driving all night. I took a room at the only motel and called her. She sounded as if I'd answered an ad in the paper. *I be at the church for the service, if you care to attend.* If I cared to attend! Where was the Lila of the letter?

I sometimes look at what we're going through as if it were an old painting. The town and all of us have a nice new surface, but the old leaks through and the colors and shapes of the past bubble up. For example, the motel I stayed in stands less than a block from the site of the old Gregory Hotel, where in the '30s and '40s, salesmen stayed during the week, with their black suits and bow-ties, their orders and demos for the store owners, and where Grandmother and every white woman in the county of a certain age—and purse—used to "take" dinner on their cook's night off. They wore hats and white gloves and their faces were paled with rice powder.

The hotel was an old rambling place, always smelling of paint and onions and fried okra. It burned down one night, and much later, Grandmother, who was in the hospital dying of old age, saw a newspaper picture of flames shooting up from a burning building, and screamed: *The baby—oh she was burned, the baby was burned!*

Who? What baby?

Long silence. *Gregory.* Tears ran down her face. It took me days to figure out that she surely meant the old hotel. I never did learn who the baby was. No one was reported killed in the Gregory fire. But an era ended. A very ugly era, never mind the nostalgic inventions that are so entrancing. People even then knew the truth, but white people hid it under layers of rules.

At the end of that first visit—after I'd "attended" Lila at the church and jumped through hoops—she said, *Next time you come, you stay here in my house. You don't want that motel trash takin' your dough.* And there was my invitation.

"Tell me about the black doctor," I asked today as I always do. "Is he someone you can talk to?"

"A good one too," she said. "Went to the same school as your daddy." Cutting her eye at me. Black students at the University of Virginia Medical School are certainly a welcome sign of changing times. "Liz-bet go to him. One of these days when Uncle Chillus leave me something, I'll do what I want."

Liz-beth is Lila's favorite niece. I remember her from my childhood, when we knew her as "Hard," short for "Hard Rock." She'd fallen out of a tree and hit her head and swore it didn't hurt.

"Lila, I'll take you. You don't have to wait till your uncle dies."

No response. Just like Grandmother. Only Lila was mistress of the art of deflection long before Grandmother got caught in a time warp.

In that exchange, reconstructed, I see another sign of my dilemma. Lila and I are, in our separate ways, careful of language. But in my words, there is often a whiff of condescension. I should have *asked* if she'd like me to take her. As I said, we treat all the old with disrespect. We disguise it as love. It's involuntary. I do not feel or believe what my words imply, but I also don't know how to correct them.

"I'd go to him with Liz-bet, but she charge me two dollars to go to the Piggly Wiggly," she says. "Two dollars and the Piggly just up the road. What she go charge for the doctor? Six month so-sa secu'ity?"

Lord. If Liz-beth acts like that, what can her other niece and nephew be doing? They all take after their mother, greedy fat Haddy. It was always Haddy this, Haddy that. It used to be whenever I called Lila on the phone, it was what Haddy'd been up to or how Haddy had taken some little thing I sent Lila. She called me one night a couple of years ago. She seldom calls me. "I lost Haddy," she said. No hello, just, *I lost Haddy.*

Lost? Wandered off?

"She fell out at the store. Say to me, 'Wait up, Sistah, lemme catch my breath.' Next thing I know, she's flat on the ground. And then *gone*." A hollow cry echoed through the phone wires.

Howl, howl for all the ones who've *gone*.

Couldn't say no to Haddy. Can't say no to anybody. Not even me, but that's part of what we're building up to face. Meanwhile, what can I do? Not much about the stuff that's over and done with, but let me tell you, next chance I got, I marched myself over to Liz-beth's. "Hard Rock!" I bellowed from the steps. Precious Eddie, now I remember, was the one who named her that. He was there when she fell out of the tree. Eddie said: *Liz-beth break any rock she hit with her head.*

"Hard, what's this about charging Lila to drive her to the grocery store?"

"Lawd, Willis!" Hard has Lila's oval face and that springy hair drawn back in a fan, but she has a squeaky little voice, unchanged since babyhood. She can't bellow, *"Whatever you doing, stop it."* And she rolls her eyes in the manner of a frightened pony, which is completely un-Lila. "I aint charge her a dime. One time she go with me to Danville to the discount store and I aint had money for the gas. She *offer* to pay."

Sure, Hard. "Well, if you need gas money in the future, let me know. Lila's old and poor and can't walk to the store. She's *helpless!"*

"Helpless like a *fox!"* Hard, plump as a pullet in the hen yard —her eyes went round and shocked—she couldn't believe she let those words slip out of her mouth. To *me.*

Dr. Brackson is peeling the blood pressure cuff from Lila's arm. "Normal. Heart sounds just fine." Unwinds the stethoscope from his neck and hands it to me. "Little murmur in a valve is all. Listen for yourse'f."

"My bladder runnin'," Lila complains. Sits up, fumbling for her glasses, which she wears on a chain around her neck. They make her eyes leap up in her face like magic. One—the one she's had the cataract operation on—is larger than the other. Magic lopsided vision!

"Bladder run like a brook. Got to get up in the middle of the night, and sometime I don't make it to the toilet. Got to go in a slop jar by the bed."

"Well," says Brackson while I stick the ear-pieces in, "we're not as young as we used to be. Don't drink an hour or so before bedtime. Don't drink tea or beer after 12 noon. You not supposed to have beer anyhow, with the dia-be-tees, you know that." He knows she likes her bit of beer.

"Here, Lila," I say, my voice echoing up through the scope. "Let me listen to your heart." I used to listen to hearts with

Daddy's stethoscope. I'd start with his, then Mother's, then the dog Rumpy's. And on to Lila's and finally my own. All different tones and rhythms. *Listen to that—that's the thing,* Daddy would say. *People will tell you life is the brain. Life is ideas. But this is life, the sound you're hearing right now.*

Thuh-*thub*—thuh-*thub*.

When that stops, that one little sound—

Daddy. It hits me sometimes. I can never see him again or call him on the phone. *Daddy? What's up, Baby?* Or Mother. Though Lord knows I wouldn't call Mother on the phone. Maybe I wouldn't even call Daddy. Blood ties are not always what they're cracked up to be. Particularly blood that is borne on waves of bourbon. But Precious Eddie—so many things I want to ask Eddie. I would love to call Eddie on the phone.

Lila's heart is not loud. *Ub-bwish—ub-bwish.* That's the leaky valve. She's breathing on me, breath warm and rich, like fresh bread. She's looking at me, shadows in her eyes.

My mind goes back years—to the fish, the sound of the fish that's haunted me forever. It occurs to me suddenly that fish have to live in two separated worlds, each contained in the other. Her face wavers in my vision. "Lila! Don't *leave* me!"

Did I say that aloud?

"There's nothing the matter with *you*," I sing out. She smiles. I smile back and without thinking, I wave. As if I'm on a boat sailing in to shore—closer and closer, waving hello to this woman I have loved, and hurt, all my life.

3

1945

EDDIE

"This where Eddie was born," Lila says, pointing to a falling-down house in the middle of some weeds. The roof is nothing but holes, trees poke up through the porch. Nobody could be born in such a place. Especially not Precious Eddie, Eddie the One and Only.

"Cut it out, Ma," he mutters. He's sitting there on a rotten step reading his comics. Every now and then, he flips the car keys up in the air, catches them. Eddie drove us all the way here in Daddy's car, miles out of town, a dirt road, too. Eddie has his license. He's only thirteen but he gets away claiming fifteen.

Hot stuff! I stick my tongue out at him. "You were born here in this rotten place."

"Eddie born in the back room." Lila straightens up, pointing at the ghost of the old house with a jerk of her head. Her hands are full of little Christmas-green leaves with white veins, blood-colored stems and roots. She makes a tea of it. *Good for heart troubles, good for women's troubles.*

"Cut it *out*, Ma!" Eddie gets really crazy when Lila talks about him getting born and stuff. "Make me sick!" But he doesn't say it very loud. Not even Precious Eddie will *really* talk sass to Lila.

"That room has briars growing in the windows," I whisper. "And holes in the floor. Anybody born in that room is a *spider*. I was born in a hospital. I was a fish."

Eddie puts down his comic. Pop-eye the Sailor Man Poop-Poop. I can read better than Eddie, and I'm only eight. "Con-fab-u-lation," I read over his shoulder. Eddie slams the comic down.

He can *drive*. And he is Lila's. "My boy," she says, and smiles the Precious Eddie smile. Oh, I just want to die. "I'm your girl," I whisper. And she smiles at me too, but it's different. The P.E. smile's curly and full of sweet sugar and a little vinegar. Her smile for me, when I've been acting up, is a flat tire.

When Eddie was my age, Lila used to smack him when he did bad. Afterwards she'd hug and kiss him. He's too big to hug and kiss now. Too big to smack too. He's taller than she is. She has never smacked me, but she doesn't kiss me either. When Eddie's around, she won't even hug me. I do all kinds of tricks to make her. I'll snuggle—she almost has to then. Or I'll pout and pretend to cry.

"*Ed*-die was *born* in a *room* with *spi*-dahs. *Bri*-ars in the *win*-dahs, *holes* in the *floor*." I sing it very softly, so Lila won't hear.

But she does. She pokes her fingers in the red dirt to pull out a bloodroot. "Bri-ahs? Honey, my gramama had this house fix good—this whole fa'hm was something." She points to a collapsed gray building, one end sagging like an old horse on three legs. "Tobacca curing barn—mmmm!" She breathes in. "Uncle Chillus light the fiy-ahs and cure the tobacca. Cows in the field, plowing mules in the shed." Her face goes all dreamy when she talks about her gramama and the *fa'hm*. "Flowers growing all around the yard, just like Miz Roberts." That's my grandmother, whose yard has flowers everywhere. Her flowers win prizes in Garden Week.

"Nothing left now but these old buttoneggs. But my gramama make good money, sugah. Birthing all the babies, knowing all the herbs." She shakes a root in the air. "Sometime now she come to me at night, sit herself on the bed, just shaking her head—the sorry state of this place have put a nail in her heart."

Lila talks to the dead. *Lila's foolishness,* my parents say. Not even Precious Eddie can stand it. He groans now and rolls his eyes.

"Did you hear Eddie inside you?"

Eddie rattles his comic book. "Y'all hysh up, now!"

Lila's shaking her head. "Gramama didn't have your daddy's contraption. But she could coax a stubborn baby out like nobody bidness."

"Was Eddie stubborn?" I hope he was. Nobody likes stubborn.

Lila smiles over at Eddie. Sugar and vinegar. "Stubborn? I *reckon!*"

Eddie's listening now, pretending not to. Always scared something will embarrass him.

My parents talk about Eddie, right in front of him, as if he can't hear. Even I get embarrassed about that. Grandmother's the worse. *Eddie was cute as a button when he was little. All dressed up in a starched white coat and bow tie and white gloves. To serve the table. Just like the little houseboys when my daddy was alive.* Her father had three plantations and a lot of slaves. She talks about all that whenever she can get anybody to listen. She even has old brown pictures, which she brings out to show, and a black-and-white one of Eddie in his serving coat. I know that burns Eddie up because he whispers a curse. Grandmother wouldn't notice if he yelled it. But I wouldn't tell anyhow, I whisper it along with him.

Now he's flipping the car keys again. Clinkety-clink. "What

so great about this place, anyhow? Why's it such a wreck, if it was so *fine*."

"A wreck because after Gramama die, Uncle Chillus didn't look after it. Too many folks, too many claiming cousin. Uncle Chillus say, 'I work this fa'hm for all us folks, but I aint holdin' up the old house for the whole of Mattaponi County.'"

Precious Eddie and I are one-and-onlies. One-and-onlies, says my mother, are smarter and sassier than other children. I wish Eddie wasn't an only, except I'm glad he's not two. I'm not allowed to wish he'd kick the bucket.

That's another thing Daddy hates—if something's dead, you have to say *dead*.

Do I wish P.E. was dead? I've seen chickens Lila kills for our dinner, and wild animals smashed on the road. There was a dog one time with rabies and Daddy shot him in our street. He made me go inside. Wouldn't even let me look at the foam in its mouth. No, I *don't* wish Eddie was dead.

But look at him sitting there. Little burnt cabbages all over his head, fingernails chewed to the quick. Doesn't that *hurt*? If I did that, Mother would paint nasty stuff on my fingers. Red, so everybody knows what you're being punished for.

"Gramama was a slave, you know," Lila says suddenly. "And she have three boys with the man who boss her. When he have to free her, he give her this farm, just for *them*. She tell him, *Think your kids go stick round listen to you call 'em nigga?* And soon as they got big, she give 'em some money and they lit out. Never sent a word back to her, not so much as thank-you-dog. Chillus, now, he's the son of her black husband. My mama come from her Inyun husband—Gramama part Inyun herself. Call themselves Redbone. Fifteen chil'ren down to three today. Still squabbling over every little thing. Gramama go take a stick to us all, one day."

"She's dead," Eddie yells. "Ma, she's *dead!*"

Lila flaps her hand at him, "When you were born, Eddie, no

23

briars growing in that room, no-sirree. She have a long table with a white oil-cloth cover and a little bed with a pretty picture hanging over it, angel with rainbow wings. Gramama come to Mama's house to get me. *You 'bout to pop with that boy,* she tell me. She know Eddie was a boy, don't ask me how." Lila nods to me, to remind me how Daddy can't do that. Daddy thought *I* was a boy. No white doctor can do those magic things.

Eddie whoops. "Bet I was a pistol!"

"Hunh. Pistol. You like to never come atall. Gramama had to *work,* getting you in this world."

I know about working to get a baby born! "What did she do? Did she have to cut you open? They cut Mother open to get me out," I shout at Eddie. "Mother like to died just gettin' me born!"

Lila shoots me the Look. She doesn't want anybody to know she told me the big secret, not even Eddie. I slam my hand over my mouth.

"Aunt Haddy the one . . ." Eddie starts. I kick him quick. Haddy told us both together. And we swore to die before we told.

"No cutting," Lila says. "Eddie finally wake up and come the reg'lar way. Your daddy say, *You almost too little, have a baby.* But Gramama say Eddie a lazy baby, was all."

I poke my tongue out at Eddie. He pokes his tongue out at me. His is big, like a giant pink slug wiggling in his mouth. He can make the tip curl up to his nose. "I won't no lazy baby."

Lila sinks down on the rotten stoop beside Eddie. I stand over the two of them. "Lazy baby lazy baby."

Lila shakes her head at me. Puts her hand on Eddie's knee to make him look at her. "How you come into the world is stuff you got to know, one day or another." Eddie squinches his eyes shut. He doesn't look a thing like Lila. He's so black he's got blue lights on his face. He's big boned too, and his eyes are like garnets. Lila is little bitty and cinnamon red like an Indian. Her eyes are green. Eddie has her long upper lip, though, so he *is* like her a little. Mule lip, Grandmother calls it. *Stubborn as mules, both of them.* And their mouths are identical straight lines.

"I hurt my mother when I came." I cut my eye at Lila. "But it wasn't my fault."

"Won't my fault neither," Eddie says.

"Was too. You were lazy."

"Enough now," Lila says.

"I didn't do nothin'," Eddie yells. "She all time pickin' on me."

"I was a fish," I start to cry. "Inside, where I shouldn't of been able to breathe but I did and they listened to me swimming."

"After Eddie come, Gramama wrap him in newspaper and hand 'im to me." Lila sighs.

A laugh sputters out of me. "Babies are wrapped in blankets, Lila. Everybody knows that."

"Used to wrap babies in newspaper 'cause the ink kept off germs."

Eddie moves off, kicking the weeds. I open my mouth to sass him good. Catch Lila's eye.

"Them was hard times, honey." She raises her voice a little. "And newspaper or no newspaper, Eddie was my Precious."

I try to say, "I'm your Precious too." But all that comes out is a squeak. A lump is growing in my throat. And when that happens, I go all hot inside and choke up. Something awful— my heart beating—fills me to the brim and stops me from breathing. *The child is holding her breath again,* my mother says. She says I do it on purpose.

The lump is growing.

I was born in a hospital and put in a blanket. Eddie was born in this falling down place and wrapped in paper. But Eddie is Lila's.

Lila is looking at Eddie. "Gramama take you up and say, 'This one name Eddie, make me think he didn't want to come into the world atall. But he *had* to. He was *called* to come.' "

"She nothin' but a crazy old thing." Eddie lashes out with his foot.

"Well you won't lazy long, whooeee! Your lungs plenty active." She laughs. "One look at the world and you let fly."

"Eddie cried?" I yell. The lump bobs and sticks. I'm *choking*. Can't Lila see?

"Honey, did he cry. Used to tune up 'bout supper time and shut up when the cock crew."

"I didn't cry. I never cried."

"Hah! You was a fish. You said it. You won't even a human being!"

Now my throat closes up completely. I want to yell that he's nothing but a—

"Both y'all hysh now! Eddie here a boy. Boys s'posed to cry, work their lungs, let you know they here."

"Hah!" Eddie shouts again. The line between us twangs like a bowstring. "I am *he-ah!*"

I open my mouth but nothing can get out.

"And this boy Eddie," Lila says, "better drive us home, time for me to fix some dunner."

Eddie tosses the car keys high as his great-grandmother's broken chimney. "Ya-hooo!"

Planting my feet in the dirt and locking my knees—I hurt all over inside. There's a hole in my middle. My lump fills my throat with fire. "Not going."

"Come on, honey. 'Fore you know it, sun be down."

Sure enough, the sky's got red streaks and purple clots. Bruises, all over.

"Storm coming," Eddie says, running to the car. "We go leave you, you got to hide from the thunder in the room with the briars." He shouts with laughter. "Hants! Hide from the hants."

I don't even want to hit him anymore. Eddie isn't allowed to hit me back, but he can say I'm not a human being. I lean over and throw up on my feet. The stink spills onto my shoes.

"Oh, honey," Lila says. "Here, Eddie, wet me this hanky at that old pump." She puts her arm around me.

"You can't leave me!" I croak. I can hear the pump squealing. Lila is wiping my face with the wet hanky. So cool. I shut my eyes. She won't dare leave me to the hants. I can make us all stay here till dark. My stomach heaves again and my throat tastes hot. "I don't want to throw up any more," I whisper to Lila.

"Talk 'bout stubborn," Eddie mutters.

Lila shakes her head at him, makes him a sign with her hand, looks at me hard. She can read my face. She knows when I'm play-acting and when the lump is real. Throw-up is always real. She starts gathering her bag with the herbs, the heart medicine, medicine to help a woman with a baby. Help her when she hurts in her stomach. She'll cool the herb tea with chips of ice in the glass, and my mouth will fill with a clean flower taste.

"Bloodroot," Lila says and starts humming, moving slow. To calm me, make me "reasonable." *Do something, Lila, make the child reasonable.*

First she pretends to look around for her hat. Finds it, puts it slowly on the porch by the bag of roots and Eddie's comics. Then picks up my shoes from the grass, one at a time. Cleans the throw-up off. Then the socks, one by one, scrubbing, wringing it out, folding it into her purse.

Time to settle, she always says to Mother. *Chil'ren need time to settle their feelings.*

Humming now, "Hmmmm-hhm-hmm hmmm," deep and

twangy in her throat. Last of all, she puts on her apron and smooths it with her palms. Everything is in order.

"Come on, honey lamb, pick some buttoneggs for your mama." I'm glad to hear the lamb. That means she is thinking good things about me. "Your mama will love you to bring her a bowkay. And after dunner, we make some vanilla ice cream in your gramama's maker. It'll be so cool." She puts her cool hand on my forehead. I shut my eyes. The lump is melting. "Vanilla your favorite."

"Will Eddie get some?" I love the wooden ice cream maker, with its ice and salt and the silky sweet cloud of cream that clings to your tongue. It almost makes me forget the hole in my middle. But will Eddie get some? Do I want him to? Or do I want him to never have ice cream again as long as he lives?

"Lawd, child, don't be like that. And Eddie got to go on now, got to get home, feed the chickens. Go start up the car, Eddie."

My knees unlock. "Will you help me pick flowers?"

She takes my sticky hand in her cool firm one and we go off to the side of the old barn, where pools of daffodils with scrambled-egg centers light up the weeds and the shadows. "Watch your bare foots now. Stay on the grass where there's no rocks."

Eddie starts the car, and sits in it, smoking a rabbit-tobacco cigarette. I can smell the spicy smell all the way over here. Precious Eddie, Big Man.

"Good long stems," Lila cautions. "Don't bust 'em off at the heads." She holds a bloom under my chin. "My girl like butter?"

I hold my breath. "Am I your precious, too?" I whisper.

"Course you are."

That shrinks the lump in my throat better than medicine. The hole in my middle closes up. "Well, how'd you get me?" She couldn't have me out of her body, the way she had Eddie, no matter how much I want that. "Tell me how."

She takes the flowers and puts them on the porch step and

reaches to straighten my hair. "Enough now. You know that old story. Right now, we got to go. Dark coming." A glance back at the car. "Eddie waiting."

I choke again. Can't help myself. Gagging.

Lila sighs. "Honey, your mama stay sick a long time when she bring you home." The rhythm of her voice rises and falls. "She call me into her room. She laying up there in her big old bed. She hold you out to me." Lila's empty arms go out straight, and her face has a yearny look.

"Lila, this is my heartstrings. My one and only. Who go look after her for me? Lila, you promise me. So I taken you in my hands and held you." She pulls her arms close to her breast and cradles the air. Then her arms are around me, rocking me, like the baby I was. "I give her my solemn word."

She lets me go and straightens. "So that's how you and me come together. Just when you were born."

Actually I know that Daddy got a trained nurse in at the beginning because he thought she'd know for sure how to keep me from crying. But I cried and cried, never mind the fib I told Eddie. So Mother brought Lila and I didn't cry any more.

She was there almost from the start.

"Well, honey, I stay there night and day till you could sleep through." She looks over at the car where Eddie has the radio going, head bobbing to the beat. "Till you lie quiet in the morning and wait for me to come and give you your bottle." I can see the bottle—glass, streaky white with milk, Li's hands with the creases all dark and wrinkly.

She picks up the bunch of daffodils from the porch step and hands it to me. Then she bends down so I can lock my arms around her neck, and piggy-backs me to the car so I won't cut my foot on a rock. Puts me in the back seat and closes the door without slamming. Then she slips into the front next to Eddie.

"Now get us home, boy, so I can fix us some food."

4

1979

THE FARMER'S TALE

"I f that car of yours any good, we could drive out see Uncle."

"The car got me here all the way from New York," I remind her. Though it's always a question, the car's so old. But when I come on the bus, we can't go on our rambles. We like to explore all the back roads, every twist and turn of the river.

Lila's eyes are green marbles behind her magic glasses—they make that one eye, the one that had the cataract removed —twice the size of the other. She hands me a cardboard box of home-canned beans, okra, and her special baby onions, the jars wrapped in paper secured with rubber bands, and two six-packs of cold Bud. On her head goes a white straw hat, which she ties on with a pink chiffon bow under her chin. Then she puts on a fresh-starched white apron and finally turns her eagle eye on me, top to bottom: stand-up hair, old T-shirt, faded jeans. She gets to my scruffy feet and frowns.

While I change my shirt, brush the dust off my sandals, and comb my hair, Lila changes her shoes. Off with the laceless sneakers, on with a pair of too-tight patent-leather pumps. Her toes are lumpy with corns, which she got from "breaking in" my grandmother's shoes eons ago, scuffing around in those pinch-me's till the leather could cradle small, pampered white feet.

Now she straightens with a snap in front of the old blued mirror and pulls me beside her. Little brown elf topped with a white bell and pink bow. Tall shaggy hippy in jeans and faded silk shirt. Lila gives her half smile and nods. "Now, child, let's go see some *folks!*"

She closes all the doors and locks Eddie's old room. She does that whenever we leave the house. I got curious and—couldn't help myself—peeked in. It looked the same as it had years ago. Posters of prize fighters on the wall, and a picture he'd drawn of his girlfriend tacked inside the closet door. Titties and pubic hair! Oh, Ed!

An old Pro-Keds tennis shoe sits in a rickety chair. I had a pair of Keds when I was about five and Eddie taught me how to tie them. It was a job too. I've always had trouble with spatial relationships. He tied and untied my shoes several times and every time I tried, I flubbed. Finally he knelt behind me so I could see exactly what his fingers were doing.

The shoe on the chair is a high top, black with a red stripe. Eddie was on the basketball team, but our schools were segregated so I never saw him play. It looks—forlorn.

Lila calls, "Come on, gal!" So now, the house properly battened down, we head out. I drive up Main Street, then up Walker past my parents' old place. This is one of our new rituals, marking our dual world. Our pentimento. I stop the car in the middle of the street, with Grandmother's house on the right and our old house on the left.

Grandmother's hasn't changed on the outside. The new owners keep it shining white, glowing in the center of the dark oak grove like a beacon. They've even matched the old black-green of the shutters, so on the outside it looks the way it did 75 years ago. Miz Coleman is forever stopping me on the street, begging me to come see it. "You'll like what we've done." "Yes, ma'am," I tell her. But no memories on earth can survive a stranger's furniture. Liz-beth says they've carpeted the old random-width wood floors.

Across the street, our little house, once white, is now red. The front door and new shutters are white—like false teeth in an open mouth. Half the old maple trees are gone. I used to climb one way up to the shaky top, where I could look out over the whole town and not be seen. Hard Rock fell out of it that time. But she wasn't at the top.

"Yes ma'am!" Lila murmurs. "Used to have some times in this little house. You and me."

Lawyer Perkinson lives here now, with his daughter. His wife was killed in an automobile accident, and his little girl was hurt.

Lila says, "Us got to go round see that Mr. Perkup one day, fix me a will."

Mr. Perkup! But I can't face even a joke about wills.

We cruise on off. Where? The car is in my hands, I'm in hers, her pointing finger my compass. Out of town, on the back road to Henderson, the jack pines begin to take over from the town's oaks. I love their pale candles of new growth, but I also miss the old sense of forest, with its medley of oak, yellow poplar, hickory, tupelo, red maple. The history of trees has been sacrificed to greed.

Stretching out on either side of the road, the tobacco fields are raw, plowed but not yet planted, rows of giant red curls that someone has combed and brilliantined. The tobacco seedlings are sheltering somewhere under canvas covers, waiting for the right moment for transplanting.

Guided by Lila's finger, I turn onto the old Lunenburg Road, which has no sign and to my knowledge no other name. Her grandmother's farm is out here somewhere.

"Turn—*turn!*"

"*Here?*" Wild spray of gravel and red mud.

Then we go on and on, crossing other smaller roads.

"Now where?" No answer.

"Are we going to your gramama's?"

She settles her hat more firmly on her head.

We rumble along in a curl of dust, following the river where we used to fish. Now I almost know where I am. We're near the bridge where Precious Eddie used to leave us off. He'd help us out of the car and zoom off, spraying gravel. Not to the farm. Eddie hated the farm.

"Does your uncle live at the farm now? Is it all fixed up?" And how will I ever find it? By some deep memory, feeling my way? She won't—can't—direct me. If you don't drive, you don't get road-wise, and Eddie used to enjoy getting us lost.

But here, 'round a bend, is the Old Mill Bridge, green metal with wood treads. Someone told me once that all the good land was on one side of the river, the town side. And all the no-good land was on the other. White vs. Black. And before it was black and white, it was settlers and Indians. Most of the native people here aren't even a name anymore. Just labels in books. And all lumped under Five Nations, Cherokee, Shawnee. The small tribes are completely swallowed up. I know the name of one— Mattaponi—only because the county and the river have its name. A friend of my father's collected *relics* and displayed them in a little cabin on his property. One label on a grinder identified it as *Mattaponi, a tribe inherited by Chief Wahunsenacah of the Powhatans*. That's the famous one of the Captain John Smith and Pocahontas tales. How one tribe could be *inherited* by another doesn't bear thinking about.

I stop in the middle of the bridge. Eddie would let us out right here, and Lila and I would struggle with our paraphernalia down to the river, watching for Copperheads. Lila would step high and call out, *Git on, Mistah Snake, git!* We'd put our stuff down under an oak tree and set up a little camp—a tattered blanket, an old cooler, a picnic basket.

This was her favorite spot, *"fishes got to slow down, take this river bend."* I asked her once who taught fish to swim. Their mamas, she said.

Instinct, said Daddy. Instinct, the way he told it, was a kind of automatic machinery that did the job of real brains. It took me half a lifetime to learn some of the complexities of that. Instinctive responses are enviable, stored capacities that let the creature blessed with them get on quickly with its life, rather than spending two decades in school. We have a few ourselves, powerful for good and for ill.

I start the car moving again. We rumble across and in a minute—the farm.

"Lila, no one lives here!" The house, wood slats covered in sky-reaching sloes and briars, has lost even its rags of tarpaper. But the old dry-stone chimney is still standing. Built for a thousand years, she used to say.

Lila walks around, purse clutched to belly. Weeds snag her stockings. Her feet spill out of the fancy shoes. "Here where I grow up. Here where Eddie born—"

Rack and ruin! Maybe it was like this in the old days and I had just dreamt life into it. The buttoneggs are blooming under the poplar tree. And there's bloodroot—*for what ail you, ail you in the heart.* And the old iron pump, where Precious Eddie wet Lila's handkerchief. I can see and feel it this minute, cool against my burning distress. The pump is lying on its side in the weeds. Lila pulls on the handle. Creak! It's half-frozen with rust. "This this be *something*, set up in my yard!"

I grab the body of it—huff and strain. Can't budge it. But while she wanders the yard, I find an old tin can and, using my pocket knife, dig up some buttoneggs and put them in the trunk.

She is going round and round, muttering. Maybe to her grandmother. I never met Miz Crowder, who died just before I was born. There's a picture of her stuck in the mirror on Lila's dresser, a black and white photo of a tall woman in a fancy 1920s pleated-front dress. White hair in a bun on the top of her head, little pipe in her teeth. Her seamed face stares out, unflinching. She's leaning against a 1950s-style Chevy. The photo has been cut right at the edge of the car, removing something or someone. I asked Lila about that, but she just shook her head.

Lila's mother was still alive when I was little. Lila says Mother knew her—Cora Neal—but I never met her. She wasn't part of Lila's mythology. And I don't think I ever heard Lila mention her father once. Only her gramama. I asked her one time where she was born. "Honey, in a shack along the railroad."

That got mixed up in my head with rail-road sparrowgrass —escaped garden asparagus, which she picked and cooked for my father. And poke salit, a poisonous plant with magenta berries that stain your fingers. I used to take a berry and rub it on my fingernails, like polish. She'd warn me a hundred times not to put my painted fingers in my mouth. But she wouldn't have allowed me to touch those berries if they were violently poisonous. The leaves, picked and cooked with extreme care, made one of Daddy's favorite dishes. He used to call it "Indian roulette." Or maybe that was wild mushrooms.

Years later, Lila told me that, like Ed, she was born at her grandmother's. So what was that rail-road shack story? No answer.

The original old lady Crowder, Lila's great-grandmother was also a wise woman, midwife, herb doctor. She was born in one of the Indian villages near the Stanton River and captured as a young girl by the *paterollers*, vigilantes who chased runaway slaves. She was taken to Crowder's farm and sold as a slave. She wouldn't go back home, even when she was no longer locked up—she was afraid to bring the whites down on what was left of her people.

"Swamp folks," Lila calls them. *"Paterollers git you if you don't watch out!* Used to be a song went like that." She told me stories about the old trackers who went into the Dismal Swamp to find lost hunters. Even earlier, those Indians had been hired to find run-aways. Each slave earned the tracker so-many sacks of corn or a ham. And they never caught just one. When I heard that, I cried.

She heads now down a path that leads to the river. I hope we are not going there today. It's hard to walk in sandals through those weeds, and there's poison ivy. After a couple of minutes, we come to a large open field that's neatly plowed and has rows of little green sprouts coming up. It must be five acres and the rows are arrow strait, the strips between them free of weeds. Someone's working it hard.

"This is our garden," Lila says. "All Gramama's fam'ly have us a piece. I too old do much work, now, so Liz-bet and her chil'ren do mine along with theirs." She points out each row of little amorphous plants: beans, squash, tomatoes, greens, watermelon, cantaloupe, corn. *Cawn*, she says, her voice soft and musical. Food is a sacrament.

"Let's go get Robert, he knows where Uncle Chillus at," she says now. She means Dance. Long ago Robert Tisdale was our gardener and Grandmother's chauffeur. I named him Dance when I was three and into naming folks, because he let me stand on the tops of his feet while he did the two-step. He has recently come back from Jersey City, where he worked for years in a factory. His house is a long way from the farm. "Well," says Lila. "We got *time!*" And then we're in the car again, going back the way we came.

Long ago, Dance's heart was broken by a little dog—funny old Rumpy. He was Mother's dog, and he used to run away from us every chance he got. Daddy and I would find him in Dance's shack, curled up on the bed. For a little dog, that eight miles must have been like a hundred for a human. And all for love.

Dance lives in the same little cabin now, but he has changed. A carefully lettered sign by his mailbox says: WOOD-CUTTING and Demolitions. RIDES ACCEPTED. As if there could ever be any driver but Dance! He knew more about cars than any other person in town, drove anything with wheels, fixed anything broken. But oh, the dancing man is himself broken now. He was big and quick, and now he's drying up like jerky.

"The porch here was made out of the wood from your daddy's office." He points at the worn tongue-in-groove we are walking on. "See this here?" Wood beam thick as my thigh. "One solid piece, not many left anymore. From your daddy's *daddy's* house, built before 18 and 90." Grandfather built it when he married my father's mother. Not "Grandmother," who was Mother's mother and lived across the street from us. The other grandmother I was almost never allowed to visit.

During the Depression, Grandfather turned their big house into a barter clinic for the farmers, and built a smaller house next door for his wife and five children. That grandmother was a Temperance Union member and openly disapproved of my mother, who drank and smoked and, God help her, was divorced before she married my father. My mother had her revenge, though. She let that grandmother see me no more than twice a year. That must have been hard because we lived only a few blocks apart. If Daddy fought the decision, I never knew. He dutifully took me to visit his mother on her birthday and on Christmas. I remember not knowing really who she was or what to call her. At about three, that era when I named everything, I came up with Bom Bess, for Mom Bess, I suppose, and so she remained, twice a year, for the rest of her life.

Inside the shack Dance's little wood stove is going, though the day is warm. Dance sits on a busted old vinyl and chrome chair, and Lila and I sink into a rump-sprung couch. She talks about the weather and her health. "Willis took me to that old

37

Brackson." Then, "Willis drove to the fa'hm a while ago. Things coming along pretty good out there." At last she works around to her uncle.

"Chillus out at the Brown place, his second wife's peoples," Dance says. "Miss Lila couldn't find it if it was a frog (*frawg*) in a jar." Lila's chin goes up a notch. And Dance begins to wheeze—laughing. I remember that laugh.

"Old Chillus, he went to his own folks, when the doctors let 'im out of the horsepital." Dance's years up north show up when he talks. He pronounces some words slightly differently from the rest of us. Horsepital, not hosspital.

"They like to kilt him, trying to git his money." Dance's voice is smoky and heavy. "I aint saying Browns is all that much, now, but they put food in his mouth. Reckon they figger keeping him alive is about the onliest way *they'll* see any dough."

"Git out the judgment seat and fetch along your guitar," Lila says. "Sing Uncle a song."

So it's back to the old Lunenburg Road. Dance leans from the back seat, touching my shoulder with his warm, long fingers, his slow voice giving plenty of warning before a turn.

"Chillus got a Comet-T," he says.

"At his age—*driving?*"

"White lawyer over to South Hill."

Ah. Commit-tee. One who commits. Or is committed to caring for another—

"Mistah G. Falcon Spauldin Junior."

"Sprawldins," Lila snorts. "Buying or stealing every piece of land they get their hands on."

Suddenly I can hear Mother: *Spaul-din, Lila. Not* Sprawl-*din.* Did Mother really miss the joke? Or was it that the Spauldins, who were supposed to be our kin, were not fit subjects for Lila's irony? But I suspect Mother wouldn't let herself acknowledge the irony. White people still laugh at the way black people talk. Yankees don't do that, but they "clean up" the talk, when they repeat it. That misses a lot of good stuff, not just jokes, either. The deep intelligence and perfect deflection of the enemy.

Dance sings in my ear: *"Lawd, don't ya lemme git old! Old folks say every day a rainy day, Lawd don't ya lemme git old.* Too late to sing that to Chillus."

I'm feeling more and more discombobulated. Speaking of missing things—what do they want of me that they aren't saying? Lila, anyway. Dance doesn't want anything that I can see except to be with Lila.

Chillus's Comet-T, a shower of shooting stars.

At last Dance sits back. "Mailbox say Brown!"

A falling-down gray house, two stories high, perches on a little rise. Warped never-painted boards rest on cinderblocks. One upstairs window is carefully mended with cardboard and tape. There's life though. Smoke shoots out of the bent chimney pipe, and dogs and chickens poke around the rusted farm machinery. In the back, ancient gnarled peach trees are dancing in the breeze, a vibrant pink chorus-girl line.

Dance slouches down in the back seat, pulls the hat over his eyes. "Y'all go on in. I got enough old folks looking in the mirror."

UNCLE CHILLUS MUST HAVE BEEN BORN 10 years or so after the Civil War—the first child by Lila's gramama's second husband, the black one. Her first children, the white ones, I knew had left. Now she told me they'd moved to Ohio and *passed.*

"As white?"

She snorted. "What else? Man in the moon?"

"Do you see them, ever?"

Another snort. "Think they go keep up with a bunch of hick

niggas?" And I remembered her saying nobody ever heard from them, *not so much as a thank-you-dog* for the money to run.

Chillus is indeed ancient. I have never seen a person so old. He's swaddled in faded blankets like a long skinny baby, and propped in an old aluminum lounge chair. Beside him, even though the day is warm, the woodstove sizzles. Lila, Dance, Chillus, all are what Lila calls *cold blooded,* which in her parlance isn't an indication of unfeelingness, but purely what it says—their bodies get cold.

I take the offered hand—skin soft, long fine bones firm under my fingers.

"Missus Bray-awn he-ah," Chillus's voice is so low I can hardly hear him. "Missus Brown—the Lawd bless her—keep me wahm, give me what little I eats."

"He got the appetite of a bird," says Miz Brown, neat and quick as a wren herself. "We tempt 'im with all his favorites, ones he got the teeth for."

Pwoosh! Lila opens cans of Bud, warm now, and passes them around, wrapping Chillus's in a handkerchief before tucking it into his hand. He's whispering with laughter. "You go blip up my spirut, Miss Lila. This he-ah be-ah fly me to the middle o' the week."

Chillus's head and hands are long and elegant. The bones, after a century in the dark, are pushing to the surface. Little lacy snowdrops slip from his head down onto his chin.

"Chillus skin so delicate, he can't be shaved," Miz Brown says.

No one except Chillus has looked at me. Lila hasn't introduced me or even mentioned my presence. I feel like a fish out of water. *Not even a human being!*

I slurp my beer too fast and it smacks the back of my head. I set the empty can on the floor by my chair. Oh Lord, I cleaned my sandals but forgot to wash my feet. I tuck my toes out of sight.

The silence tightens.

"We brung some jars, Uncle," Lila says at last. "Just some vegetables I put up last year. Soft enough you can gum 'em."

Chillus's eyes are shut, arms straight and stiff on top of the blanket. He's asleep. The stove hisses and pops. Sweat trickles under my arms, breasts, hair.

"Us come in Willis's car." Lila names me at last. "Willis drive me." Allowed to notice me at last, Miz Brown bows a little in her chair. I bow back.

"Willis live a long way now, you know, up in New Yawk." Lila is saying my name more in these two minutes than in the last two years. "She drive me all around when she here, to the store, the doctor. I depend on Willis."

"Aint that a blessin'," murmurs Miz Brown.

I stare at my feet. From Fish to Blessing—one minute, twenty seconds.

"I first (*fuh-est*) work (*woik*) my mama fa'hm." Chillus's whisper is sudden and harsh. It rumbles through him like an earthquake, every syllable a tremor. "I woik it for huh sence I war a child. I have been a *fa'hma!*" As if he were saying: "President!"

The voice is old and cracked, vowel sounds curled and resonant. People, white and black, talked like Chillus a hundred years ago. Even longer—from the time my people came to this country, the 1600s. Cyar, gyarden, woik.

"I am one-hundred-aught-one yeah old, fa'hmin' sence I was *eluven*. I *fed* them! Many many peoples." His eyes are open and fixed on me, dark and stern. "Dey set me—set me out in de winter." Now the whisper cuts like ice. Chillus's chest is heaving. "Put me neked in a chair (*chay-ah*) in the middle o' the cawnfiel.'"

Naked, in winter? Someone put him out to freeze? This is what Dance was hinting at in the car. "*Lila?*"

She flaps a hand to hysh me. Miz Brown, looking embarrassed, turns her head away. Chillus hisses. Shakes his arm in the air, like a bone.

Lila pats his shoulder. "Don't think on it, Uncle. Turn it over!"

Miz Brown leans toward me. "Us found 'im, me and my gals. Setting naked in a chair, just like he say. Frost on the ground. Crying like a little bird."

"Da-yam *they*-em!" Chillus shouts. "Cuh-*ur*-se *they*-em!" His cheekbones make hollows in his face. His mouth shapes each harsh, slow word.

"Lawd, Uncle," Miz Brown shakes her head. "Now we looks after 'im the best as we can. That lawyer, though, that Comet-T, don't give us much—not even food money sometimes. Say he got to pay the hospital bill. Oh, now, Uncle, look at you. So upset you slobberin'." She gets up and hurries out of the room.

"Buh-uds will feed up-on me," Chillus whispers, skewering me with his eyes. "I war a *fa'h*ma but I out-live ma time."

Grandmother, senile and in pain, said, that. *I have outlived my time.* But no one put her out to die—though maybe sending her to a home, old and out of her head, amounted to that.

Miz Brown comes back, wipes Chillus's chin with a diaper. "He got the state aid and the Medicare, you know." They sound like diseases. "But that law-yer say—"

Lila stands up. "Honey, we got to go!" She is clutching her purse to her belly in a gesture I'm coming to understand. "Robert Tisdale out in the car."

Chillus gives a little crow, waves his elegant hand. "Please ask Mr. Tis-dale to step in for just a minute." The past, the terror, have blown away like mist. "I 'preciate it if he play me a song."

"Something lively, Mr. Tis-dale," Chillus whispers, when Dance, guitar in hand, eases into a chair beside him. "Something to set my toes atingle—mighty long since I dance with a guhl."

Dance looks at me and laughs. "Want to sing our song?"

My heart nearly stops. In my brain, the little song suddenly blooms: Hoppagrass settin' on a railroad track! "For heaven's sakes, Dance."

He shrugs and swings into "Irene Goodnight." Chillus waves his hand to the beat, leans his head back and closes his eyes once more. But I am so jangled I can't listen.

When I was maybe five, Dance taught me to sing and dance while he played the guitar. At that age I had no inhibitions, I'd show off in front of anybody.

After one last "good night," when Leadbelly takes his morphine and dies for Irene, Dance and I slip out to the car, while Lila, the one who leapt up to leave just minutes ago, lingers at the door with Miz Brown.

"Dance, who put him out to die?" No answer. "Am I supposed to do something?"

"What *can* you do—return him to his vigah?"

"That white lawyer is robbing him."

Dance grunts. "Well, that happens around here. He got his vittles and a fi-yah now, not much time."

Lila eases herself onto the seat beside me and I let the car drift downhill, over the ruts, and onto the county trunk. I pop the clutch to start it.

The first loop of the river goes by. The second. Here comes Lila's grandmother's place, again. Where Chillus farmed his life away. A hundred and one years. Child and man, the weight of a family on his back.

What did he make of Lila as a little girl? Or the birth of Eddie, right there in his house? Mouths—mouths to feed and with such pride! *I war a fa'hma!*

I stop the car in the old drive. The smell of the sharp-scented weeds drifts in the window. The car pings as it cools. Aside from that and the sweet whistle of meadowlarks, the spring evening is silent.

Lila looks out of the window. Dance is asleep in the back.

"Vegetables," she says, "we take some of whatever we get out the garden to Uncle. Enough for the Browns, too, since they keepin' 'im."

What a cycle of feeding. Chillus to Lila, Lila to Eddie. And me. Feeding *me*. The fa'hm feeding everybody. What happens to the feeders?

In the back seat, Dance's breathing deepens.

Sleep. Then feeding. Then sleep. Lila, eyes closed, relaxes— her arm is warm against mine. But she keeps her other hand pressed hard against her heart.

5

1946

GRASSHOPPER PROMISES

Hoppagrass singing—hot summer afternoons the air shimmies, and your heart beats in time with his song. Stretching a willow leaf between my thumbs, I play that song, and the hoppagrass sings back.

Grasshopper, Daddy says. *Not hoppagrass.*

"You nothin' but a hoppagrass yourself," Lila says to me. "He got eyes bigger than his stomach, sing and dance all day."

Screeee! The leaf harp flutters between my thumbs. I can make it wail, *wa-wa,* just like a harmonica. "Daddy says the grasshopper is lazy, good for nothing."

"Hah!" Lila snorts. "You want to know what a hoppagrass good for, ask another hoppagrass."

The clock on the mantle chimes *bong bong bong bong.* Four times. Mother calls this "the maid's hour." Cleaning, washing, and lunch all done, something delicious slow-cooking on the back of the stove—we can go out. Mother sometimes drinks something to make her sleep in the daytime, because she needs rest. And Lila and me are just slipping out the door when— "Where are you two going?"

"Little walk," Lila calls back to Mother. "Stir us up a breeze." And we scurry. "Else we gotta go on that walk for sure."

Every day, we go the same way to the same place. Down the hill, past the old brick tobacco warehouses, dark as caves and spicy with tobacco smells. Past the whining saw mill. "Cut oak smell bitter," Lila says. "Cut pine smell sweet." On across the railroad tracks into Lila's end of town, to the Jefferson Davis Café in Sugar Bottom. From a block away you can hear the shouts and laughter and the music from the jukebox.

Daddy hates the Café. *"Wastrels,"* he cries. *"Lazy good-for-nothings."* My father, who works all the time being a doctor, doesn't like anybody to do nothing. But at the Café, something is going on all the time. Nobody is ever doing nothing.

Mother wouldn't allow me to come here, if she knew, so we make sure she doesn't. We wouldn't tell a lie. We just don't say the word. *Only Nigra sluts hang around places like that,* Mother says, whenever anybody mentions the Café. She cuts her eye at me, expecting me to ask what a slut is. Grandmother calls every black woman except Lila a slut, and about half the white women, too. Mother says I'm too young to hear all that. So I'm not going to ask now just to give her the satisfaction of not telling.

"Howsomever," Lila says, half-closing her eyes, "nothing bad in the Café in the daytime. Just don't you tattle."

"Tattle-tale tit, your tongue shall be split, every single dog in town will get a little bit!"

Lila snorts. But I haven't even told Eddie. He never goes with us. Lila's friends come to the Café, though, wearing starched white uniforms like Lila. I don't know all their names. They all know mine of course.

We have till five o'clock to drink Co'cola and dance to the jukebox. Then the maids have to go back to the white side of town to cook dinner. And Lila and me too. I always help Lila when we get home. She says not a soul in the café would tell any white person a thing. No other white children come with the maids either. Lila says I get to come because I can keep a secret.

The Jefferson Davis is long and dark with just a single window in the front. It always smells like beer and cigarettes. Rows of bare bulbs sway like stars and make the corners of the room wobble. In the very back is a door that leads to the undertaker's parlor where Mr. Davis, who's the owner, looks after dead people in his spare time. I always hope I'll see inside but I never have. There's another entrance to it on the back street. Lila never goes that way.

Oh, don't you just love the jukebox? A Christmas tree with flashing jewels. Dance—Robert I'm supposed to call him—says the jukebox is so lively, the dead are going to come out of the back room one day and do the jitterbug.

"Will they really? Will Lila's gramama come?" I would love to see Lila's gramama.

Dance is a tease but he knows things. I named him Dance because he used to waltz me around when I was a baby. He and Lila taught me to jitterbug and he's teaching me to play his guitar. "One of these days, you'll see 'em," he says. "Keep looking."

Dance wouldn't be scared if the dead came out, and if Dance or Lila was there, I wouldn't be scared either. I'd never be scared of Lila's gramama. I'm only afraid of the Zombies— the mean, unhappy dead people who want to kidnap you. Daddy says they're nonsense. But Eddie's seen them. And I actually felt their breath on my neck one time when I ran. I heard *feet* coming after me.

"What would they do if they caught you?" Daddy asks, and laughs and never listens to the answer. Eddie says they would eat me. I don't want think about it.

Mother sometimes says, "Don't act like a Zombie!" when

I'm not listening to her. But she doesn't mean our kind of Zombies, Eddie's and mine.

Inside the Café, it's like night all the time. The pretty colors from the jukebox whirl over the walls and ceiling like magic lightning bugs. We dance in the open space in the middle. Nobody ever sits at the little wobbly tables on the sidelines. They just put their drinks down so they can dance or sing, or go lean on the old bar, telling stories with Mr. Davis. I'm allowed to call him Mr. Garland, like Lila does.

Lila always sits me in the back on the pool table, which is covered up with a board and an oilcloth. Only the men get to play pool, and only on Saturday nights. Mr. Garland takes the board and stuff off and charges a fee per game. Then the table is covered over again. On Sundays and funerals, the church ladies put out a big buffet.

From my perch, I can see all the action and smell the smells. Delicious!

Mr. Garland brings me a Coke with a straw—another secret. *Cokes rot your teeth,* my father says, and brings out his demonstration—a piece of steak covered with Coke in a jar. The meat is blue and eaten away wherever the Coke touches it. *If that poison will do this to a piece of steak, think what it does to your teeth.*

Waste o' good food, Lila mutters.

My father is popular with all the maids. He jokes with them, and they tell me how he has set their broken bones and cured them of boils. Now that Lila's gramama is dead, he even births their babies. Lila's friends see me sitting up there and call out, "Here's Doc's little golden-headed prin-cess."

Lila buys a beer, digging into her apron pocket for change. Mr. Garland never charges her for my drink. Every time she takes a swallow of the beer, she makes a funny face, squinting her eyes and puckering her lips. "Nas-ty!"

"Why do you drink it?"

"Good for what ail me."

"What ails you? Lila—what ails you!"

Sly sideways smile.

After the beer, she chews some Teaberry gum. I hold out my hand and get a half a stick.

The women are swaying together in the middle of the floor, scarves tight around their slicked-back hair—slow dancing, the way they do with the men. Only most of the men are still off to the Army. The ones here are working in the daytime. They come in at night and on Saturdays. Then there's always fighting. Specially if the soldiers from Camp Pickett come to town. I wish I could come on a Saturday and see the fights.

Some fast, bopping music comes on now "Our jitterbug," Lila says, poking me with her elbow. "Lets us show 'em."

She whirls me onto the floor, holding my hands in hers, swinging my arms out and back to the beat. My head comes up to her bosoms. At home, when nobody's around, Lila and me and Eddie do this. Eddie and Lila are really good. But I have to talk it through under my breath. "Toe in, toe out, heel-swing-*left*, heel-swing-*right*. *Kick 'em!*"

"Ha ha ha, you and me! Little brown jug how I love thee! How I love theeee!"

"Show 'em, honey," Lila whispers. And swings me up on the pool table. "Shake it now, like we been teachin you."

Sudden silence. The jukebox song ends and the dancers are staring up at me. I can feel myself going red and a scream bubbling up. "Li-la!"

Lila flaps her hand. "Oh well. Show time another day."

"No sirree!" Dance, but not in his driver uniform, appears under the light bulb, which makes his pale, freckled face shine. "She up there—she gotta *go!*" He waves his guitar at me. "Missy and me *really* show y'all how to cut the rug."

Bobbing his big chest, he strikes a soft chord and beats a slow time with his foot. "Our song, Missy: *Hoppagrass settin' on the railroad track, pickin' his teeth with a carpet tack. Play all night and sing all day. What he go do on the judgment day?"*

Heel, toe, kick left, kick right, shimmy left, shimmy right. Fist in the air!

I'm on the tabletop dancing for the whole world. Maybe the dead will see me and come out at last.

Fist in the air! Switch to the left. Fist in the air! Switch to the right! Turn all around, and stamp your feet! Stamp your feet!

The crowd applauds and laughs. "Do it!"

I wish Eddie was here. He'd swing me right up in the air.

"You now." Dance hands me his guitar. "You play, I dance."

"Da-ance!" My triumph dries in my throat. "I ca-an't!"

"Sure you can." He puts the guitar strap around my neck and places my fingers on the strings. "You just got to git the chords. This is One. Strum with the other hand." I strum. "This here's Two." Moves my fingers. I strum. "And this here's Three." I strum again, almost remembering.

"One two three."

I play: One. Two. Three.

"Faster now." I go faster. "Now sing it."

"Hoppa-grass settin' on the railroad *track.*" Strum! "Pickin' his teeth with a carpet tack!" Strum. Dance nods and grins at me.

"That the way, now." He heaves his big barrel chest up and down, slowly, like a dancing bear.

"Sing all the day—night!" I croak. Oh Lord!

"Steady," Dance whispers. "Find the beat."

I strum on time. "Sing all the day."

Dance bobs himself around in a circle, his arms floating out and to the side in a beautiful slow-motion twirl.

"What he go do come judge-ment day!" *Strum!*

Dance stamps. Loud and slow and true.

"One more time, now, we 'most got it." Dance has his arms up ready to start. His loose overalls, hanging by suspenders, stand out from his skinny body. His hands are long and his fingers wave back and forth like the feathers on a bird's wings.

A flush goes through me. The world is watching! "I'm *doing* it."

"Over my dead body!" And Daddy is there in the light of the bulb, his face red and swollen, as if his bow-tie is choking him.

"Get off that table, Missy." To Lila, "You know better than to bring the child here. What were you thinking?"

Dance takes the guitar out of my hands and pulls the strap slowly over my head.

"Down, young lady." But I can't move.

Dance swings me off the table. "Mistah Doc, we aint—"

"Hush!"

"No harm done," Dance insists quietly. "Just *fun*."

"They were *laughing* at her. That's your fun, Robert." I can smell the familiar ethery hospital smell of him. And cigarette smoke. And bitter anger.

Lila draws me toward the door. Dance vanishes into the shadows. My father is slicing toward us and the crowd melts away in front him. Outside, the light is a knife blade in my eyes.

"Don't you cry," Lila whispers. "That make it worse."

"The child made a spectacle of herself. With a bunch of do-nothings laughing at her. Where's your dignity, Missy?" He's so mad, he says Dance's name for me.

Lila pulls me along backwards. I am still frozen.

"Be thankful I don't tell Miss Anne. And I won't as long as you promise me my daughter will never come here again."

Oh—don't promise. Lila, don't *promise*.

"Promise me, or Miss Anne will have to speak to you." My father's face is still red as a turkey wattle and his pink hair stands up on top of his head. His white shoes are dotted with dark spots—blood, from cutting people open.

Lila's hand tightens around mine. Say no. Say no! But how can she say no to *him*?

"Yessuh, Mistah Doc."

"*Yessuh* what?"

"I promise." Never come back to the Café. Never sing and dance again. I look to see if her fingers are crossed. But her hands are locked around one of mine, against her stomach.

He bores right into her. "Promise what?"

Lila sighs. "She aint go come here, Mistah Doc, not if I the one bringing her."

His face relaxes and the red fades to white.

"All right."

He's gone.

Lila keeps my hand as we walk up the hill. I've started to shake all over. "Don't cry, honey. Take a breath."

I breathe as deeply as I can. "Lila, what's a *spectacle?*"

"Some kinda eyeglasses, I reckon, where folks sees things ugly. You did good, honey. Your daddy just don't want you there, is all."

"Why?"

"He want you to play with some little white girls, you know. That Florence Lee."

"*Farrence*. She can't even say her own name. And snot runs out of her nose."

"She can't help that."

"I know. I'm sorry." I am, too. "But Lila, *were* they laughing?"

"Honey, they laugh to be sure. They laugh because you make 'em happy!" Lila laughs herself. "You some hot stuff!" She bounces herself like Dance and throws her hands up in the air. "Shootin' your little fists up and stompin' your feet. You coulda been stompin' a snake up there!"

This almost makes me happy again. But then I remember my father.

"I can't go back. Not ever. Can I?"

Lila shakes her head slowly. "We got to do our dancing in the kitchen, I reckon."

I will never dance on the big tabletop again and hear the crowd clapping.

"Oh Lila, I'll never get to see the dead come out and do the jitterbug—with their sheets all around them. *Why* did you promise? We could of gone back if you hadn't *promised*."

No answer.

"He said you'd have to talk to Mother. You talk to Mother all the time."

She sighs. "*Talk to*, honey, don't mean talk to, like you do all the time." She sighs again. "This *talk to* mean maybe your mama have to say she don't want me with you anymore."

What? How could Lila not be with me? Lila *is* with me. Even in my dreamland, where she and I have a house together and we are never apart.

"You promised her. When I was born, when I was just a fish, you gave your solemn word you'd be with me forever!"

"And have I break my word? Have I? But some folks forget. Hoppagrass promises."

"*I'm* the hoppagrass. And I want to dance in the Café."

But it's no use. Lila has promised.

"Did somebody tell on us?" Haddy told on us. Bet you anything.

We walk on home without saying another word.

6

1980

WAKE UP! STAWM GOT US!

Crash! goes the thunder. The walls of Lila's little house shake and chatter, the wind whines and howls like a banshee. Now the rain rattles and drums on the tin roof and blows in through drenched and billowing curtains.

"Lila?" Her cot is empty, covers flung back. Is she under the bed? She used to go under the bed whenever there was a monster storm, but her old knees won't let her now. And she makes me take her big bed. I gave in on that finally because the argument was distressing her.

I run to the window and, in a blast of cold and wet, slam it shut, snap down the shade.

When I was little, her terror of storms rubbed off on me, and I'd shiver myself down under the quilt—then slither, thump, under the bed. Just like Lila.

One stormy night at home, Mother forced me out of my hiding place and into the back yard. Lightning, spiked with ozone, danced about our ears. *"Look up! Willis, Open your eyes! Look up!"*

My eyes were full of rain. The sky exploded and my whole body quivered. What was she *doing*? I just wanted to die and be done with it. Water plastered her nightgown to her flesh, and under it, her huge dark nipples were like eyes, blind, under ice. Her arms were raised like a witch calling down demons. Sizzle zap!

"Lila?" In the dining room, a little oil lamp is gleaming. She has unplugged everything, she always does. Closes all the doors and blinds. She's sitting at the table in her flannel nightgown, eyes shut, hands folded in her lap. Clutching—a *pistol?* "Lila, what on earth are you doing with that thing?"

"Bad folks, honey. *Baa-ad* folks come in the storm when you can't hear 'em."

"Oh Lila!" I look around to assess stealability. Her house is a cock-eyed museum. Everything from somewhere else, some other lives. Things from our house and Grandmother's and people I don't know. Left behind and rescued by Lila. She collects abandoned things, things with other people's bad memories trapped in them.

I suddenly hear, in Lila's voice, which often lives in my head: *Anybody steal these, goin' home with a ghost!* The thought makes me laugh aloud.

Here's something of mine. A glass horse Daddy gave me just before we moved away. Thick and sturdy as the Trojan horse in *Bulfinch's Mythology*. Light plays through him like magic. And Daddy told me something else magic that day: glass is a liquid, flowing forever. You can't see it, it's slow. But it happens—the epitome of transformation. I remember trying to tell Lila, but she laughed. *Honey, hush! Take a million years to do that. Ever see a busted glass grow back together?*

But she'd saved him.

Actually, I left him deliberately. Mother said Lila had been *let go.* And though no one said so, it was *my* fault—I loved her so much and Mother hated that. So I had to sacrifice something, to make up.

Her collection is not complete, though. There's nothing of

Eddie here. His room is the way he left it and on her dresser she has a picture of him, solemn and handsome in his big-brimmed Army hat. But there are no little presents he gave her, things he made for her in school. I remember a paper napkin holder with a dowel that let you pull out just one.

She has her eyes closed. Then as a thunder roll fades away, she gets up from the table and fetches a box out of the corner cupboard. It's covered in velvet and shaped like an Irish harp, little mirrors twinkling between braided strings. She opens the clasp on the front and turns it so I can see. Stuck in the frame with some military pins are little photo-booth strips. A hand-some young man—Ed, staring at the camera. A beautiful porcelain-faced Asian woman is sitting on his lap. When I look closely, I see not a hint of the boy I remember. The boy with bitten nails. The skinny boy fast dancing with Lila and me in the kitchen. Later, he taught me to play mumbley-peg with his little pocket knife. I was never any good at it.

Here he is, a stern-faced *man,* cradling a woman. There are several of these pictures, a different pale China doll in each one. All their faces are still, composed, no young couple flushed with new love. Realists who've struck a bargain, presumably satisfactory to both.

What do I feel? The man, the women, all foreign, exotic. I wanted to see Ed, I wanted to see the boy I was so jealous of, whom I loved and admired even as I envied him. Lila has given me the man. The life that was and is completely closed to me.

I get up and light the burner under the pot on the stove. "I'm just going to turn on the gas—no electricity." If I plugged in even one small light, she'd have a fit. *Callin' the fiyah down on us!* The blue flames under the kettle flicker and there's a faint tinge of propane in the air. The indestructible perfumes of this little house—kerosene, propane, Clorox. Chantilly body powder. Fatback.

When I get back to the table, the Irish harp box is gone. And the storm has returned. With each crash, her knuckles on the pistol get tighter. "Lila, what are you so scared of?"

"Sugar Bottom bad boys!" Sudden harsh whisper. "From Jersey. The folks—Liz-bet and the rest—went Nawth, lookin' for the high life. Night clubs, dance halls! Hunh!" She snorts. "Now they crawlin' home, and chil'ren used to runnin' the streets up there. Go wild. Knockin' on doors, bustin' windows. *Trash!*"

"Preying on old their old aunts and uncles?"

"Too chicken to go after the whites. Dope fiends," she goes on. "Steal you blind you don't lock up everything."

I slip a cup of coffee, sugared to death as usual, under her nose. She opens her eyes. With her free hand, she pours a little coffee from cup to saucer to cool it. She used to do that with old dog Rumpy. Gave him his morning coffee in a cup, putting in condensed milk. She pours the cold coffee back in her cup.

There's that sneaking finger, again, rubbing the spot on her chest.

"Put you out to die," she says suddenly. Chillus—left out like an Eskimo for the bears.

"Nobody's going to put you out to die." I start to say, *I promise*. But that smells of my parents' lies.

"Lawyers. Comet-Ts." Her voice is high and tense. "Liz-bet and them try do that to Haddy." A kind of terror is in her that I haven't seen since the afternoon Daddy caught us dancing in the café. These are the true nite-crawlers of her soul. "Sheriff brother, the one work for Leggett's, come to put in my hot water heater and left with a pair of your mama's old silver candlesticks."

The sheriff let his brother do things like that? "Did you tell anybody?"

Snort.

Would she really shoot a person?

After Mother died, I lived alone with Daddy out in the country until he remarried. He was always on call. A neighbor, an old crippled veteran from World War II, taught me about guns. "If you need to shoot," he told me, "shoot to kill. And be sure you drag the body into the house. If he's too heavy, you call me, I'll come drag 'im in."

If Lila shot an intruder, a white intruder, it wouldn't matter where she dragged him. Or what he'd done to her. They'd kill her.

The soup and corn pones left over from supper are hot now. Rich peppery Brunswick Stew is best on the second or third day, but the pones get hard. She puts her pistol on the table, covers it with a napkin. Breaks her pone and puts it in her soup bowl.

She cooks all the old dishes when I'm here. I no longer say not to bother, that I'd be happy with anything, because this Memory Food is one of her ways of communicating. Exactly what, I don't always understand, but words, even Lila's, aren't nearly as rich and subtle as a prime sauce.

The wind drops for an instant again and new sounds start up. Rustling and knocking. Hell, she's got me doing it—listening for the enemy. What did I call them when I was a child—the boogey-men who make the dark a terror? It was a game Ed invented. He used to scare me silly, jumping out of shadows. "The Zombies are going to get us," I say now, and laugh too loud. Lila doesn't laugh.

Plink plink, rain drops ringing on the roof. Each one makes me jump.

The wind dies and Lila straightens up, calmly slurps warmth and spices from her spoon.

I'm the one holding the bundle of fears.

She chews and suddenly snorts again. "Old days, *nothin'*

scare me, honey! Old Li-lu-lie twist the devil by the tail!"
Laughs. "Got my North Ca'lina pistol! Ha!"

"You've had that pistol that long?"

"Honey, North Ca'lina pistol is what we have back then—
our folks not allowed to have guns—a foldin' razor! We call it
our North Ca'lina pistol. Kept it right here." Pats her bosom.
"Naw. I won't scared. Your mama and your daddy look after me.
Didn't have to worry about a thing. Nobody mess with me, or
they'd of sic'd the law on 'em."

"That's—" I start to say, *that's a lie.* Lila's own husband sliced
her to ribbons. Probably with her own North Ca'lina pistol.
And Daddy and Mother did nothing. Well, Daddy sewed her
up and saved her life. But nobody put the man in jail or
punished him in any way.

This is the kind of talk that gives "whitewashing" a whole
new meaning.

I always felt, in my deepest heart, that Lila abandoned me. But
the actual facts are that my parents simply went on with their
lives, and left her. *We'll take care of you, Lila,* and then they forgot.
Or never meant it to begin with. When I think of it, I curdle inside.

"Your mama have to start a new life," she says now, reading
my mind, as usual.

"What new life?"

"She make sure I got the so-sa se-cur-ity. Long time ago
when it start up." Lila shuts her eyes again.

Long silence. Then, like a fist, the wind thumps the roof
again and thunder rolls from wall to wall. The damn storm has
circled us. We both jump out of our skins.

Rain rattles. Wind picks at the door. Lila reaches for the gun
and once more holds it in her lap. She hasn't told me where she
got it or when. And she won't.

"Your mama had to get him back." Her voice cuts through
the storm.

"Who. Get *who* back?" But I know who.

"When she come from the Beach that time, after she took you and run off, he didn't want her. He say to me, 'Lila, I got my child back, and with your help, we can raise her.' "

Virginia Beach. Mother took me there and I ran away from her. Mother always drank, but at the Beach, she was out of her head all the time. I found my way back home, and I was punished to a fare-thee-well too. But—my father, plotting to take me away from Mother? This was new.

"I tell him, 'Miss Anne been good to me, I can't be part of taking her baby from her.' "

Sometimes Lila talks in parables with roots you have to dig out. But at times like this, she states the bald truth and it peels the skin right off.

I'm suddenly remembering a whole chunk of my life. I remember the first time Mother blamed me for her suffering when I was born. I remember her other machinations—I was by no means the sole victim. She exerted no effort to make people glad to be around her. Or even to stop drinking one single night.

"Mother cut all my hair off, that time we were away. To get back at Daddy."

She shakes her head. "Don't do to talk down the mama." Her eyes are suddenly open and dark. Blue shadows over her cheeks in the dim lamplight. "Don't nobody badmouth their mama to *me*." And it's true. I know she didn't get along with her own mother, but she has never breathed a word against her.

"I wasn't," I said. Only in my heart I was, and Lila knows my heart. "I just now saw that she did things to me to hurt him." And to hurt me for loving Lila more than I loved her. Somebody, somewhere, needed to belong to Mother. Today I understand that kind of emptiness.

"Your mama say to me, 'Lila, what you want most in the world?' "

Lord. Here's what I want to know. Lila's wishes. And something is coming. Another turn, a new twist of the blade in old wounds.

"I say to her, *'I want me my own house.'* I just rent this here place then, you know, when Eddie was a baby. Well, she say, *'If you help me get him back and we can be a fam'ly like before, I'll buy you this house with my own money.'* And she did."

"She bought this house?"

"So I work on the problem. I talk to your Daddy. He the one I fault the most anyhow. He did bad by her, and she won't strong. She already been divorced once, she couldn't go through that again. I didn't say none of that to *him*, though. I talked to him about you, and how you have to have both of 'em. And at the end, they got back together and she buy me this house like she promise." The general on the battlefield. "She say, *'You hang on to this place. Don't you ever sign nothin'. This is your se-cur-ity.'*"

Her finger is back at her chest, pressing, pushing the pain back inside. "I work for other folks, fancy cooking. I do pretty good. And I was a home-nurse. Your daddy taught me. Used to say to me, *'Lila, this Miz So-and-So, got the cancer of the breast. I know you can help her.'* And I do it. One of 'em was that Miz Hutchens. I scrub her cancer with peroxide every day. She was well on the outside, but it got her on the inside."

Tears prickle my nose. "She bribed you, Lila. Mother bribed you." She could have had everything, with Daddy and me. I shut my eyes. What would my life have been like, my teen years with Lila? Without Mother and her illnesses. Her sorrows. The wrongs done her all her life by the people she loved. Daddy wrote me, years after Mother was dead, *"The Furies pursue me for the way I hurt your mother."*

Guess they gave him a pass on Lila.

They got him in the end though, the Furies. Thirteen years later, he was dead himself. They got Grandmother too—

lost in her own mind, dreaming about fires and burning babies.

Guilt. Guilt is what makes us Southerners different from animals.

"At your daddy's house, you don't rember this, but I never have a room to myself, no place to wash the dirt off. And your daddy won't about to let Eddie live in that house with you and me." Lila's voice is slow and sad. I can't say a thing. The biggest house on earth wouldn't have broken down my father's barriers.

So they left and Lila was in real poverty. She had the house, but no job. Eddie went into the Army then, to make a life. Send her a little money. Probably the only way he could.

The emptiness of those years overwhelms me suddenly. Not just for her, for me. Long days, frightening weekends. Sundays were the worst. Mother and Daddy hissing and drinking. And me—slipping away to climb trees and hide in the woods. New place, far from this town. Far from Grandmother, though that didn't bother me. And far *far* from Lila. And nobody noticed. Lila, her Precious Eddie a world away. He didn't live to come home again. Nobody noticed that either. Not even me.

Daddy's new wife hated Lila, whom she knew only as a person in stories that did not include her. She wouldn't let Lila visit. She didn't like me much better, and before long, I was out of the house too, at college. Then wandering. I never went back. We were stick figures, blown apart in the wind.

"Well, you chose right." You traded me for a house, I am thinking. But it *was* right.

"Where could your mama go, he kick 'er out and keep you and me? Her mama's? And do what? Creep around him and you, peepin' in the windows?"

God. I hadn't even thought of Mother. Something—a little slipstream of truth, of understanding—washes over me.

The rain slams. Wind screams. Thunder roars. The past is ripping me apart, with its new truths.

"Lila, what would make you safe, right now? For *you?*"

I don't have much, but I'm certainly more secure than she is. I have a job and what she calls my "piece of a house." What *I* want is the same as ever. Her. But I'm conscious enough now to want most of all for her to be happy. To feel safe and loved, wherever she wants to be.

"Oh, if I could buy your grandmother's farm—"

We could live there. Dance could be with her, with his pigs and chickens and his bad leg. His DEMOLITIONS. And I could come and go. Making money to support us, somehow, somewhere. But coming *home.*

"Storm dream, honey! What you go do with a falling down fah'm? It might feed a few folks, but it eat up more money than we could get out of it in a million years." Ah the general has returned. The Gazelle of Perfect Deflection.

Probably there isn't any real safety. And nothing anyone can do to heal old wounds.

"Sign me a papah." Her voice breaks into my thoughts.

"What?"

"A papah, honey, keep 'em from taking my house away from me."

The damn house.

My god! She means a real paper. A legal document.

"Something keep 'em from kicking me out if I git took." Took sick, she means. A medical power of attorney, she means!

I hear myself saying, "Well then, *okay!*" As if it were the simplest thing in the world.

Lila throws her head back, laughs aloud. She lifts her pistol one last time, and holding it in both hands, aims at the kitchen door. "Ka-pow," she whispers.

Then gets up and opens the door, as you would if you'd really shot a gun through it.

The wind has calmed and the smell of the rain, clean and rich, wafts in. Like a child's freshly washed hair, a tinge of animal, and soap.

Then the wind whips the house again, and shakes shakes shakes.

7

1947

LOST IN THE JUNGLE

I want to go away with Lila. I want to live with her in a new house. Just us. Not Eddie, not even Eddie's things. Eddie will disappear (he won't be hurt, though) and I'll have a new room, because even Eddie's *room* will disappear.

Our house—Lila's and mine—will be lot like her house now, but the two bedrooms will have a door that opens between them, two closets where our dresses and blouses hang, blue and yellow with flower patterns. No uniforms or boring white. Sweet-smelling from the pomander balls. We will have special cups and bowls and dishes, with flowers and gold on the edges, which I'll buy because Lila doesn't ever have any money. And special silver forks like Grandmother's, with birds on the handles.

In our house, we will be able to do all the things people always tell us we can't do. I'll cross my legs if I want to. Go off the property without asking. Go to the Café and stomp a snake. Lila can sit with me at the soda fountain in Leiter's Drugstore. Also she won't have to say yes ma'am, yes-suh to white people who are rude to her. We'll have a radio tuned to our favorites—gospels. Which Lila can sing whenever she wants, not have to keep her voice down and not disturb my mother. We can do the jitterbug all night long. I guess my parents will have to disappear, too.

I know better than to tell her this, of course. Those bits about Eddie and Mother disappearing? Trouble on a stick. But I *could* tell her about our garden. My favorite flowers are honeysuckles because you can drink the nectar. Hers are vincas, white vincas from a graveyard. Why a graveyard? She won't say. She will make a spell with them probably. Or keep someone from making a spell on us.

Lila's palms are pink with dark lines in them, dark creases in her finger joints. "What makes these?" I spread her hand out on the kitchen table and run my finger along them. Would the brown come off like melted chocolate if I scratched? "Where are *my* chocolate lines?"

The brown fingers close over her palm. "You don't need 'em."

"Why not? Why don't I need 'em?"

"You not lost in the jungle." Lila laughs and gets up from the table.

"Jungle! What jungle?"

She just laughs again.

"Li-la!"

"Well, look at you. Just go look in the mirror! You're no jungle bunny. Now enough of this foolishness. I got your mama's chicken to pluck."

In the pantry off the back porch hangs a little broken piece of mirror. Whenever Lila passes it on her way to empty a pan of water onto the garden or toss some crumbs to the chickens, she smooths her hair as if someone's waiting for her in the yard. Turns quickly and neatly from side to side to be sure no crinkles are escaping the stocking that holds her slicked-back bun. And every evening, after the last dish is dried and I'm bathed and in my nightgown, the very last thing before she leaves to go home—to Eddie—she gets a lipstick out of her purse and paints a bright red line on her mouth.

She doesn't look like a bunny either.

I drag a chair over and look at myself. Icky pale. Puny lump of a nose—almost no nose at all. Beige face, beige eyebrows, beige eyelashes. Only the top of my hair is gold and nice. The plaits are okay, but I like my hair better when Lila unwinds them and my hair falls in ripples.

Ugh. Those cooked-fish eyes.

Lila, now, is rich red in her face and other places. Like cinnamon. Delicious! And red-black hair that crinkles like a halo till she makes it straight and shiny with Vaseline. But she's got dull scaly brown on her legs. Her legs look as if she rubbed them with ashes, until she puts Vaseline on them too.

"Why do you grease your legs?"

"'Cause I got the scales from the rickets when I was little. My legs bent like willow twigs. Your mama told me drink milk and grease my legs with Vaseline so I do it."

I know what rickets are. Your bones bend because you didn't eat right when you were a baby. "Is rickets something jungle bunnies get? Lila, are jungle bunnies a name for country folks? Country folks don't always eat right, Daddy says, and they get sick."

Lila snorts.

Now Eddie. Eddie's skin, with no rubbing at all, is as dark and satiny as fudge. "Doo-doo," I whisper to him when no one is listening. I like Eddie's skin and wish mine looked just like it. But I say doo-doo to him anyhow.

The only things I like about my boring face are the freckles over my nose, cheeks, and eyelids. My mother hates them. When she remembers to notice she rubs my face with butter-milk and lemon juice to bleach them off. But it doesn't work.

I like them because I want to be—dream of being—brown like Lila, so I can live with her in our new house. Grandmother is always telling me that if you want something with all your heart and soul, and pray for it, you will get it. Well, I've wanted this *so* hard, it's making the brown pop out. Someday the brown will spread all over my face. I've been praying like sixty. My freckles are larger and darker every time I look.

You're not lost in the jungle.

But I could be. Well, not the jungle. That's far away in a book with pictures of giraffes and elephants and dearly beloveds. But I *could* go out and get lost in the yard.

That would be silly. But how about beyond the vegetable garden *beyond* the yard. Even beyonder. Through the garden gate, out into the Victory Garden, where all my mother's friends used to work during the war. *"Too bad we can't raise coffee and sugar,"* Mother used to say. *"And chocolate. Now that would be worth all the effort."*

Now I'm out the tall gate, so tall the deer can't jump over it into the gardens. Mother'd have a conniption if she could see me walking away. I'm never allowed this far by myself.

Am I scared? What about Zombies?

But Zombies only come out when the sun goes down. Lila says nothing can get me in the daylight and when other people are around to watch over me. "Honey, hants and stuff only get you if you been bad to 'em. They get you from the inside."

So—are there any dead people I've been bad to? I don't know any dead people. Both my grandfathers and Lila's gramama died before I was born. How could they be mad at me when they never even met me?

Across the fields, where the town ends, the high grasses stick up, with spicy rabbit tobacco. Lila smokes it. I sneak a puff too every now and then. It's nasty.

Now the dark lemony cedar trees close the path. When you get close, the path opens between them like a secret door. Little rustlings and squeakings, mice and things. Bigger rustlings mean rabbits. Or deer. I always think: "Zombies!"

Daddy says, *Stop that foolishness! It's only deer. You don't see them because they always smell you first and run away.* We must smell very bad to wild animals.

The creek—one hundred-percent forbidden. *You could drown in a teaspoon of water,* my mother says. *I don't care how good a swimmer you are.*

Daddy tut-tuts. He taught me to swim almost before I could walk. Threw me in the river and I had to dog paddle or I'd of drowned. Well, he says he'd have pulled me out before that but he was glad he didn't have to. Mother always has the knock-out punch. *The child will fall and break her head on a rock.* How could my father stand up to that? Me, dead in such an accident. Not even Lila could stand up to that.

The jungle would be dangerous. And noisy. The book has tigers roaring, with gleaming teeth, and snakes as big as my legs, wrapped around tree limbs. Ugh.

But at the creek, it's all cool and shadows. Silent. A hoppa-grass bends a weed stem. I reach out to touch him. He has googly eyes and he can see out the back, so he makes a clicking noise with his legs and pops away.

The damp of the stream bank soaks into my underpants. Oops.

The Zombies *could* get me now. I'm away from everyone. But they don't like sunlight.

"I don't know any dead people," I shout as loud as I can. I make the finger-cross Lila taught me to keep away hants.

Water purls and tinkles. It makes me want to pee. But where?

Twigs crackle.

The bark of the tree I lean against is rough and thick. Ants stream up and down the trunk, carrying things in their mouths. And my legs are hurting from hard old walnut shells, so hard you have to smash 'em with a hammer. Even squirrels can't crack 'em, they have to gnaw gnaw gnaw until they make a little hole.

I can pee in the bushes. Lila and I do it all the time. Mother would have a fit. *"You must wipe thoroughly every time you u-rin-ate."*

Above me are the young nuts, all wrapped in green with seams like baseballs. When you pick at them to get the nutmeat inside—don't eat it, you'll only throw up because they're not ripe—a sharp acid smell comes out. And your fingers burn and turn brown!

Brown?

Yes!

I open as many green nuts as I can using a rock and spread out the bits in a circle. It takes forever and my fingers have turned mahogany and burn like crazy. I mush the skins some more with the rock. And I rub the mush on my face. Down the nose. Cross the forehead. Down the cheeks. Chin, throat. Up under the eyes. That spot feels like fire.

In the creek water, where it's almost still, I can see a brown-skin face bobbing on the surface. White hoppagrass goggles round the eyes. It worked! My face is dark like Lila's.

Wait'll she sees me—toe in, toe out, shimmy to the *left*—

But. What will my father say? My fingers are cracked and streaked. The brown isn't rubbing off in the dirt. I remember now—the brown from walnuts doesn't rub off at all! Trou-ble.On.A.Stick.

Maybe they won't notice. Sometimes my parents go for weeks without looking at me. I'll tell them I was painting a clown face. That way they won't mind.

But in secret, I'll be like Lila, and we will live in our dream house.

. . .

"WHAT ON EARTH you done to yourse'f!" Lila cries, dropping a spoon. "That aint mud."

"Tell the child to wash," my mother calls from the living room. "She knows better than to track mud in the house."

Lila leans me up against the kitchen sink and scrubs at my face with a soapy dish towel. "Stop stop, my skin is coming off!" I hiss.

"What is this here? Ink?" She sniffs my mottled fingers. She has a nose as keen as a fox's. "Walnut juice." She groans.

Oh. Maybe this is not so great. "I was—I was playing clowns."

Lila shakes her head. She sees right into my heart. "Your mama have my hide, she see this. And you been down to the creek, to get walnuts." Sharp eyes still boring into me. But the corners of her mouth are twitching. "Walnut juice take a month to wear off!"

Over and over me goes the rough wet towel like a cow's tongue. Next, Clorox. The fumes sting my eyes and make me cough. Lila marches me over to the chair on the porch and lifts me up to look in the mirror. "You tell your mama I had *nothing* to do with this."

A stranger is staring back at me. Pale rings around reddened eyes. Streaky blotchy face. Not rich and brown the way it looked at the creek. Ugh. A sickly yellow, like the cigarette stains on my father's fingers.

"Go show her, now. And tell her what I say."

"If I don't go, maybe she won't notice." I hate it when I upset Mother. She cries and rolls her eyes up in her head and pretends to faint. And tells me that I am breaking her heart. If it was a real faint, I'd feel terrible. But it's a pretend. After the first time or two you can tell. When Grandmother faints she keels over and bumps her head. Sometimes she leaves a little puddle on the floor. But Mother always slides down a wall or tips over into a chair.

Lila gives me a gentle shove. "Get it over. Don't mention the creek if you can help it."

My mother is a skinny woman with a fat stomach and a shelf-bosom. She is wearing a green and white seersucker dress that hangs on her arms and bulges the giant pearl buttons across her middle. Reading in the living room, stretched out in her favorite lounger chair—its bottom swings up into a footrest—with the dog, Rumpelstiltskin, in her lap. Rumpy growls at me. "What?" Mother looks up. "I thought I told Lila to see that you washed."

In the bathroom, Mother scrubs. By now I have no skin left at all. And my whole face is raw. But in Mother's mirror it's the same sickly yellow color. That yellow must go down to bone. I feel like screaming with the pain, but Mother's mouth is drawn into an ugly line.

"Why?" she cries. "Just tell me that. Why *why?*"

"I was playing clowns."

She glares at me. "Clowns have white faces."

Without meaning to I start to sob. "I wanted to look like Lila. I wanted to—"

Mother's hand drops suddenly over my mouth and stops the words. Her fingers pinch. In the mirror her eyes are very bright.

Now my father is staring at me from the bathroom doorway.

"Did you hear that? This child has broken my heart." Mother starts to weep. Dramatic sobs, to show how much I have hurt her.

On the side porch my father opens his doctor bag and takes out several bottles of stinkums. "What were you thinking?"

"I was playing clowns." The lie hurts. It hurt—a little— when I told it to Mother. But it was the worst when I told it to Lila.

I'm being eaten up by Daddy's medicines. Each thing he puts on my face smells sharp and stings my raw skin, though he doesn't gouge at me the way Lila and Mother did. Between swipes, I open my eyes. He has the tip of his tongue stuck out in concentration. And his freckles are just like mine.

The hot-cold-hot of alcohol. I squinch my eyes shut. Now the sick sweet of ether, like the time I broke my leg. I keep my eyes shut, lips tight sealed against the nasties.

"I'm going to look just like the meat in the Co'cola," I whisper.

My father sighs. Sometimes he says, *You are not very popular with me.* He said that the night after he made me and Lila promise not to go to the Café again. Now he only sighs again and says, "What'd you use? Not food coloring. Pecan rinds?"

We have a pecan tree in the back and I should have remembered that the rinds turn your fingers yellow. I nod. And cross my fingers. This lie is for Lila, so she won't get into trouble because I went to the creek where the walnuts grow.

"These shenanigans have really upset your mother."

"I know. I wasn't *thinking*."

He says, "Hmmph."

Finally, when I can't help sobbing, he gives up and takes me back into the kitchen. Lila is putting little white stockings on the roasted chicken legs.

"Do you understand all this?" Daddy asks her.

Again the corners of her mouth twitch. She knows I haven't told that I went to the creek. "Just chil'ren's foolishness, I 'speck."

After he's gone she laughs outright, but noiselessly. "You a mess," she whispers to me. "A *mess!*"

Well, a mess is good. A mess, for Lila, is somebody tough, somebody you can't beat down. Folks you admire even when you're mad at them.

She reaches into her purse where she keeps the evening lipstick and takes out a box of powder. The oval lid has a picture of a woman with an almost bare bosom, a mountain of white curls, and a black spot on her cheek. My mother has the same box.

Lila stands me once more on the chair by the mirror. I squinch my eyes shut. I never want to look in a mirror again. Ever. But I peek. In the evening light, my sore skin glows purple and red where Mother and Lila and Daddy have all scrubbed it to death.

Lila begins to dab on powder. It's cool and it's pale, like Mother's powder. "Why isn't this brown like you?"

She dabs a bit on her nose and it makes a for-real clown spot. She sticks out her tongue. After a minute, she has covered over most of the scuffs on my face and paled the yellow. She tilts her head to one side to inspect me. Nods. I will do. "You go say 'Sorry' to your mama, now. Then come back eat some dinner with me."

"Mother hates me."

"She loves you, honey. You her heartstrings, I told you."

"Maybe when I was a new little baby." My voice squeaks and my hateful throat lump is growing.

Lila considers me. In her eyes I can see that she knows what I'm feeling. "Well, eat first then. Let things settle."

She sits me like a baby in the little breakfast nook in the kitchen. Then goes to serve my parents. They have to eat chicken and gravy. She gives *me* a honey biscuit and a cup of warm milk with a pinch of chocolate in it. "This little pinch got to last us till Mr. Perk get in some more." She looks around to be sure no one is watching us. Then sits across from me and eats the chicken feet—ugh—they're all pebbly and dead. She sucks the toes and lines up the little bones on the edge of her plate. Then she pops the pope's nose in her mouth and winks at me. I hear the juicy fat squish against the chicken's little tail bones. Double—*triple*—ugh. Now she gets up quickly, goes out and comes back with my parents' dirty plates.

I lie on the bench, my head on a little pillow. Nibbling the biscuit. Warm milk is so delicious. Makes my eyes shut and my mind swirl.

Rattle go the dishes in the sink. Bang goes the ice-box door. Lila hums softly to the gospel station on the radio, turned so low you can't hardly hear it. She sings lead alto in her choir and likes to practice whenever she can.

After the dishes are done, she bathes me in the bathroom off my bedroom, careful to keep water away from my face. When I am in my nightgown, she touches up the powder again, tilting my head to get it just right.

"Do what you got to do, now. Remember your mama's sick. It's hard, being sick. So just go say you sorry."

I creep to my parents' door. Daddy went out after supper. I heard his car start up. Mother is by herself.

"Mother." No answer. "Goodnight, Mother." I haven't decided for sure that I will say "Sorry."

Lila, in the kitchen doorway, makes shooing motions with her hands. "In," she mouths. "Go *in*."

I turn the knob and go in. Sure enough my father's bed is empty. Mother is lying on her matching bed, a damp cloth over her eyes. Rumpy is sleeping beside her. He doesn't growl this time, but cocks his ears and stares. Mother's breathing is the breathing of crying, not sleep. And a sour smell is in the room.

"Mother."

"Yes."

"Goodnight." Usually I kiss her cheek and she hugs me.

"Goodnight."

"I'm sorry." Is feeling bad the same as sorry?

Silence. I creep out. Lila nods, satisfied.

"Listen, honey," she whispers, when we are back in the kitchen. "Listen good. Black peoples and white peoples is not the same. Nothing you do can change that."

"But I went to the jungle. I wished and prayed for something with all my heart and soul."

75

She shakes her head. "Some things *nothing* can change. Not even a mountain of prayer."

Tears are hot and salty on the back of my tongue. My dream house is crumbling away. And it's not because of Precious Eddie this time.

"Long time ago one of the black folks way off in Africa there got lost in the jungle. Went to a part where he have no bidness. So many little paths runnin' through the bushes, where the animals make their roads. Can't find his way home. And he git scared, dark coming and everything. So he start to cry: *'Lawd. Oh Lawd, I so lost, help me, Lawd!'*"

Lila's voice goes up to a squeak, to make the scared talk. She's sponging off my face, gently, wiping away the face powder, dabbing it dry.

"So the Lawd look down and say, *'What you doing in there? This here the animal place. Dangerous for you. Didn't I tell you to stay to your own? The black folks got a place, the white folks got a place, the animals got a place. You aint listen to me. Looka here.'* And the Lawd taken the man's hand in his big one," Lila opens my palm flat. " *'This here is your way home. This here your life road. I go fix it so you won't forget it again.'* And he bear down with his finger on the man's palm like so." Lila's finger scratches, hard, across the lines in my hand. For a minute, I hold my breath hoping a black line will pop up.

"The Lawd got a hot heavy hand, child, believe it. And he mad too, so his hand just shoots out the heat. He make the life road in the man's palm, and where he traced was *burnt.*" She opens her own palm and points to the lines. "That charcoal mark stay so we can always find our way." She hands me another cup of warm milk. "Drink up, honey, so you can go to dream land."

"White people don't have a map," I say. "We'll get lost."

She laughs. "Well, honey, that's the breaks."

She stands up from the table. Her knees pop. She gets ready

to go, putting on her line of red lipstick. In a minute she'll take me to my room and put me to bed.

Dream-land. I want to go to my dream *house*, the house with Lila. But instead I'll be stuck here with my mother. I will lie in bed and listen to her. She'll make noises like crying but not crying. And wander around the living room. She'll open my door. A bar of light will shoot in and I'll squeeze my eyes shut, so she'll think I'm asleep. Sometimes she comes all the way in. Sometimes she just stands in the door. Sometimes I fall asleep waiting for her to close the door and go away.

"Don't go, Lila." I want to tell her I'm scared, but I can't.

She sighs. "This here where we got to have our two different roads, honey. I got to go home now, feed Eddie. And you got to go into your bed and sleep."

"I want to go with you. With you and Eddie. So I won't be lost." Even Eddie. Let me be with Lila, God, and I'll never be mean about Eddie again.

Lila leads me into my room. Rubs Baby Oil on my face, using just the tips of her fingers. My angel-shell night light, the one Daddy brought me from Florida, is making a soft glow. She winds up my music box, "Heigh-ho!" from *Snow White*. Before I know it, I am under the covers. "Sleep tight."

For a second I cling to her hand. Lost in the jungle —

"Tomorrow," Lila says, smoothing my head. "Tomorrow, everything be back to normal. Wait and see."

It won't, but you can't say anything to grown-ups when you feel like this. Not even Lila.

The light becomes a golden crack, smaller, smaller. Black darkness. "Night, Miss Anne." Back door shutting. Creak of the porch step.

She's gone.

And I'm here. In the place where I have to belong.

8

1980

NORTH CA'LINA CHILD

"This is a simple document, really." Lawyer Perkinson pushes a typed page across his desk. He too grew up here, a few years ahead of me in school. "I'm disappointed you don't remember me," he says. "Your father was one of my ideals."

He and his wife, who died in the automobile accident, bought our little house not long ago. As a lawyer he's welcome in the neighborhood. But in the old days, the grocer's son wasn't "our kind," as Grandmother used to say. She said that about most people and I didn't think anything about it. But I was kept away from working people and country people. And black people, except those who worked for us. In school I used to try to make friends with girls from the farms. They weren't as snotty as the townies. But they rebuffed me time and again. People down here "know their place." And the idea of whites and blacks being friends? I'd never have met Lila if she hadn't worked for my mother.

I look down at this *simple* document. What on earth is simple about Power of Attorney? The very sound and the weight of those words—

"This'll do it, honey!" Lila murmurs. "No nursin' home for me, no ma'am. Liz-beth and all say to Haddy—their own mother who looked after 'em, fed 'em, changed their didies—they go send her away if she get sick. *'For your own good!'* For them to get her house, is what!"

A house, a house. My kingdom for a house.

"So I say to her, *'Haddy, who go get that good?'* But Haddy fool 'em!"

And so she did. Haddy died before any of it could happen. Liz-beth, that is to say Hard Rock, and her siblings are still squabbling over the pots and pans and matching bedroom sets. At the very mention of her sister and brother, Hard cries, *"Hawgs and weasels!"*

When my high-class grandmother died, my family did exactly the same thing. The language was more refined, but the greed was just as crude.

What on earth will Hard call me when she finds out about this paper? What will all of Sugar Bottom think of me?

"This doesn't mean a thing right now," Perkinson is saying. "Can't go into effect until or unless Lila is incapacitated. You'll be called if she gets ill or injured, but as long as she seems clear in her mind, she'll make her own decisions."

Does Lawyer Perkinson have any idea who he's dealing with?

A faded man. Soft around the middle, soft under the chin. His wife's death has made long furrows down his cheeks, funnels for tears to flow. Or maybe he always had those. Rumor has it he's seeing another woman, an out-of-towner—a Yankee even. That he knew this woman before the accident. Of course they said the same thing about my father and his second wife, and when he died they said she'd killed him. Rumor is a living breathing ogre in this place. I've never come across anything quite like it anywhere else, and I'm not sure I understand its place in the lives of people here. Fairytales! Creating impossible enemies and sometimes heroes. But always some kind of twisted message at the heart.

"I had a Lila when I was growing up. My Bessie." Perkinson nods at me now. "I know how responsible you feel."

Everybody white in this town says to me, *Oh we know how you feel about your Lila!* It's what lets them tolerate me. And if they didn't, I'd be a problem and they don't want a problem. They'd make Lila pay in some way. Interesting how no lawyer in town except Perkinson would draw up this paper. And interesting that he would do it. Maybe because of "his" Bessie.

"I think about my Bessie a lot," he says. "After my wife was killed, Bessie offered to come and look after my little girl. My little girl has a brain shunt to drain fluid out of her head. From the accident."

His face gets whiter and the furrows deepen. The newspapers said the baby was in the back seat, in a baby restraint. Or she'd be dead instead of injured.

"When she's grown up a bit, she'll be fine. I have a nurse 24 hours a day."

Not Bessie? Bessie wasn't "nurse" enough?

Suddenly I feel like weeping. That baby needs Bessie, not some 24-hour rotation of nurses.

Dear God. What if something happens to Lila? What will I do? She'd have to stay with me or I'd have to hire someone to look after her here. What would *she* want? And how would I pay for any of it? I live on next to nothing. Free-lance editing—no fortune there. Seems I inherited my parents' monetary fecklessness, if nothing else.

Perkinson is looking across the desk at me. I must have said something out loud. Lila's face is closed. Purse clutched to belly.

"She has your old room. My wife loved that little house. We fixed her room up with antiques."

Oh, this whole house thing.

"You should come to see us. You'd like what we've done."

Why do people think you'll like the changes they've made to your memories?

I lean over to sign the paper. Medical Power of Attorney. So that Lila can be like Lawyer Perkinson's baby daughter—taken care of. Never have to go to a nursing home.

God help me keep my promises.

Lila reaches for the copy Perkinson hands her. She smiles at it as if it were a living thing. Tucks it into her bosom where she used to keep her North Ca'lina pistol.

Perkinson laughs. I laugh. Lila laughs.

And then she sighs, a sound so long and deep, it's as if she has been holding her breath her whole life. That sound, that long sound, makes me completely glad I've done whatever it is I've done. And I vow inside that I'll figure how to make it work when the time comes.

Walking to the car she tosses her head. Pats her dress front. "North Ca'lina papah!" And reaches for my hand. Hers is warm and firm.

In the car my hand tingles still. Lila doesn't touch me much. I hug her when I arrive, I kiss the soft fuzz on her cheek, aware of every nuance of her skin, her smell. Another hug, which she endures, when I leave. Closing my eyes and breathing deep to take in her scent, the way I did when I was small.

"Let's go somewhere to celebrate. This is a big moment."

But where? Leiter's Drug Store that has such a good soda fountain? She still wouldn't be allowed to sit with me there, the law be damned. We'd be frozen out. The old Davis café where black and white can sit down together? I really just want to go to her house.

She points me down the rutty street to Sugar Bottom. Waves me past the turn to her house and on to the back streets. "Want you to see somebody," she says. "You rembers Bessie."

"Mr. Perkinson's Bessie?"

Lila snorts. "Bessie's Bessie. Uncle Chillus cousin, on his first wife side."

"Who left him out to die?"

"Lawd no! More to that story, honey, than you been told! Bessie used to cook for the other Miz Roberts, you rember her."

Grandmother's sister-in-law, also named Bessie. Lived across from the elementary school, large white house with cool green awnings. Creaky metal swing on the porch.

White Bessie and Black Bessie. But I never knew that Black Bessie was Lila's cousin. Or that she'd ever looked after Mr. Perkinson.

We pull up to a little neat house with a picket fence around the front. Bessie greets us on the porch, holds my hands between her cool ones for a long minute. Then I sit in the freshly painted white metal chair. Bessie and Lila sit side by side in the swing. Creaky-creak they go, in their circumscribed arc. Lila eases her lumpy toes out of her ever-too-tight shoes. Sips the offered lemonade.

"I made some of your favorites, Miss Willis." Bessie smiles at me and passes me a huge plate of cookies. Gingersnaps! It's a set-up! I try to catch Lila's eye. Why did she tell Bessie? I never knew they were special friends. Lila is scrutinizing a crack in the porch ceiling.

Bessie is not a bit like Lila. Pale, a smooth tan color with a sprinkling of small pinkish freckles over her cheeks and chin, even her eyelids. I can hear Daddy saying to Mother, "Old Gus Ferguson, can't you just see him every time you look at her face?" Mr. Ferguson was a white man. "Look at those freckles," he'd say, "that long expanse between her cheek-bones and jaw." He'd measure that section on his own face, and hold out his fingers, as if Bessie had been painted by old Mr. Ferguson, rather than sired. Measured out and put into a picture.

"Your daddy," Bessie says, shaking her head and closing her

eyes as if even now, ten years later, she can't believe he's dead. "Your daddy save me. He save my boy too."

Again I glance toward Lila—whose eyes are now shut.

Creaky-creak goes the swing. The wind sighs.

"Well, I been paining for a whole day with the birth, uhm-hmnh!" Bessie spreads her hands across her belly as if she feels the pangs right now. "And Harriet, Lila's gramama, the midwife down here, you know." I nod politely. "She call your daddy and he come, taken me to Farmville to cut my boy out of me. Say to me, '*Bessie,*'" Bessie's voice goes high in imitation of my father's light tones, "'*Bessie, you in a peck of trouble here. But you got your papa's bulldog heart to see you through.*'"

Old Ferguson's secret heart.

"And he wouldn't let me go. Would-not-let-me-go. Set by me and held my hand. '*You hold on, Bessie, we get this baby in the world.*' I come to in the hospital bed, he settin' there still, holdin' my hand." Bessie nods and falls silent.

I realize I'm holding my breath. My heart is sinking. Please, God, let there be a good ending.

"'*Bessie, your boy have a problem.*'" The voice is so sudden—and so Daddy—that I flinch.

"'*Got a problem with his skin,*'" Bessie goes on, still in Daddy's voice. "'*Could be a simple problem, could be not so simple, we won't know for a while.*'"

Oh, that is so like him too. Giving the good and the bad in one double-whammy. And what do you hear? Some of us hear just one thing. The good or the bad. The optimist and the pessimist go into a bar—the old joke.

"Well, I reckon I start to holler and cry, because he tighten up his grip. '*Hush up, Bessie,*' he say sharp, like he do, you know, when he mean what he say to the dot. '*You pray for a livin' boy and you got one. And you can't have any other. So just recollect when you hold him—he is one of a kind.*'" Bessie rocks the creaking swing. She and Lila nod in unison.

"One-of-a-kind. And he was."

Creak-creak. Creak-creak.

I know I have been hit by a high-speed bullet, I just don't feel it yet.

Bessie is smiling. Lila's off into the blue.

The perfect child, the one and only. Lawyer Perkinson's baby. Me. Precious Eddie. Now another. Eddie went into the Army, was sent to Korea and got shot in the kidney. And died. The rest of us are—marred. Mr. Perkinson's baby is hurt and will suffer throughout her life. I guess you could say I'm marred, too. Unfit for life in this world. All of us one and onlies.

Oh! Dear lord—Bessie's son is dead! I sit up suddenly, unable to speak. Sometimes, the very awfulness of life sneaks up and knocks the breath right out of you.

"We come by Mr. Perkinson office," Lila says. "Willis sign me the paper." Pats her bosom.

"Aint that beautiful," Bessie murmurs. "How he doing?"

"Fine," Lila says. "He look just fine. And the baby coming along, he tell us, didn't he, Willis? He mention you."

Bessie looks down. Her silvery crinkly hair is lit by the late light, like a halo. And her face has gone still. I see Perkinson suddenly as a boy on her lap, lolling his long thin head against her pillowy bosom. A child face marred with sorrow lines. Merging with a baby with a stent in her head and another baby who had a maybe little problem, maybe a big problem.

The minute we are in the car—"Snake baby," Lila hisses, before I can get the question out. "Bessie's baby covered all over with scales *exactly* like a snake!"

"My god! What happened to him?"

"Baby Oil! Bessie and me rub that child with Baby Oil five times a day. He got better. Wont ever right, though. Skin tight like plastic. Live to be 32 years old. He stay home with her, never marry. And he have a good job, construction—work for that construction man who pay even our folks a good wage. So she buy her house, have a little savings."

Ah! The perfect child. But dead at 32. Dead of what—I can't bear to know.

On the way back to Lila's, I circle the block, driving slowly, looking at the houses. Lila says nothing, though she must wonder what I'm doing. Or maybe she knows.

What I'm doing is, I'm absorbing what I can of the people who live here. Her people. If we were uptown, I wouldn't need to—I know white life, even if I don't know the people, even if they're rich, poor, religious, awful. I know most of the possibilities.

Here in Sugar Bottom, I don't know the life. Or only a little corner of it, the corner Lila has shown me. "Who lives there?" I ask, passing a house a block from Bessie and a block the other way from Lila.

"That Stickpin and his wife Nettie. He work up at the Ford place."

"What does he do?" Expecting her to say "mechanic."

"He clean out the cars. They got a carwash around back, he do that."

So we go from house to house, all down her street, past the man who has the barber shop, the couple who "do for" old Miz Hutchins up town. Past the woman who cleans Dr. Brackson's clinic, another who does "fine laundry."

"What is fine laundry?"

"Delicate lady things, you know, lace and all, needing sunbleaching and a cool iron. Silk and like that."

"No men's things then."

She laughed. "Honey, you be surprise what men get up to."

Next is a street sweeper who also cleans chimneys and his cousin drives a semi. All the women cook, sew, and clean "Uptown."

All the yards on this street are clean and tidy, even if the house has peeling paint. This is Sugar Bottom's "Uptown."

And no doubt, they all know about our "papah." I'm feeling cranky. But it's a North Ca'lina papah. A protection. And if it's going to work, everybody in town really has to know about it. Even if they don't like it, it will exist, a sword and a shield. *Maybe.*

Finally we are at Lila's and I pull in back where I always park my car. She gets out—hesitates—sighs the way she did in Perkinson's office. Long, long sigh. Shuts her eyes. "Thank you, sugah," she says again. And softly, "And thank you too, Sweet Jesus."

❧

AT NIGHT, in bed, I hear her murmur, "Um, umph," as she's rubbing her legs with Baby Oil—the great cure-all, next to Vaseline. The combo plus Absorbine Jr is working on her arthritis now. It was once for her rickets. Sometimes she lets me massage it into her back and shoulders when the pain gets really bad. The ghost smell of it penetrates me. And the babies —the onlies—march through my head. Myself, Precious Eddie, Bessie's scaly baby. The hurt Perkinson child. All of us rubbed and polished to a glow.

"Bessie couldn't have any more chil'ren, just that one, and he die before her." Lila's voice comes in the dark. I know she has her paper under her pillow. "Your daddy took her womb, said he had to. Took mine, too, that time I got cut so bad." Eddie's daddy cut her. *Sliced her to ribbons,* my father said. But did he *have* to castrate these two women? Without giving them a choice? Medicine—the Holocaust of America, then and now. Blankets to the Indians salted with small pox. Tuskegee syphilis. An Austrian friend once said to me, "Our parents did

86

things *we* would not dream of today." And I was shocked into a kind of recognition.

God, I hope we won't do such evil. But people did. People do. And we're people. Makes me wish I were a dog. Any animal whose loves and battles seem so much simpler.

"Bessie all alone now. Sick too. She won't say so."

Not like Lila—Lila who also had only one child from her body, yet who now has a paper, gets taken to the doctor and looked after. Lila won't end up like Bessie. Or Haddy. Or Chillus. I have promised, I have signed my name on this paper, Lila's Black Hen's Egg of love and belonging, which promises she won't be forgotten.

Lila has orchestrated this. And thank God for it. It's brilliant. With all my love, I would never have thought of it.

Bessie's last sad look hangs in my mind. "Lila, what about Perkinson, does he give Bessie anything? Does Bessie Roberts's family give her anything?"

"Perk-upses?" She snorts in the darkness. "Climbers! His mama move to Florida, and nobody so much as give Bessie a call when she left. The Robertses all dead themselves. You know that, your gramama was the last of 'em. And *she!*" a new emphasis, a new *she,* "never set Chillus out in the field."

This is a family story I will never know except in its shadow form. Who? Someone who wanted a field to raise food or tobacco for money? Someone with an ancient grudge? Someone who would—I can't finish that sentence—

We are trying to sleep. A glow from the streetlight outlines the window where the old black-out blind is pulled down. Swish flump! Lila turns over and over, like an animal shifting to find just the right spot. So do I. Swish flump!

Do your stuff, papah!

"Scales all his life? No ma'am!" Her voice smiles in the dark, shines and sizzles with triumph. "Baby Oil!" The night fills with the odor, buttery and thick. "Bessie and me—didn't we turn that snake baby into a human being?"

You nothing but a fish, not even a human being!

No, Eddie. I'm a North Ca'lina child.

Glowing with the warmth of this thought and the memory of touch, I curl up in Lila's bed, thinking of my own little bed in that room where the wounded baby now lies—and drift almost fearlessly into sleep.

9

1947

WRITE MY NAME ON THE BLACK HEN'S EGG

My mother is going to Richmond to the hospital. She says, "Lila will stay with you at your grandmother's until I come back."

I beg her a hundred times, "Let me stay at Lila's house this time. Please please. I'll be very very very good. I'll do everything the way you want. I won't be mean to Eddie." Which I promised God, too. "It's my greatest wish."

I really expect a no. Mother hasn't forgiven me for the walnut juice.

"Sniff!" says Grandmother. She doesn't approve of me staying at Lila's. But I happen to know that she wants to go with Mother to the hospital. "Anne needs rest," she says, "and I am the one to see she gets it." Also she'll get to go shopping. Grandmother loves the big fancy Thalhimers store. She'll be on my side this time.

My father carefully settles my mother in the passenger seat and then swings the driver door back and forth. "As long as she doesn't get up to any foolishness, I don't care where she stays." By foolishness he means superstitious tales and people he doesn't know coming to Lila's house, and of course the Café. "Whatever you decide, decide it and let's go."

I beg so hard, I use up all my best ideas—how I'll be good and all the things I will do to make her happy when she comes home, so at last, just so they can be off, Mother says Yes. And Grandmother hurries home to pack.

"Don't rush," my father calls after her. "Robert will have to drive you over later."

Mother stares at me, then hands me a bag through the window. I peek in. A box of sugar wafers. Chocolate. "Special," Mother says. "Because you love them." I say, "Thank you, Mother." I really only love the vanilla ones, which are so sweet you have to eat them in a hurry or your teeth will ache. Eating them fast makes a sugar waterfall in your throat. Delicious! Mother likes the chocolate ones because *chocolate is a rare com-mod-ity.* Eddie likes them too.

Mother is giving Lila a thousand instructions. A thousand times.

Finally she calls me back to the car window to say goodbye. After she has told me to be good and mind, she fixes me with her large sad blue eyes. They hold me stronger than if she had grabbed my hand in hers. She whispers, "I will think of you every minute. I will hold you in my heart and mind without cease as long as I am away."

Her eyes have a ring of yellow next to the blue. The yellow is speckled like a cat's eyes, a ring around the little black hole that sees you. These eyes say to me without words, "I know you will forget me the instant I have left. You will not give a thought to me, suffering in the hospital. You are already thinking only of the good times you will have with Lila."

I cover with my pointer finger the funny place on my cheek that's still dark after what Daddy calls the Pecan Caper. She always stares at it when we are facing each other. I know it proves that some of me is Lila'a. And she knows it too.

But I make my eyes as sad as hers. "I *will* think of you, I promise."

Good-bye, good-bye! Her eyes let me go, but she turns around to watch me out of the little back window. Even though she always says she can't twist her head, her neck is too delicate.

"Dance coming to get old dog Rump," Lila says. "He can drive us and all this paraphernalia your mama load us up with."

"But he can't—Dance and Rumpy are taking Grandmother to Richmond. We can take my wagon." We'll go along Main Street bumpety-bumping and everyone will see us and know where I am going and why. "We'll need my wagon at your house, won't we?"

Part of me wishes I *could* ride with Dance and Rumpy. When we're alone in the car, Dance and Lila and me, we sing. The harmonies are so beautiful, I end up crying and we have to stop.

But walking to Lila's is better.

Lila brings the wagon and we load it up: cod-liver oil—ugh! —my pillow, a *decent* blanket, some food from the icebox. I have added a stack of my favorite books and Nora Gordon, who has real hair, short and curly and soft, and a wet-hole. My suitcase will sit on top and hold it all down.

Suddenly Eddie runs up! "I'll carry that!" Snatches the bag away. It's an old doctor one of my father's, made of black pebbly leather with the letters ATG Jr. MD in gold. Eddie only wants to carry it because people will think he's been given an important thing to do.

Stamp, rumble, clatter. "Step on a crack, break your mother's back!"

"Hysh," Eddie whispers. "Aint your mama in the sanitarium?"

Oh! To have already forgotten her. And to be reminded by

Eddie! I have to fix my mind on Mother immediately. Not on her eyes, though—her nose, which is long and straight, not at all like my stumpy nose. Her hair is dark and short and curly, sort of like Nora Gordon's. Mine is blond and long. I need to remember her voice, too. Every word she's ever said to me. And I do. The words but not the sound. I can whisper the words in different patterns and kinds of voice and make them mean different things.

You must not be alone. You will not be safe in in the front room. Someone could break in. You must sleep in Lila's room. In her big bed.

Sometimes at home she says I have to have the windows open for my health. At other times, closed—so no one can get in to kidnap me. *No wonder the child talks about Zombies!* Daddy says.

Daddy has patients to cut open and take the bad parts out of, he has to be scientific. He says patients are called patients because they have to lie still and do what he tells them. Mother will have to be washed by the nurses and sit on a bedpan. When I broke my leg, I tried to be patient, but I couldn't. My leg jumped all over the place. Grandmother said, *That thing has a life all its own.* A nurse told me it was *a wayward nerve* and she had to tie my leg down. Then Daddy put on a cast and brought me home and Lila watched me and put me on the toilet and pushed me around in my old baby carriage because I refused to walk on the crutches Dance made for me.

Rumble, rumble, we're on Main Street. "Eddie, stop swinging my bag!" If I look sad and worried, my parents' friends who pass us won't say, *Look at that heartless child, her mother's in the sanitarium and she has forgotten already.* Instead, they will say, *Look at Anne's little girl, so sad over her mother. Anne is lucky to have so loving a daughter.* In fact they will be concerned and want to do something nice for me. Miz Leiter will come out of the drugstore and invite us in for sodas. This time, she'll let Lila sit at the counter next to me. She'll probably draw the line at Eddie, though. Eddie will have to sit in the back.

But we cross the tracks and no one sees us at all.

Lila's wonderful little white house is shaded by a big dark cedar tree that smells like lemons. Possums climb it at night. You can see their eyes, glowing like ghosts when you shine a flashlight. There are beautiful shooting-star cut-outs in the shutters on the side windows. The back ones have no shutters atall. And the one front window always has a blackout blind covering it so nobody can see in.

The rooms are like train cars, one behind the other, and you could look straight through except a curtain blocks the dining room. In the back sticking off the kitchen is Eddie's room, which used to be a pantry.

The kitchen smells of fatback and collards—fatback is like bacon and collards are bitter. There's also kerosene and that funny smell other people's houses have. You could blindfold me and I'd know Grandmother's house. And this one of course. But my house has no smell at all, except for Mother's room.

I am trying to remember the first glimpse I had of the inside at Lila's. But everything is turned around now and smaller. There are shelves of little china animals and things, all of them chipped or missing legs or ears, their bad sides turned to the wall. Some are almost familiar. Maybe from Grandmother's, or even my own house. When they broke, they probably got thrown away and now they live in Lila's and Eddie's house. It's kind of a hospital for them.

Eddie flings my suitcase down on the linoleum and runs into his room. Slam!

I knew it wouldn't really be like my dream house.

"Lila! I want to call the hospital." Lila has a phone in her dining room, paid for by my father. *You never know when I'll need to call in the middle of the night.* Lila keeps it on the good lace tablecloth where most people put flowers. It's polished black, with shiny metal finger holes. *Nobody in Sugar Bottom but me have a phone*, she says. *Me and the undertaker*. But she's also scared of it. Holds the receiver away from her head and shouts into the mouthpiece. Sometimes she asks Eddie or me to call for her. *Call up Mr. Perk at the store, see if he have any such and such.*

"Your daddy call us when he know anything," she says now.

"But I want to call."

She shakes her head. "They not even there yet."

"It's Daddy's phone!"

She looks at me almost as sadly as Mother, and starts to set the table, her back stiff with my meanness.

Eddie flops down at the table and scoops fried pork chops onto his plate. Four of them, stacked like pancakes ringed with fat. Ugh!

"I won't eat meat ever again. Not ever. I mean it."

"No argument here." Lila has fixed me my favorite, honey biscuits and warm milk with a pinch of sweet chocolate.

"Probably I won't eat anything ever again."

"You watched me chop the chicken heads," Lila says. "Didn't I tell you go back in the house?"

What Lila does to chickens is too horrible for words. Worse than forgetting to think of your mother when she's in the hospital. Worse than breaking her back a hundred times on the sidewalk. She chases them into the pen, catches them, takes them to the wood pile, and—whack! Cuts off their heads with the axe. Then they start to dance. Without a head. Sometimes I peek through my fingers at the dancing. But I can't watch the chopping part.

Daddy says such thoughts are foolish. *People are more important than animals. We are aware and they are not.* But he didn't see the chickens running. They *knew.* He says, *They are here for our use.* That makes me feel funny. I like to pretend I'm an animal,

94

but then I'll remember him saying that and it gives me duckbumps.

Eddie is trying to make me throw up. Opens his jaws wide with every chew and rolls the food around in front of his teeth. Hides this from Lila by sitting sideways in his chair. And I can't say anything because of my promise to God. My biscuit turns to dust in my throat.

"Eddie, go fire up the water heater," Lila says.

Roar of the gas going on. Then the rush of pee in the toilet. If I can hear Eddie pee, he will hear me too. In this house you can hear and smell everything!

"I want to go home."

"What's the matter, honey?" Lila puts the back of her hand against my forehead to see if I have a fever.

"I want to go home!"

Eddie laughs. "Thought you so hot to come here. Be with *Li-lah.*" He mimics my voice, makes it squeaky and dumb.

I will not let Stupid Eddie see me cry. "Can I please be excused from the table please?" I run into Lila's room and slam the door.

Instant cool and silence. My suitcase is at the end of her high bed, and my shorts and shirts and underpants are spread out on the counterpane. Nora Gordon is sleeping on Lila's pillow, eyes closed.

"Come on, Nora, we are going home!" Scoop the clothes into the bag. Open the window wide and push the screen out. Squeeze my legs over the sill. Lila will be beside herself and serve her right. Her and Eddie.

I ease the window up higher until I can duck down and get my head out. The window presses against my back, trying to push me over. It's a long way down. It didn't look so high from outside. And it's dark.

Zombies! They'll get me, I'll be slowed down by Nora Gordon and my suitcase. I've been thinking such bad thoughts!

The window sticks and I can't bend over low enough to get my head back in. Oh, what do I do? I'll have to scrape my legs in one by one. Sideways. Holding on tight.

I'll have to stay. Am I glad? Or am I sorry! At least no one can see me cry.

I made it. Sneak on tip-toes to the door and peek into the kitchen. Lila and Eddie whispering! About me.

On the ice-box door, Lila has taped the paintings I made for her. Redbirds to sing her a sweet song. A tiger with golden staring eyes and stripes all over, to eat her up when she frowns at me. And a list in my mother's careful printing.

Don't forget Willis's cod-liver oil. Yuck!

Don't put Willis in a cot. She must have the bed.

I want the cot—all plushy with a sag in the middle to snuggle in, and soft pillows and blankets tucked in. Blankets smelling of moth balls—so sharp and clean!

In the night I know I'll get nervous about Lila's magic bags, little cotton sacks hanging on the four posts of her bed. Against bad spirits. They smell musty, and what's in them? She won't say. Feels like bones. One of 'em squishes!

Grandmother says there are mice in Lila's house. She doesn't know about the sacks. She says you have to be high off the floor or the mice will make dirt on your pillow. She uses that word, *dirt*, to mean a lot of things.

Lila snorts. *Miz Roberts the one have the mice on the pillow!* Which is entirely true. I've seen their turds right by my head. Ugh!

Not 'turds,' Daddy says. *Feces.* Until he said that, I thought only people had feces.

That would be on Daddy's list if he had one: Use the right names for things. Respect scientific facts. *Co-cola is 85 percent acid. It eats your tooth enamel.*

Mother's list isn't as interesting and it always has things I don't like. *A teaspoonful of cod-liver oil every morning. Don't forget to brush Willis's hair a hundred strokes every day.*

Cod-liver oil is an em-in-ation from hell. And that hateful brush pokes holes in my head.

Lila's dresser has five little pots on it. Safety pins. Buttons. A box of old watch heads that all say different times. They run too. I wind them up and dot them among the pots. Tick tick tick. Seven old watches ticking.

One pot has a wad of hair in it. Lila keeps all our hair from our brushes. And buries it in a hidden place so nobody can find it and make a spell against us. There is a conjuh man in town. He makes the spells with magic. You have to pay him a lot.

Oh, a powder box with a ballerina on the top. The key is rusty and the music part doesn't work anymore. The dancer twirls slowly to the beat of the ticking watches.

Lila opens the door behind me. Picks up my suitcase by the window, shakes out my clothes again, and hangs them on hangers. Humming. Passes me, feels my forehead again. Forgives me!

In the bathroom, rusty water in the tub. I won't sit in that! The old tub has a pebbly, scratchy bottom too. And chipped lion's feet. I like those.

Lila lets me stand. She soaps me all over. "Once you all clean and nice, in fresh clothes, we play some cards."

"I won't play if Eddie plays."

"Don't be like that, honey."

And I remember my promise. To God. If you break a promise to God, really scary things happen to you. Oh but I'll give Eddie the chocolate wafers Mother gave me. He will love them and it'll be like saying "I'm sorry" to God.

Lila rinses me with a pink hose with a rubber shower nozzle. The soft droplets tickle, but if I wiggle, I'll fall in the tub and break my head.

Now comes the towel, which has been warmed on the water heater. Smells of hot cloth, like Lila's ironing. Delicious!

Lila rubs my hair, knuckling into my skull. Joggling my head—uh-uh-uh-uh. And Mother's eyes find me. *Didn't I tell you you'd forget? You've broken my heart!* I stand straight and bite my lip as hard as I can. *I didn't forget*, I whisper to her—oh that's a fib. *I'm even going to give the chocolate cookies to Eddie.* I wish they were vanilla. To make up for bad things, you have to give up something you want. I need to make up for everything bad I've ever done.

"*When I in awe-some wonder,*" Lila sings. A beautiful quaver in her voice, a quiver on her lips and cheeks. Even the fuzz on her cheeks trembles. She lifts me out of the tub and wraps the towel around me. "Run, run!" We run through the kitchen, Lila holding my towel together at the back.

From Eddie's room, the screech and rumble of his no-music. I wish he'd play be-bop. Jitterbug!

Lila makes a face and closes her door.

Now to the dresser. First the body powder from the dancer's pot. So tickly on my legs, under my arms! Then the brush. "We got to make you your daddy's golden prin-cess." Lila nods at me to keep the count so she can go on singing.

I have to call out the brush strokes. "Twenty," I say at 17. Lila is so busy with her gospel, I can cheat more than usual.

"*Then sings my soul! My-Savior-God to thee. How great thou art! How gray-ate—*" She is singing the alto. I sing the melody with her on this "sings my soul" part. Our voices are so beautiful together, tears clog up my throat and make me squeak. And I've lost count of the brush strokes.

"Can't squeak like that on Sunday," she says. "Spoil the song." I nod and don't say anything. But I'm so happy! I'm usually not allowed to sing in Lila's church. Mother didn't mention it when she left, but she's said it many times before, listening to us practice and hearing me beg Lila to sing with her one day. It isn't that Mother doesn't like Lila's singing. Or even that she thinks I don't sing well. She says it would be disrespectful for me to *push my way in.*

Mother herself has taken me to hear Lila sing in the choir. We sit in the back as quiet as mice. But the preacher always sees us and says, *We offer welcome to our honored guests!*

Lila must have asked her special, this time.

The hymn and the braiding come out even. Lila gives a tug on the finished plaits to make them hang straight. Then she brushes the ends.

She braids my hair so tight, one day my eyes are going to pop out. In the speckled blue mirror, sure enough, the skin between my ears and my hairline is stretched and my eyes are bulging. Lila pushes my hand away. "It'll loosen. Turn to a thousand snarls. Lawd knows how you do it."

How can I be a golden princess if I'm scalped?

Whoosh, an undershirt goes over my head, mashing my nose and eyebrows and the plaits. "Should of put on the shirt first," she clucks at herself.

"Now," she sits me on the bench and sits beside me for serious talk. "I know it's hard to come to a new place, you not used to being away from home at night. But, honey, too late to back out now! I aint made arrangements about Eddie."

Oh! Eddie. I know very well he stays with Haddy when Lila sleeps at our house. And I know Daddy thinks Eddie won't be here now, while I am. He won't let Eddie even visit our house. He lets Eddie drive us places, though. Daddy's rules are confusing.

"Your mama go be fine. Need a little rest, is all, then she be home." Lila's eyes go to the picture that hangs over her bed, Jesus holding a lamb. A string of dried garlic is wrapped around the frame. "Lawd knows, I pray for her."

She puts her hand on my knee. "Let me tell you how I *know*

it be hard. I been knowing your mama since I was a little girl. Your mama *raise* me."

"Raised you?" Lila is "raising" me.

Lila nods. "For a little while. I was a sick girl and she took me in and cure me. She used to work for her stepdaddy, down by the tracks, a rail-road lawyer, you know. And she was a sport, lemme tell you. Laugh and play all the time."

My mother, laughing and playing? But she's sick, now, of course. From making me born and other things—too sick to laugh or play.

"My mama," Lila guides my legs into my underpants, "used to wash folks' clothes. Walk down the tracks with a basket of laundry. And I come along with her sometime. Slowed her down, because I couldn't hardly walk, I had the rickets so bad in my legs. Your grandaddy call me 'little bow-legged fool.' Your mama say to me, 'Do your legs hurt you? Does it hurt to walk?' And she say to my mama, 'Good food, rest, and sun will help the rickets.' She say to my mama, 'Let me have Lila, for a while, I fix her legs.' "

"How did she know she'd cure you?" Daddy would have known. But Daddy didn't know us till three years before I was born.

Lila flattens her mouth. Her mule lip, beautiful lip with the soft pale hairs on it, crinkles. "Honey, she work on my legs. Rub 'em with lineament and oil, make me lie in the sun—and cod-liver oil? Whew!" Lila stretches out her scaly legs and rubs them. "You could shoot a ball through 'em!"

They're still crooked at the bottoms, but the tops mash together just fine.

"But listen to this now: I was living with your mama, sleeping in a cot in her dressing room, and I miss my mama so bad at night, I used to cry myself to sleep. Used to pray, 'Lawd, lemme go back home to my mama and my gramama. I don't care if my legs bow in a circle.' " Her voice is bumpy and the words come out like crying. "My gramama tell me, 'You comin back to me one day, don't you worry. I writ your name on the black hen's egg.' "

"What's the black hen's egg?"

"A way the old folks got of making everything come out good. Bindin' you to 'em forever, honey. For *ever!* But now your mama start getting me to do some things, helping her make me some clothes on her machine. And she teach me to cook beaten biscuits and little cheese rolls, like the white folks like at parties."

Each of these words rounds her tongue, hangs on her lip, like a soap bubble. "I got so I didn't cry at night. Your mama make me go to school too. When my legs bad, the kids push me down and laugh at me. I never went inside a school till I near ten years old. But she help me. 'Just stick your nose high in the air, Lila,' she say, 'you just as good as they are. Just as good.' She taught me to read."

A sigh. "By and by I come to like living up there in your gramama's house—your mama and me was some good-time gals." Voice drops lower. Goes sad, sad, sad. "And when I did get back to my mama, look like nothing would satisfy me. Nothing go right."

Her face looks like she's about to cry. I rest my head on her knee. "If I'd of been there, you wouldn't of left. I would put your name on the hen's egg!"

"Gotta be a black one, honey, a black hen," she murmurs, patting my braids.

Eddie's awful music goes up suddenly and thumps through the walls. "Eddie! Shut up! Shut up!" Silence for a second. Then the music comes back on, even louder. I am going to *bust!*

Lila wags her hand at me. That means: *Go easy. This Eddie's house, he can do what he want, even if you don't like it.*

Eddie's house.

Lila puts her hand on my arm. *Stop. Swallow. Take a deep breath.* I know all the steps now. She nods. "That the way."

She turns on her radio—gospel music to almost drown out Eddie. She pulls me into her lap. Her front warm against my back, her crooked legs bony under my behind—she rocks. Up and back. I get up and fetch Nora Gordon, put her onto my lap, so she'll get rocked to the gospels too. It feels so good. Up and back. Up and back.

"Li, I'm going to write your name on a whole dozen eggs. Keep 'em forever."

She hugs me tighter.

"Do the eggs really have to come from a black hen?"

"Yep. They *got* to."

"Are the eggs black?"

"Just the hen be black, sugah. The eggs be brown."

"Did you want me in Grandmother's house, when you were living with Mother?"

Her bosoms bounce in and out against my back. Laughing. "To be sure!"

"Really—did you?"

"Honey, back then, you won't a gleam in a eye yet. Nobody know your name!"

Bad eyes, not to have me in them. How can I not have had a name? "Is that because I was a fish?" No answer.

We go on rocking, but now half my heart hurts. The smiley part of my heart is warm with Lilulie's arms and her breath. The frowny part hates a time when nobody knew my name.

How *can* there have been a time when Lila lived in my mother's house, and nobody wrote my name on the black hen's egg?

10

1981

SKINNING THE DEAD DEER'S HEAD

I am doing the damnedest thing. Still wearing my go-to-church skirt, paper spread out and Dance sitting with me on Lila's kitchen floor—I am skinning a dead deer's head.

It's dark in the room and we are working by a kerosene lamp, tilted in the chair by our heads. Dance's bad leg is sticking out at an angle. He's given me the knife on this job. He grabs a fold of skin and fur with one hand and steadies the head by holding onto an antler with the other. Then I take the knife and slice at the white rind between the pelt and the meat.

When we started, the head was just a stage prop. Eyes calm and glassy, fur all stiff and cold. And no blood smell. As we go on, these things begin to change.

It's hard work, Dance's part especially, since he's supplying the tension. Opals of sweat bead his upper lip. I haven't been this close to Dance since I was little enough to ride on his back or sit in his lap and fit my fingers onto the strings of his guitar. He's gotten smaller.

The pores in his nose are perfectly round, like pinholes. Root ends of the sparse hairs above his ears show blue under the tan skin. He has little tight curls, each separate from the next, with rows of flesh between, like gray bushes on a rust-colored field seen from up in a crop-duster. Eddie's hair grew like this too.

That Robert Tisdale over seventy, Lila keeps saying, *near wore out.* She's in an odd mood, when she calls him Robert. And odder if she says "Robert Tisdale."

Today, far from worn out, he looks happy, dead deer's head and all. Yesterday he said to me, "I ask Miss Lila to marry me."

"What did she say?"

"She say she poor enough all by herself." Dance wheezes with laughter.

A little while ago, before Dance and I started on this project, Lila asked me if our paper would hold up if she had a husband, so maybe she's considering it. I told her I didn't know, but I'd ask Lawyer Perkinson. "Husbands have rights," I told her. "And if Dance marries you, he'll earn 'em." We both laughed.

"Hold that there," Dance says. A piece of pebbled gray slime by the mouth. Takes the pliers, grabs the fur I've cut loose and, nodding to me, pulls, ripping the hide away, like a New York butcher skinning an Easter lamb. The deer holds onto his fur better than lambs, though, or else his skin is more brittle, because it comes away in Dance's hand in a little strip. He grunts.

"You ever skinned a deer head before, Dance?"

Laughs his laugh. "Naw. I don't hold with wild meat."

From the doorway, Lila snorts and moves into our line of vision. Without lifting my head, I can see the hem of her dress and her skinny bent legs, the soft slippers with the toes cut out. All that fancy carving Brackson does and still the nails stick up like wads of old gum.

"Wild meat! You wish you had some meat on that thing. I aint notice you turning your nose up at rabbit, when you get the chance."

Behind her, in the dining room Hard Rock shuffles papers.

She has brought some legal documents, and she and Lila are in a confabulation. Hard, with a hundred little sly remarks, makes it plain she wishes I were a million miles away so she could get something, whatever she wants, out of Lila. And Lila wants to ask me to help her figure out what's in Hard's papers, but she can't: First of all, she's scared for Hard Rock to find out about *our* paper. *Liz-bet do somethin' to spoil that for me,* she says, adamant even when I reassure her. But Hard is Haddy's daughter, after all. Schemer genes. She knows all Lila's tender spots, too.

The second reason is that Hard gave me this deer's head and I've roped Dance into helping me with it. Lila knows I can't stop now.

Well, it's a mess all right. A friend lent me his car to drive down here from New York—mine's in the shop. My friend wanted to come with me, but I said no. I always come alone. Not that Lila wouldn't welcome my friends, and they'd appreciate her. But the rest of the town, black and white both, surely would have problems. Especially with a man friend. Can't you hear the tongues flapping now?

But this is the 1980s, my friends say to me. Well, yes, in New York it *is* the 1980s. But we are here, in perpetual Jim Crow land. Whatever problems I kick up will come to roost at Lila's door. I suspect I'm creating a problem just staying here all the time. But I think our "paper" gives us some legitimacy. *We know how you feel about your Lila.* Bastards!

I could have taken the bus and avoided this whole gratitude thing, but that would have meant no driving the country roads and we look forward to our outings. So I said, "What would you like me to bring you from the Old South?" Expecting something like a Virginia ham, which is "in" right now.

"A deer skull," he said. "To hang on my wall."

I keep expecting this whole scene to get horrible, but it doesn't. The deer is made in layers—off comes one, revealing another, each with its own design and function. I thought I might get sick when the skin came off around the eyes—eyes are sure-enough *balls*—but after a minute I got used to it. And then the teeth, set in the jaw, now without lips. A ghastly smile. I got used to that too.

Being around Daddy gave me some tolerance for and curiosity about how we're put together. In addition to the usual cuts and broken bones, which I was familiar with by the time I could talk, he let me watch two operations when I was fifteen. I saw a white woman have her breast cut off for cancer, and a black woman have a baby cut out of her. Its head was big as a watermelon. It was a little boy, and Daddy said he'd die right away, but I found out later he lived six years. His mother rolled him around her farm in a wheelbarrow and suckled him all that time.

Daddy apologized to me for letting me see that. He knew the baby would be hydrocephalic, but not so extreme. I said I thought he ought to apologize to the woman for the breach of her privacy. It was one of those exchanges where he and I completely lost each other. I wonder sometimes what he'd make of my life today, not least my relationship with Lila. He'd be uncomfortable. He'd disapprove, like all the white people in this town.

This morning, as Lila and I were dressing for church, here comes Liz-beth, in her fancy high heels and hat, toting a brown paper bag. "I heard you lookin' for something like this, Willis."

I opened the bag, and there was the head, fur and all, staring up at me. I almost dropped it. I'd asked Lila where I might get a deer's head, and of course while I said "head," I meant "skull." I certainly couldn't say any of this to Hard. I just thanked her. And she laughed her sneaky laugh. Somehow in the family genes, Hard got Lila's keen intelligence but not much of her wisdom. A minute later, Lila beckoned me into the bedroom. "You better give me twenty bucks for Liz-bet," she whispered, "that thing is valuable."

"Why don't I give her the money myself?"

Lila snorted. "It was a present!"

I can't fathom Hard saying no to twenty bucks in the name of social niceties, but I handed Lila the money and Hard laughed some more. Watching us through a crack in the door.

Valuable. A dead deer's head. Look at it closely, now: Wouldn't you have said they all look alike, every one you've ever seen over the cash registers of country stores and cafés, and hall mirrors in farm houses? But now I'd know our deer anywhere, even if I met him in a New York bar. The way his eyes are close together alongside that funny bent nose.

Lila has coaxed Hard Rock into reading her document aloud.

"Com-mon-we-all of Vir-gi-ni-a, cir-cu-it co-ert of Matt-a-pon-i Count-y." Hard reads each syllable separately and gives each the same weight, so that the words run together. Once out in the air, they wind around slowly like the old Mattaponi River when it's swollen with rain, pulling things into its sluggish stream.

"Sub-po-e-na in chance-rye. Liza-beth Mc-Pleasant and Li-la Neal Dog-gett."

Dance and I both stop cold, our hands dangling. It's a summons! And chancery, I believe, has to do with property. Lila and her fears for her house!

"Eh?" she says, almost shouting. "Speak up!" Lila's about as deaf as an owl. She just wants to be sure Dance and I hear every word. "Go on, Liz-bet."

"Your com-plai-nant, G. Fal-con Spaul-din Comet-Tee for Chillus Crowder, an in-comp-e-tent ad-ult. Comp-lain-ant's in-comp-e-tent has been con-fined in Com-mun-it-y Memor'al Hawspital and has in-cur-red large med-i-cal ex-penses..."

Hard falls silent. Lila's skirt hem whips by my nose again. The very starch whines in distress.

"Chillus over there in the hospital," says Dance. He has commandeered the knife and is sawing away at a strip of deer. "Got the pneumonia last month. Miz Brown call the doctor and the amb'lance took him away."

"I tell you, aint I?" Lila asks me. "I call and tell you about Uncle?" Sometimes she doesn't tell me things, when I'm in New York. As if I were worlds away.

The Commi*tee* G. Falcon Spauldin. Chillus, his incompetent! God! Legal language really can really peel off the pretenses, can't it, even as it euphemizes.

Hard starts to read on, but I get up, wash my hands, and ask for the papers. She hands them to me.

"At this time the personal estate of complainant's incompetent has been exhausted yet his incompetent is the owner of the following described real estate to wit: *All that certain tract of land being in Buckhorn Magisterial District, Mattaponi County, Virginia, lying north of Highway 47 near Wightman, and on the east side of State Road 662, containing 48.39 acres, more or less, bounded on the north and east by Robert and Ruth Thompson and on the west by Old Pough's* (Pug's, Puff's?) *Mill Road.*"

"Old *Pooh's* Mill Road—run right by Gramama fa'hm."

"That property *is* your grandmother's farm."

Lila stares at me. "Read it again."

"Forty-eight-point-thirty-nine acres, more or less, bounded on the north and east—"

"What they mean 'more or less?' That farm always been fifty acres."

"Lawd lawd," Dance mutters, "they have skunt that po' old man." Pulls himself slowly to his feet using the chair as a prop, wipes his knife on his overalls, sets it on the chair by the lamp. Goes to the door to light a cigarette and blows smoke outside. Lila doesn't permit smoking in her house.

"Sun tomorrow," he says. "Been rainin' three days. Never yet see a Sunday, though, without a little patch o' blue."

Lila glares at the deer mess all around us. "You ex-perts go have to scoot down my floor with the garden hose when you done, look like."

We're suspended—all of us.

Chillus. His hands. Dark, bony, blue-nailed, eons of earth in the dark seams left by his labors. But then it's Daddy's hands, cutting into flesh and yellow fat—the woman's breast coming off clean and round in his fingers. He must have learned to do that by doing just what Dance and I have been doing, only on a dead *person.* Following each piece to its end.

Dance shakes his head and sits down again and I join him on the floor. He takes up the knife, upends the deer head by the antlers, and shakes. Out falls the tongue.

Snort from Lila. She stomps over to us and snatches up the tongue and sniffs it. "Not a thing wrong with this!" Carts it off to the sink to wash it. "My gramama taught me to use every piece of deer meat. Tail bone and all."

"They won't let Chillus go back to Miz Brown. He want to die at home but—"

On the farm, wild sloes and briars are taking everything. Nothing there could possibly interest Mr. G. Falcon Spauldin. God, even the name is predatory. House is entirely gone now. Even the old barn, which was better built, is getting holes in it. "What does that man want?"

"Some folks want 'cause somebody else got." Dance is looking down at his hands, as they work automatically over the fur and flesh.

That farm is dreams. Storm dreams. Some good ones, about building and restoring. Keeping, cherishing. Once when we were talking about it, Lila said, "We oughta go get Chillus so he can see where he was raised one more time."

Hard Rock is standing in the doorway, looking down at me.

"Us used to drive by that old run-down place with boys." Snickers. "To smooch. You ever done stuff like that, Willis?"

What am I supposed to say? When we were little, she'd worry me about sex all the time. Boys sticking their tongues in her ear or her mouth or whatever. I'd get so confused, I'd cry. How many years ago, now? I'm an adult, right? But I feel just the way I did then.

Dance shifts, easing his bad leg. Then we go to work on the really last bit. The cords that bind the bones to one another, and muscle to bone.

"They go sell Uncle's fa'hm," Hard says. "I told you."

"That aint Uncle's fa'hm!" Lila suddenly wakes to passion. "That's *Gramama* fa'hm. And my fa'hm and your fa'hm. She *promised*."

Lila's feet come down bang! with every step. Back straight as a rod. Shakes the pages in front of my nose again. "Read!"

Hard mutters, "I read perfectly fine."

"You aint know B from bull's foot."

I try to catch Lila's eye. *Don't, don't put me between you and Liz-beth like this.*

"Willis!"

"Okay with you, Liz-beth?"

She grimaces. "Just don't get blood on it."

My hands are gory still. I wipe them on my skirt and rub a spot of blood off the paper. "Complainant believes that the other parties aligned as defendants herein are complainant's incompetent's heirs and next of kin. (That means that he knows you have an interest in Chillus and the farm.) Therefore complainant prays:

"(1) That his Bill of Complaint be filed herein. (He wants the court to decide.)

"(2) That a copy be served on the parties of the defendant. (You and Liz-beth have to go in and say that you do or don't agree and why.)"

"I *never* agree."

"(3) That a guardian *ad litem* be appointed to protect his complainant's interest. (Who knows what that means?)"

"Protect Chillus from us!" Dance snorts.

"(4) That his incompetent's real estate be sold and the proceeds used to pay his debts."

Lila lets out a long breath.

"(5) That complainant be allowed a reasonable fee for services rendered his incompetent." This I *don't* want to read.

"(6) Any and all relief as the nature of his cause may require. And he will ever pray."

Lila growls. "Pray? What he go pray?"

Dance's laugh. "I pray ever myself, I rich as Falcon Sprawldin. He say old Chillus got no money left, aint that so? So they aint go put Miz Lila in jail, only go rob 'er."

Hard Rock comes over, stepping gingerly around the deer parts, and takes the paper out of my hands, rubs at the now invisible blood spot.

Dance bends his head, tackles the last of our job. This dead deer has held onto its skin and meat very tightly indeed. We could pick all night and never get it down to pure bone. "What we need now is a good old ant heap," he says. "By-gone days, ant heaps used to clean up everything: dishwasher to graveyard."

He stops, leans back, lights another cigarette, right here in the house. And Lila doesn't say squat. She looks from me to Dance to Hard and back. But she won't say a word as long as Hard is here.

"Picked clean. A ant will pick anything you want him to. And some you don't." Dance nods, gives a little cough. "Willis," using my name for the first time since I was about three, "I aint go truck with these deer eyes."

"Y'all crazy," Hard Rock says, scornfully. "I may not read too good, but I got better sense than to dig at a dead animal."

Out of its cavities now comes a kind of thick sweet smell, like a child's wet unsoaped hair. The blood on our hands is clotted and stringy, like Jello.

Time for this to be over. Time to get up, find a plastic bag, wrap this head—all red and white, stark staring and smiling a smile of grace. Tie it tight and neat with used string, the way Lila always ties garbage and charity packages.

Here's a vision: I hand this bag to G. Falcon Spauldin—my mother's second cousin once or twice removed, so he would conceivably accept a present from me. He opens it. Sees those naked creature-eyes looking right at him, takes in the power of that lip-less smile.

Suddenly Lila starts bustling in and out. Muttering how busy she is.

Work usually drives Hard to the door in a flash, but this time she doesn't budge.

Lila's rattling pans, opening cupboard doors. Then moves to the closets. Tactical mistake. Hard would walk a mile for a hint at what's really in Lila's closets. Sure enough, she anchors herself tight to the seat.

"We'll go to Mr. Perkinson tomorrow," I say. "We'll see if we can get a copy of the will. Hospital bills, bank accounts. Spauldin has to keep records."

"They can't sell Gramama fa'hm," Lila insists. "She left that to Chillus and me and Liz-bet's mama and all of we."

"*Perkinson* go do all that?" Hard says. "Accounts and hospitals and a old will?" Caws like a crow.

Lila looks at me. Dance looks at me.

"If we hire him to."

Dear God! What am I talking about? I have barely enough money to get down here and back and meet my bills and some of Lila's. I just paid her house taxes last week. She was worrying that spot on her front with her finger, when I walked in the door, saying: *Lawd, where I go git the tax money?* And I said, *How much?* She said, *Twenty-two and some.* And before I could faint at twenty-two hundred dollars, she said, *Twenty-two dollars fifty cents.* I paid two years' worth with a giant sigh of relief.

"Oh hell! Look at this! Hair and bits of meat all over the linoleum." I want to scream and stamp. Hit something or somebody! Sweeping, sweeping, furious broom! Just makes a smear. Down I go on my knees, squooshing around a hot wet rag. Wish I could scrub holes in the floor!

Suddenly, from Lila, a little sound, round and hard with rage. Disdainful toe nudges the deer in his plastic bag. "Hah! Now y'all done, let me tell you I could of cleaned 'im up in a hour, boiling 'im on the stove."

She's angry at *me?* What have *I* done? "Hell! Why didn't you say so?"

"Well, Miss Know All, you aint ask me! Just set there picking at that thing. Both y'all," she glares at Dance. Then, *flip-flop, bim-bam, bang!* Bedroom door slams behind her.

Hard stands up, smiling. "Well, Miss Lila got a lot on her mind, I better git myself on home!"

Yes! Are you satisfied, now, seeing Lila and me fighting?

The bedroom door stays shut. Not a sound leaks out. But I know all too well what she does when she's this hurt and mad. Sits with her Bible open on her lap, muttering at the wall. Finger pressed to her chest.

Dance and I limp to my borrowed car, rain coming down now in a heavy sheet. And I'm still in my skirt, all cold and wet and bloody. Damn damn damn. "Where's your spot of blue?"

Dance eases into the seat beside me. "Comin'. Aint quite Monday yet."

Wish I could say something to Dance, how I'm sorry for yelling at Lila.

"Nothin you can do," he says, suddenly. "Mark my words."

Is he talking about Lila's rage? Or the farm and Chillus? All of it, probably.

Neither of us says anything else till we get to his cabin. Long ago, I'd sit by the stove here with old Runaway Rump on my lap, and Dance would tell me stories his grandmother told him that her grandmother told her. That takes us back to about the time of Mozart.

Dance loves to build things. Shacks, sheds, neat stacks of firewood, sturdy handles for tools. Gets tired of looking out on one spot, boards up the doors and windows, and opens others, onto another spot.

"Change of view," he says.

And so he goes round and round, from the old view to the new and back again a hundred comforting times.

His favorite building materials come from the remains of Grandfather's old Barter Clinic. My father's father, a country doctor of the old school. Lila has the other kind of remains, the small, forgotten, poignant objects. "I rember the Barter," Dance says, reading my mind. "Used to take a bushel of turnips and greens up there with my mama when she havin' another baby. Not even a parking lot there now." The new clinic—Brackson's—is clear out of town. And Liz-beth would charge Lila two dollars to take her there. Even though she swears she wouldn't.

Chillus is more than a century old. Newspapers should take pictures of him and ask him the secrets of long life. He should have his farm, all fixed up, to leave to his niece and grandniece. Good farm, wonderful farm, in the family forever.

Didn't he ever have children?

I should have stopped the deer head stuff and offered to read the paper and hugged Lila and raged with her. Promised to try to save the farm. Save Chillus. Save history.

Instead, I'd yelled.

"Dance, you ever have kids?"

He looks at me keenly, and slowly shakes his head. "Don't reckon. Don't reckon I ever got married!" And he laughs his slow laugh.

Midnight. Red flames twinkle between the cracks in the old stove. The rain has stopped. Dance and I shake hands goodnight. Then laugh and hug.

Back to Lila's. The bedroom door is open. She's fast asleep on the cot. But the big bed—her bed where she insists I sleep—is turned down, my nightgown is spread out, waiting for me.

Her chest goes up and down. The room is filled with her warm rich breath, tinged with the sourness of distress. She's straight as a piece of string under the cover, face turned away, arms warm in flannel, which she wears to sleep in no matter what the temperature, neatly on the outside of the covers.

What will we do? Chillus is gone. In the hospital, done for. The farm is gone. Once when we went there, long ago, Lila and I picked buttoneggs to pacify my mother. Why on earth are they called "buttoneggs?" Gone and forgotten. Why did we pick them?

To make Mother to forget—she'd never forgive—my love for Lila.

I want to save that farm. For Lila. For us.

What can I do? Tomorrow—Perkinson. Surely there are *some* reasonable people here now, reasonable laws. Not Spauldin's law. *"And he will ever* prey.*"*

Rabbit runs over my grave.

I WAKE. Still dark. Smells—Clorox. Kerosene. Coffee. Lila moving rhythmically in the kitchen. I was dreaming. Chillus, in the field, in his chair, not naked as he described himself—the way I saw him last, bundled up, tucked in.

Except, under the blanket covering him, I know that he is in pieces like the deer. In layers. And that there are more parts and more layers than are his.

Lila. Dance. Liz-beth. Me. Layers and parts of us all.

11

1947

STRIPPED

Dance is in Lila's kitchen, and they are talking about Precious Eddie. Dance talks low. I am only pretending I'm still sleeping so I can hear: "He over at Miss Laura Keene!"

Lila snorts. "Trash!"

Laura Keene is Eddie's girlfriend, I knew that already. My mother says you aren't supposed to let boys kiss you or touch you. You have to be married to them first. And what girl would possibly let Eddie smooch her? Hard Rock says Laura Keene is 22 years old and has another boyfriend.

I hope Lila's making corn cakes—so soft in the middle with lacy crunchy edges that sizzle with butter. Delicious.

"The ani-miles goes in, two by two! El-e-*phant* and kang-a-*roo!*" Dance is starting to play his guitar and I know he wants me to get up and say "Good morning." I hop out of the bed. Then I remember Eddie might come in, fresh from smooching his girlfriend. I can't sing and dance in front of Eddie. He laughs at me and Lila lets him.

Dance dances with his guitar, and Lila swirls around the kitchen, a skillet in her hands. Dance pats her behind. Is Dance

Lila's boyfriend? Do they sleep together naked? Boys are so uninteresting. No bosoms! And Dance and Lila are old.

After my corn cakes, I go out in my nightgown to take the garbage to the bin in the alley—on the lookout for possums and foxes. I'd love to see a fox but Lila hates them because they eat her chickens.

It's shivery in the morning. I might meet the night animals. Just hearing them is scary—foxes make a yowping sound. Possums don't say much of anything. If you surprise one in the garbage can, Lila says it'll play dead. But I saw one once, and it showed all its teeth. Daddy says they have more teeth than I do. And they bite. But you don't get rabies from them. Why? Even Daddy didn't know why.

"What'll he do when he's playing dead?"

"Fall over, shut 'is eyes."

Well, that's just silly. Playing dead would make it really easy to bop him on the head. Play dead, get dead, that's what I think. Though it might be fun to pretend with Mother. She plays like she's fainting—how could she fuss if I played dead?

When I'm back and dressed in shorts and shirt and my awful saddle shoes—I love sandals, but Mother says my feet need support. I am supposed to have high arches, like all delicate ladies. Ugh.

Lila and I head toward my parents' house. I'm to take a bath there, a real bath, in water clear and sparkly, not red and full of rust flakes like in Lila's tub.

Have you ever gone into your own house when it's empty? Of course you know where everything is, but you still feel like a stranger. My parents have been gone for two days and the house looks deserted.

Air-raid blinds are drawn. The war's over, but Mother leaves those blinds up. Not even a sliver of light was supposed to get out at night, or the airplane pilots going over would tell on you and you'd get arrested.

The chairs look like hunchbacks in the corners. Even my favorite picture, a courtyard in a far-off country where princesses live in castles, looks cold. Like a prison.

In my parents' room, a sheet is spread over the fire screen to keep out the swifts that live in the chimney. Daddy's hospital whites are thrown over a chair. Some frilly night things are crumpled on my mother's bed. She doesn't usually wear frilly stuff. Perhaps they're a get-well present.

And my room, tucked behind the big living-room fireplace where on cold nights I cuddle up to the back of the chimney that's warm as a sleeping animal, is all different. In dim light my patch quilt is much too tidy, and Nora Gordon is gone, my books are gone. No one I know could possibly live here.

But oh to bathe in an abandoned house! Delicious! And in my mother's forbidden tub. "Please please!" It's large as a pool, with cool, gleaming white tiles. And bubbles. A fairy-tale bath. Before Lila can say no, I turn on the faucets full blast and kick off my shoes, wiggle out of my shorts and shirt, and hop in, dumping bath-scent after me. "Lila, you, too—I dare you! We can pretend it's *our* house."

Lila and I swim all the time together at the river. Only there of course we have to wear bathing suits. And Lila doesn't know how to swim so she won't let me go in over my knees.

"You go dare me? I scared even pee in here, folks around."

But looking over her shoulder and laughing a little, Lila turns her back and takes off her uniform. Her slip strap is held up by a big safety pin, and her bra is frayed under the arms. Oh! Long silky bloomers, like Grandmother wears! And then she's naked.

Animals are naked except for their fur. Baby birds are all pink and blue flesh in the nest. Except for baby chickens which pop out of the shell like yellow fluff balls. Fish are especially naked. And when we're born, we're like fish, without fur or feathers. We're naked making ready for everything.

Lila's bosoms—I've seen them before, only through bushes or a flash when she pulls her nightgown on—are large and drooping, like Mother's, but red as plum skins, with purple nipples in the center. Between them, a white rabbit foot on a chain. "For luck!" "For foolishness," says Mother.

Lila's fanny is narrow and hard while Mother's is soft and wrinkly with fat. Lila's belly is a little melon, hard and round. And there's a big brown line diagonally across her whole body.

"What is that?"

"Scar."

Mother has a scar, from my birth, running from her belly button to her private hair. "See," she'll point to the crinkled blue-white line, "how I almost died to bring you in the world?" And I shiver. It's so ugly! And all my fault.

Lila says it isn't. Mother says it is. Which do I *feel?* Today, I agree with Lila! Her scar is the gramama of all scars. Much too amazing to be ugly. Bigger and longer than anybody's.

"Where did you get it? Can I touch it? Did you get it when Eddie was born?" But I know Eddie was born in the country. Scars come from hospitals.

So smooth and hard and black! No crinkles, no tucks in the skin around it. A beautiful seam across Lila's body, a zipper into her secrets. Zip! And all that's inside will be open, plain.

"My insides all come out. Your daddy put 'em back in and sew me up."

In the huge tub, our legs touch, our feet overlap, the water is getting cold. I turn on some more hot. "Did they just fall out one day? Your insides?" But that's not right. I know enough from Daddy to be sure our skin doesn't just open up and let things slide out.

"Eddie daddy cut me with a razor."

"Eddie's—?" Not even Eddie is allowed to mention his daddy. I heard of him but never dared say anything. Eddie says his daddy always carries a knife. Maybe even a gun. And he's gone somewhere, up North. "Run off," Eddie says. "With the law on his tail."

"Didn't mean to. Say he love me. *Love me like sun, love me like rain!*"

"Were you naked?" This scar couldn't have come through clothes and underwear. Had to come straight—like the sun.

Eddie's father, cutting Lila, when he loved her! And my daddy sewed her up.

"Lila, is love—is love a great *peril?* Like in fairy tales."

Lila sits upright in the tub. "What your mama go say, she find us in her bath? 'Lila, git your black hide out of there right this minute!' "

"Mother wouldn't say that! Besides you *lived* with her. You just don't want to tell me."

"In the long bye-m-by," Lila croons, smiling slyly. "Bye-m-by!"

We get out and dry off on fluffy towels, but they're not warm like the ones at Lila's.

Still damp under our clothes, Lila heads us up the back path, under the poplar trees, toward Daddy's doctor office. "Why are we going here?"

"Dirt-ball!" Lila mutters. Oh the look on her face. She isn't calling *me* that. We just got out of the bath. Besides, none of us call names, ever. Except I slip sometimes with Eddie and he does with me. And what have I done anyhow? Nothing.

My father's nurse, Miss Fleurnoy, is at the office door, as if she's waiting for us. I hate her. She's tall and stick-like and her skin flaps on her legs and arms. Ugh! And yanked-back hair, narrow eyes, narrow lips over squirrel teeth. Even her name splinters, two nasty pieces. Lila calls her "Miz Flea Nose." And every time, Mother corrects her. *"Flerr-noy!"*

"Come in," Flea Nose says, boring her eyes into me, ignoring Lila, who stays behind on the porch. I look back, but Flea Nose pulls me inside. She leads me into Daddy's examining room and lifts me onto the table and begins to unbraid my hair, handling it as if spiders might come out. Lifting each wavy strand and peering at my scalp. Behind my ears. My neck.

"I'm perfectly clean, I just had—" Oops!

"Your father said I was to check you."

Check me? *Dirt-ball!* That I would get dirty at Lila's! "I am not dirty! I'm cleaner than I usually am at home!"

"There's dirt and there's dirt," Miss Flournoy presses her lips together. "I would have been happy to have you stay with me. Get undressed."

"No!" I will not get naked in front of Flea Nose. And what was that she said? Me? Stay with *her*? "No! No! No!"

She reaches for the phone. Dials. Hands it to me.

My father's voice. Firm and distant. "There's impetigo going around, Willis." I know what that is. You break out in blisters and it comes from not washing.

"I didn't get impetigo. I'm *not* staying with Miss Flournoy. I'm not undressing in front of her!"

"Who said you were staying with her? Now do what she tells you. For me. And don't let me hear that you had one of your fits."

I hunch naked on the table, choking. Rolling my eyes up as far as I can into my head. Frogs do that so they can swallow.

Miss Flournoy pokes around my body. Under my arms, back of my knees. Her fingers cold and hard, like the witches the time I broke my leg.

My body, my secret body, feels so dirty now in spite of the magic bath. And like someone else's body at the same time. Far away. On the moon. The bumps where my bosoms are supposed to grow but naturally aren't yet. My fat legs, the skin mottled white and purple and covered with goose bumps.

Suddenly, Miss Flournoy spreads my legs—before I can slam them shut—and touches me there. I howl!

"Someone should teach you to wipe yourself."

I gag. I can't even say I just took a bath.

I am still burning and choking when my clothes cover me again, and Lila and I are walking away. My hair is loose now, and usually I like that. Today I hate it. *I hate it.*

"She—touched me youknowwhere." Lila holds my hand very tight. "I'll tell Daddy and he'll fire her."

"What you go tell him?"

"I'll tell him—." *Now do what she tells you. For me.*

And I know I can't tell. I don't know why. But I can't.

"Tell him she lookin' for nits?" Lila glowers. "Your daddy say *take the child there be checked over tho-ro-ly.'* "

"I'll slice her up in little pieces. I'll borrow Eddie's birthday knife. I'll cut her up so nobody will marry her! Grandmother says, *'Nobody would marry that stick!'* Or maybe someone will and love will burn her up and bust her wide open."

I am never going to speak to my father again. Not ever. They can kill me. I'll do everything they hate.

We walk walk walk, and my body cools. At last. We stop in the cemetery and Lila sits under Grandfather's tree by his monument that says Beloved Physician, and makes an acorn horse. But it's not the same. Flea Nose has changed everything.

"She looked everywhere—but she didn't even find the chigger in my toe!" I whisper, leaning my head on Lila's arm. "Stupid Flea Nose." I'm crying but I hold it as far in as I can.

Dance is still at Lila's, but thank heaven Eddie hasn't come home. Dance takes my foot in his hand and smothers the itchy chigger-bump with butter. "Butter make it so he can't breathe. Make him back right out that little hole," Dance says.

A chigger's so tiny you can't see him, but he's made a little hole in my body. A place for awful things to grow.

"Ani-miles goes in two by two. Come on, Missy, show us how you shimmy!" But even if Eddie never comes back, my skin crawls at the thought. I'll wipe now—all over—till I have no skin left! I'll grow hair over my face, arms, legs, everywhere. Like the Wolf Boy in Daddy's book.

At dusk, Eddie runs in and bolts his dinner. Is about to rush out again, when Lila yells, "Hold on! You can just set here with us a spell." Eddie groans. He fidgets, looking out the window. Goes into his room and for once leaves the door open. His bed isn't made. Clothes all over the floor. Dirty underwear. Pictures of prizefighters on the walls. But I knew it already. I sneaked in once.

Eddie turns on the radio as loud as he can. I put my fingers in my ears and lay my head on the kitchen table.

When I look up, it's dark outside. A rapping at the door. Eddie jumps and runs to open it.

Expecting Miss Laura Keene! Does he love her like the sun and the rain? But it's only Dance again, bringing in some wood for the cook stove.

"Lemme teach you to play mumbley peg," Eddie says to me.

"Me?" I sit up.

"Out in the yard on the table." Oh. He wants to be where he can watch for Laura Keene.

"Go on out, honey, cool off," Lila says, pressing her hand to my forehead. I duck away. But after a while I slip out the door.

The yard's all wrapped in black velvet. I can't see a thing. I don't care if a million Zombies are watching me in the night. I hope they come and get me.

At the picnic table sits Eddie. Tossing his knife and when it comes down, it sticks in the wood. Thock. Thock.

"Come on, I show you."

My mother won't let me touch knives. I grab at it.

Eddie holds the knife away. "Easy, there! You gotta watch me."

"It's too dark."

"Go turn on the bulb by the door."

When I'm sitting down again, he balances the knife point

on the tip of his pointer finger. Then flips. The blade flashes up and comes down, sticking into the table. Thock! Eddie goes through all the fingers of his left hand; even the little one. Then the right. Thock thock thock. The knife quivers and sings at every hit.

Whee-eeww! A little whistle from the back alley. Eddie tosses the knife down and rushes off into the darkness.

If I follow him, I'll find him with his girlfriend. Yuck. Bad Laura Keene. He has a picture of her on his closet door, I saw it when I sneaked into his room. He pinned her face on the door and drew a naked body under it. With nipples and hair down below!

Can I balance the knife on my finger? Ooh. Hurts, makes a little dent. How does he flip it? I drop it straight down, I want to hear the singing, thocking. But it doesn't work.

Perhaps I'll go in and cut up Eddie's dirty picture. Make a scar across Laura Keene's skinny body. Like Eddie's daddy cutting Lila. But my daddy could never sew up that cut.

I could cut myself to pieces. And Flea Nose would be put in jail and killed. I'll write a note: Miss Fleurnoy. No—Flea Nose —is the one killed me.

I rest my cheek on the cool wood and my head becomes a jar of water, tears run out of my eyes. Nobody's here so it doesn't matter, I don't have to pretend.

Pieces of the day whirl by me. The stars speed up in the sky. My clothes melt off. I'll have to ask everyone an embarrassing question—*Do I have any clothes on?*

Daddy won't understand. Mother will cry and ask why can't I be reasonable? Grandmother will tell me to stop my foolishness.

Lila. What'll Lila say?

Baby birds dead in the nests, ants on their eyes. Chickens with their heads off flopping in the yard. Fish floating in a pail, waiting to be scaled and eaten. Salt water, like tears.

Lila with her insides out—stripped!

Without a skin I'll drown. Wash away on the river. Sink to the bottom.

Not even bones to reach the ocean.

"Will-ie—Will-*ie!*"

Lila. Standing in the light of the door. Hands locked over her stomach scar.

I wait one breath. Two breaths. Three—then I walk back inside the house.

12

1981

TRASH

First thing Friday mornings, I take out Lila's garbage the way I did sometimes when I was a ten-year-old. Thursday night, last thing, Lila sprinkles the garbage with baking soda and ties it neatly into newspaper packets, as if anything she's used, even what's beyond use, deserves respect. The packet doesn't go into the can outside till daylight on garbage day, because she doesn't want to attract "pests."

I take the packet out, put it in the can, weight down the lid with a cinderblock on a rope. This will keep out possums and raccoons. And the baking soda will discourage the neighborhood dogs. For good measure, I pour little ammonia on top.

When I was little, Lila showed me how she trapped possums in Grandmother's garbage. She used a contraption with a pulley and a brick that slammed the lid down when the possum went in. I no longer remember the other details.

When she got one, she'd kill it—never in front of me—and cook it with persimmons to cut the grease. She doesn't do this anymore.

Today I can't get the smell of garbage out of my nose. Our

deer's in there—bits and pieces of him. I can smell the process of his breaking down.

Later, in the car, Dance's cigarettes and the rich loamy aroma of his clothes make me feel a little better. Men's smells are so downright and identifiable. Lila's smells are complex and mysterious. The old Li-lulie mix of Clorox, kerosene, cooking, Chantilly bath powder.

Do Dance and Lila make love? Daddy used to take me with him to pick Lila up on cold or rainy mornings, and when she got in the back, I'd hop over the seat and snuggle up close. Sometimes a smell would waft around us, pungent and organic. Not the rusty-metal smell of blood from her periods. I knew all about those. The morning smell was different. Years later I recognized it coming from myself. The smell of sex.

Today we troop in to Perk-ups' office, all three of us. All of us smelling better than roses. Lila has Hard Rock's paper, she goes in first, then Dance, then me.

I get my first shock. Mr. Perkinson doesn't see this whole Chillus situation the way we do! "What do you want from me, Willis?" he says. "A sick old man, hospitalized. Where's the money for all that coming from? What would happen if *you* got sick without insurance?" What indeed?

"Mr. Crowder has Medicare."

Perkinson looks at the papers. "There is a balance owing of almost a thousand dollars."

"Is that a big enough balance to sell his farm for?"

"You going to pay it?"

His reasonableness abashes me. I hadn't thought of any of those things. "Yes, I'll pay it." Then I panic inside. I don't have a thousand dollars.

But my chances of getting it are better than Lila's.

Guilty look at Perkinson. At Lila, who's gone into the familiar death-grip mode, purse to belly. "Well," I say, "I am not

101 years old, being fleeced by a white lawyer who should be protecting me. At the very least, looking for alternatives!"

Silence.

"We would like to see his mother's will," I say.

"You," says Perkinson, frowning, "have been—"

What? Too influenced by these ignorant blacks who are forever crying "victim"? Oh, Perk-ups, our shining white knight, your rust spots are showing—

"—have been in New Yawk too long," he finishes. "You don't even sound like Mattaponi County any more. You think bad things of us."

I don't respond. I'm registering my second shock of the day: I am no longer "us" to Perkinson. Well, of course not. But I didn't dream *he* knew it.

So where am I "us"? Not in New York, lord knows. Until two minutes ago, I'd have said with Lila. But she's glaring. Is it my fault Perkinson is wavering?

No. *I* wavered, and she saw it. One little waver.

Perkinson finally agrees that we should see Lila's gramama's will. He sends us to Mr. Nat Hutchinson, Mother's cousin and everybody's legal mentor. "Even the Nigras go to him. He's retired from being judge," Perkinson says, "but he consults. If he says to go ahead with that will, I'll help you."

Out we troop, anger and confusion mixed inside me. Along with the feeling that I've misbehaved.

"Mr. Nat Hutchinson. My mama raised him," Lila says, shooting me the Look. *He won't waver,* that look says. *Not the one my mama raised.*

Mr. Nat is about Lila's age. I knew Mother "raised" Lila and cured her rickets. But till now I never thought about how that came about—Cora handing over her eight-year-old daughter to a white woman to treat her rickets? But Cora was off with someone else's kids, of course. Like Lila raised me while Haddy raised Precious Eddie.

Oh, the envy and hate of babes! The ones we long for and ache to be with, always belong to somebody else.

Mr. Nat still has his office, complete with law library and secretary—and odors of book dust and leather and medicinal-old-man. "I didn't want to give up the accoutrements of usefulness when I was retired," he says, waving us to seats. He's tall, rigid, pale as stone. I remember his mustache, but nothing else about him comes back to me.

Lila marches past me and perches herself in the chair nearest the desk. "You rember my mama, Mr. Nat," she says, "Cora. Cora Neal."

Mr. Nat doesn't look at her. "Ah, Willis. I miss your father to this day. Miss his humor and his counsel."

"Cora Neal," Lila repeats. "She raise y'all. You and your sister Miss Haw-tense."

He says nothing. I've never known Lila to misjudge a social scene before.

Mr. Nat is to Lila what I was to Eddie. Does he feel it? Behind that marble forehead, the thwarted infant rages? His face is dead white and still, all seams and crevasses, decorated by a neat white ring of hair over his lips—like milk. Compared to Lila—his milk sister—he looks frozen. And if there's an infant under there, or anything as interesting as rage, I can't see it. Not in his icy face nor his mottled, precisely folded hands.

I reach across the gap that separates my chair from Lila's and touch her arm. Oh yes—I wavered. For five seconds. I didn't fall away. She's shrunk back, now, purse to belly again. Dance twirls his hat between his knees and stares at the floor.

"About that will," Mr. Nat says, after reading the papers, "you will find a copy, and I suspect from this instrument that one exists, at the County Clerk's office. And if it is what it seems to be," tapping the Spauldin papers again, "you can see that Lila gets a part of the old man's estate after the property is sold."

"I aint want it sold."

He sighs, still without looking at her. "Well, we know how it goes with these old folks. Can't look after themselves. And debts. Sometimes the lawyers in charge *do* take a bit more than is strictly their due. But long as it's not too far out of bounds, there isn't much we can do." In the long silence, a clock ticks.

"They take what they *think* is their due, no doubt," Mr. Nat goes on at last, "and it's a job, looking after the old." A job, his tone suggests, that no one wants. Voice is dry and precise. The sort of voice I was raised never to contradict.

He winces suddenly, the stone lines about his nose and jaw break into gray pebbles. He's one of those old people himself and that knowledge is in his intelligent, cold eyes. "They put me out to pasture, you know. But I refused to be pastured! I consult with the poor now, free of charge."

I hear Chillus's ice whisper: *They set me out in the field! For the bu-urds and the wuhms to pick me!*

"So you know what it's like to be trashed! Mr. Crowder was..."

Lila hisses. I'm telling a secret.

Mr. Nat's dark, combed eyebrows head for the sky. His mouth puckers up, like a dog's ass. Sorry—*anus!*

"Mr. Falcon Sprawldin Senior was the best white man I ever know," Dance rasps out suddenly, saving us all. Mr. Nat's face returns to its normal stone. Not Chillus-stone—earthen stone, natural and compelling. This man is carved marble.

"Yes," he says. "He *was* fine. The old man was wise to trust his affairs to him. Who could have foreseen he'd outlive his lawyer?"

Back in the car, Dance cracks the window and lights a cigarette. "More to this than meet the eye," he says.

"Did G. Falcon Junior *inherit* Chillus? Or did someone in the family pick him when G. Falcon Senior died?"

Dance blows smoke out the window. "Nobody pick nobody. County assign 'im to Senior, then to Junior."

Lila presses the spot on her chest. Drilling a hole. "Claim Chillus been *neglected*."

All the holes in her heart—the old holes: Eddie. Haddy. My parents. The new holes: Chillus. The farm. Now Mr. Nat, who won't even acknowledge his milk-mother's name. And then there was my waver.

I want to say I'm sorry. I've many found things in myself this visit to make me sorry. I want to say I love her, cherish her. I'm with her.

~

THE COURT HOUSE is in another town, twenty miles to the southeast. The car purrs and hums. Lila is silent. Dance has nothing to say, no guiding finger over the car seat even. Their silence reeks of the death of hope. If I gave up right this minute and turned around neither one of them would make a peep.

The County Clerk is Mr. Nat's nephew, another Mr. Hutchinson, a sort of cousin to Mother, too, I suppose. Crisscrossing bloodlines here define you backward for five, six generations. This Mr. Hutchinson hasn't a scruple of his uncle's strength. A toy of a man, too small for his own ears and for the big chair in his office. Sits behind a giant desk, swinging his little feet. His is the strength of a bouncing rubber ball.

"I heard that bit of propitty was up on the market," he says.

Doesn't greet Lila or Dance, even after I introduce them.

"I know every transaction on every parcel in this county, you believe 'at?" Cackles. Of course I believe it. He's been County Clerk for eons.

"How can it be on the market, when this—instrument— hasn't been heard?"

"Oh, I expect it was heard and agreed," he said. "These

things get sent in the mail, but who knows how long it takes to go their routes? You got a mailbox?" He turns to Lila suddenly.

She shakes her head, no. "Mail come through the slot."

"Well there you are. Put in the wrong slot, I have no doubt."

Turns back to me. "You'd be s'prised at the number of parcels changed hands not once in 150 years! Now that place, worn-out land, grazed to death. Tobacco don't even grow on it. But it's got the river at the bottom, you know. Somebody'll buy it just for that. Tear down the old wrecks and put a decent road down to the water."

Old wrecks! And it's plain he's seen the place!

Mr. H sends his secretary for Lila's gramama's will. "Harriet Crowder, Harriet Crowder, freed woman. I recall that will. Did I see it recently? I know every will in this county too, you believe 'at? Read every one of 'em."

Secretary returns. The will's missing.

"Missin?" he shouts. "A will (he says *we-all*), in my care *(cay-ah)*, missin?" After a moment, he collects himself and says that perhaps Spauldin has it. "Shouldn't have removed it, mind you. But these old hand-written documents—devilish hard to copy on a machine, you know. Got to write 'em out, word by ever-lovin' word. You go to Spauldin, now, and tell 'im I sent you. Tell 'im to give you that we-all. If he has it. And you bring it back here to me."

Spauldin is in still another town. By the time this day is over, we'll have covered three fourths of the county. On the way, Lila pulls a bag from her purse and hands sandwiches to Dance and me. Leftovers. Yum. She eats half a dry ham biscuit, slipping it into her mouth and chewing behind her hand. Tucks the other half into her handkerchief. Pours us a communal cup of coffee from a battered thermos. Sugared to death, no cream, in deference to Dance's tastes.

"I guess that was the only argument you ever had with Rumpelstiltskin," I say, glancing at him in the rear-view mirror.

His eyes go round and startled. "If I remember, Rumpy liked *his* coffee with cream." Lila would pour him a saucer full and put it under the table.

Lila clucks. "Old Rump! Been a age since I thought of that old dog."

But in the mirror, Dance's eyes have turned to hollows. He's thought of Rumpy, all right. I wish to heaven I'd never opened my mouth.

Love is not "reasonable." Connected to a million pathways in our brains—a falling down farm. A dog. An old woman who is not my blood mother.

At G. Falcon Sprawldin's I get my umpteenth shock of the day. Several at once, in fact. First of all, he's expecting us. Which means that somebody called him. Second, he's furious. We don't even get properly in the door. He pushes us back out onto the sidewalk, shouting. "Take a we-all from the Co't House? That is agains' the law. You accusin' me of breakin' the *law*?"

I say no, we were sent by Mr. Hutchinson, but Spauldin's a bulldozer. His red head blazes, eyes shoot flames. Any second, his Bourbon breath will ignite!

God, does that smell take me back! My stomach gives a twist.

"You git these filthy liars outta my office, take yo'se'f right with 'em. Blackin' my good name. I'll sue you. Libel and slander! Heard of that up in Yankee land?"

"*Liars?* You're drunk, mister! You're drunk and *crazy!*"

And he swings at me—Lila drags me backward just in time to feel only the rush of air. She hauls me out to the car.

How can I drive? Shaking and sobbing, can't get my breath. Having a fit! A fit!

God, if that bastard is watching—

"He tried to hit me! I'm going to call the cops!"

"Whoa up, there," Dance says. "Po-lice don't do no good here."

"He tried to *hit* me! What the hell are the police for—"

Dance laughs his laugh. "Had a dime for every swing I felt the wind of, I be a millionaire! Po-lice take one look at us and at him . . ." his voice trails off.

Well, at least I'm "us" again.

Where are *we*? In the country of the helpless and ignored. The police would choose not to believe me if I came with Lila and Dance, complaining about a white lawyer. Even if I *am* the old doctor's daughter and the Hutchinsons' kin. I'm contaminated by the company I choose and by twenty years of Yankeeland.

When at last I pull away from the curb, Dance touches my shoulder, says, "What I say about Mr. Falcon Senior was the truth. A good white man. Only white man I ever trusted." Meets my eye in the mirror. What is he doing? I'm a million miles out of sight of land—no maps or markers. Lost at sea.

No, I am *not* wavering. But I'm out in the cold. Dance is playing peace-maker. But why to me? Apologizing. For Lila? Himself? For a world where Mr. G. Falcon Senior, a fine man worthy of trust, could spawn such as G. Falcon Junior? My cousins, the good and the evil?

"Are you saying *Senior* wouldn't of done this?"

Dance looks away.

Trash. We're trash. We what's left after the world skins us. All the people thrown out, not just the old—Chillus and Mr. Nat. But Lila and Dance. Lila living in an old house filled with three generations of my family's throwaways. Dance living in a shack with holes in the walls. Me, up in New York, scraping by. All skinned and tossed away.

What happens to me when I am with them? In New York I may be poor, but I cope just fine. I'll stand up to anybody, police, courts, whatever. But here? The people, white people tell me in a hundred little ways that I can cross back over onto the power side only by abandoning Lila.

Dear God, the farm will be destroyed. What did Mr. Hutchinson say? Tear down the *wrecks.* The old mule stalls, still faintly smelling of manure and grain. If you get up on what's left of the barn roof, you can see the shining Mattiponi weaving through bare trees. And in Lila's old room in the falling down house, full of rain-soaked plaster and dust, the feathery mud daubers' nests stand out like angel's wings on the peeling tarpaper.

When I was little, she taught me that the dauber, *dirt dobba,* she calls it, doesn't sting. Taught me the smell of mice—musty and acidy with urine and something indefinable. Organic. Mortal. She taught me the dry sour scent of snakes. And the smell, everywhere, of fear. She calls it "palpitations." She can smell palpitations.

Wrecks? The chimney, that wonderful old chimney, a dry-rock construction with two hearths? Lila, pointing up, said, "We the only ones have us a fireplace on the second floor."

History that doesn't count.

We're out of town now and I pull over, stop the car. Shall I go back to the Court House? Demand that Clerk Hutchinson pursue the missing will? Drive to Perkinson, make *him* get the will? He'll only say, *Why didn't you do what you were told?*

I'll buy the farm. Borrow the money from somewhere. Am I white enough for that? But every penny I make is spoken for. And what would we do with a piece of fallow land but pay taxes on it forever? Yet I can't get that dream out of my head.

Knuckles blue on the steering wheel. Hate in my heart.

I crank down my window, lean over Lila to open the window on her side, too. It's going to rain and the air is cool. She shivers, but I want the wind to come and blow us clean. Blow away the ashes of the day. Blow away rage and hate. *Fear!* Feel it coming toward you! G. Falcon Sprawldin Junior flew at me with the rage born of guilt. And if Lila hadn't jerked me away, he'd have hit me. I wish he had. Nothing Dance or anybody said would have stopped me from prosecuting that vile man if he'd connected with my skin.

But oh—to feel rage coming *out* of you. Consuming you.

What am *I* afraid of? That "they" can destroy me? Worse, destroy something I love. And something I value in myself.

"Let it go," Dance murmurs.

For a second I go on choking. Then the feeling ebbs and once more I am as helpless as they are. I *am* them.

Lila, I can't save your farm. You didn't raise me to think Falcon-Sprawldin-white.

Dance says, "You want to go back to the Co'thouse, we go in with you, but I ruther be home with my pig!" He gives his wheeze-laugh.

"Come on, honey," Lila sighs. "We still got our paper. Start up this old heap, take us home. Time to fix some folks some dunner."

And it's late! The headlights show just the gray road with its white line, bare trees, like sticks, whipping by.

The round of use and refuse begins again.

13

1947
RUNAWAY

"Get up!" my mother says. The overhead light bursts into my eyes. "Up. We're leaving."

It's the middle of the night! "Where—where are we—"

"Hush," my mother says. She's thrusting me into my clothes. Her voice is strong and hard. She smells of perfume, not the old sicky sour smell. "You're always spending time alone with Lila. Now you and I are going on a little trip." Pulls me to the door with hands that are strong and firm. There are four large suitcases, and the dog Rumpy, on a leash.

"Where's Lila? Where's Daddy?"

"Hurry! Robert is here."

At the car, Mother says, "Robert, I am giving you Rumpelstiltskin. I know you love him and will take care of him." She makes a little gasping sound. "You'd better take him now—"

Dance, in his driver's uniform, even though it's the middle of the night, puts the suitcases in the trunk. He doesn't look at me.

My mother and I are in the back. Whirling in a black and

white blur of love, Rumpy hops into the front seat next to Dance.

"Hurry!" my mother cries.

"Miss Anne," Dance says, "you sure you feel all right? Mistah Doc go have my hide."

"I am perfectly fine." My mother jerks herself upright. "You're driving for *me*. Let's go."

"Mother! Where are we going!" This is almost fun. A new Mother? All perfume and adventure! Dance is driving us out of town!

Mother suddenly glares at me. "Don't you *dare* have a fit."

As if I had even been crying!

"Train station a hour away, Miss Anne," Dance says, glancing at me in the rear mirror.

So I know we're going somewhere by train.

At the train station, Mother sends Dance in to buy tickets. "To the Beach. So be happy," she says to me. She gets him to buy cups of coffee for himself and her, a Coke for me. A Coke, in the middle of the night!

And the Beach! "Will we stay at our same cottage? Will Miss LeMoine meet us?" I love Miss LeMoine's old wood-sided station wagon. She lets me sit next to her and steer. She looks like a mad duck, staring down her long flat nose with her little yellow eyes. But she's really nice. "Will the war be over at the Beach too?" The war, Daddy says, was right *at* the Beach. Planes going over all the time, and ships coming in and out.

"The war is long over, Willis."

"Everywhere?"

She grits her teeth and looks mad.

"Is Lila there already?" Probably shouldn't ask, if she's mad about something, but I can't help it. Sometimes Lila goes ahead and fixes up our cottage. I always ask to stay with her in Miss LeMoine's servant's quarters, but the answer is always *"No!"*

138

Daddy joins us on weekends. Eddie never comes! He has to stay with mean old Haddy.

Mother takes her coffee from Dance's hand, "Ahhh!" Sinks back into the seat. Dance pours some of his coffee into a little dish for Rump, who sniffs it and whines. He wants to lap it up. Wants to please Dance. But he hates it black. Dance clucks and goes back into the train-station restaurant for milk.

I sip my Coke. The night air is cold, and silent. The streetlight makes shadows in the parking lot. How exciting, to travel at night! I hope Daddy and Lila will be waiting when we get there. A surprise. They never even hinted!

"You'll remember what to feed Rumpy, won't you, Robert?" my mother says. "He's yours now."

"Mine?" Dance says slowly, "For keeps?"

"For keeps."

But Rump is Daddy's too! Though now he only likes Dance.

Suddenly Mother laughs. "At least once a week he runs away to you." That's true. We find him at Dance's, curled up on the old army cot, asleep and happy. And he yearns back at Dance out of the car window when we drive off.

What will Daddy say? What will it be like not to have Rumpy? Whenever anything happens, like a fart, you can blame Rump. "Rumpelstiltskin is my name!" And everyone laughs instead of scolding.

But I guess I can visit him at Dance's. Or Lila's.

I am awakened by Dance, carrying me in his arms. The train puffs and groans, and curls of steam wreathe about us like ghosts. Dance climbs the steps and sidles with me into the compartment, eases me onto the soft seat and covers me with the car blanket.

"Have the dead come out to jitterbug?" I ask him. Dance smiles and shakes his head.

"What?" my mother says, frowning.

"Good-bye, Miss Anne," Dance says. "You sure, now—"

"Good-bye, Robert. I will see that you get none of the blame."

"Blame for what?" Have I done something bad?

Dance has gone. The train begins to lurch along, clacking, wheels singing. Sharp smell of soot. My mother, sitting in the seat opposite me, stares out of the window. It's dark. And there are two dim train cars, one where I'm lying and the other, perfect, in the window.

"Floozy," she mutters. "That floozy!"

"Flea Nose?" I ask. Her crimes have caught her at last?

She turns her head to me. "Go to sleep, heartstrings." She used to call me that whem she'd wake me up at night, smelling funny and wobbling. It makes me shudder. She's put on a sweet voice, but I can tell it's pretend. She pulls the blanket around me, tucks a pillow under my head. "That floozy," she sighs again.

"Who's *Floozy?*"

"A bad woman."

"Do I know her?" It is Flea Nose. Mother has found out what Flea Nose did to me. But why would she take *me* away for that? I don't know what to think.

But Lila and Daddy will take care of it at the Beach. Lila and Daddy.

MISS LEMOINE MEETS us in her station wagon with the wooden sides and squishy seats. I hop right in the back and flip up the little half-seat.

"I think you're very foolish," she says to my mother, who whispers. *"Little pitchers."*

"You should have thought of that before," says Miss LeMoine, and flings our suitcases into the back.

I twist till I can see Mother's shape in the dark. Something is definitely happening. "You've never had your life smashed to pieces! What could I do?" Mother sounds like she's crying.

In the morning, I wake up to sunlight. I'm in Mother's room, on a cot. Which would be okay, only where is Lila? "Why are we here? Where is Lila? Is Daddy here yet?"

My heart is sinking. They are not here at all. They are not coming.

My mother smokes and looks out of the cottage window. "We're here because I want to spend some time with you."

I sit up. "Then I want to call home!"

"You may not make any calls."

Then the rest of the rules: I am not to go alone to the yard, the beach, or the cottage. I cannot go anywhere alone, especially Miss LeMoine's office, where the phone is.

"We never have rules like this here."

No answer.

"Why am I in *jail?*"

I feel myself choking. But I stop myself, using all Lila's instructions—breathe, swallow. Breathe some more. I *won't* give Mother the satisfaction of a fit.

"What did I *do? Moth*-er!"

"Nothing!" she snaps. "You did—*nothing!*" A new kind of crime.

Well, I'll just have to spy.

Spying is easy. First you listen carefully to whatever you hear. Every word is probably a code. And you linger outside doorways when you've been sent from the room—bend over, tie your shoe. Crouch under windows. Better not get caught at that. You come back from the beach to go to the bathroom 20 times a day, when you've been sent with the children or the servants.

"Is something wrong with your bladder?" my mother asks. "Do I have to take you to a doctor?" A doctor?

Two days of snooping have given me these facts: This has

nothing to do with Flea Nose or me. My father has done something bad. And so has Floozy, who listened to my mother's opera records and slept in Mother's bed while Mother was in the hospital.

The new Mother is fading. The old Mother is crying a lot in Miss LeMoine's office (where I can't go), and when we're together, she wears her suffering-in-silence look. We don't do anything but take long walks up the beach at sunset, counting the planes zooming over and watching the spotted ships go by on the horizon.

"Think of the poor pilots and sailors, Willis," my mother says in her dramatic tragedy voice, "who *love* their wives and daughters. And will never come home to them again."

"Why not?"

She shoots me a look. "They are killed in the war."

"You said the war was over. Long time ago."

She tightens her lips.

One day I ask: "What has Daddy done? This adventure is sad and I want to go home."

I don't expect an answer. But she hisses: "He has hurt me *unutterably*. And you. He has hurt you. He doesn't deserve us."

But Daddy hasn't hurt me. Not since my broken leg.

"I want Lila."

Mother stops in the sand. "Oh god, Lila this, Lila that—I'm sick to *death* of Lila!"

Sick of Lila! Mother has always loved Lila. Even when she's mad at me.

"We'll be special friends, Willis. Can't we be friends? The way you and Lila are." She leans over me. The perfume smell is gone—the sour smell is back. My throat is tightening.

"Oh, Jesus, *don't* have a fit. I will go to *pieces*. You never take my side." Tears run out of her eyes as if she doesn't know they're there. I swallow the choking feeling.

Act like someone else, her eyes say. Be someone else. For me. Please!

At home, I can fight that. But here—

MOTHER BORROWS Miss LeMoine's sewing machine and begins to make clothes. Whirr, goes the machine as she pedals. When she sews, she seems happier, hums and sings. She makes us both blue blouses with lace collars, in which we look like pigs dressed up.

She brushes my hair till my scalp is raw. Counting every single stroke. But she braids better than Lila. She doesn't pull, and when the braids are undone, my hair fluffs around my face. "Aren't you pretty, heartstrings?" she croons.

"We won't have any secrets from each other," she says one day. "What secrets do you have to tell?"

My throat begins to close again. I don't have any secrets I want to tell her. The Café? That's over anyway.

What about her secrets? Why we're here, when we're going home. Maybe if I tell her about Flea Nose, she'll tell me things, too. "Flea Nose," I start.

"Miss Fleurnoy," Mother corrects me absently, the way she does Lila.

"No! Hateful Flea Nose!" I cry. The very name makes me feel as if my clothes are melting off. "Mother—do I have—am I *naked*?"

"What?" Mother says sharply. "Are you trying to torment me?"

What will make her feel better? "I cried every night you were in the hospital," I lie. "I was so worried."

A smothering, sicky-sour hug! "Oh, my heartstrings!"

Every morning I stand by the gate, looking for Daddy and Lila. Come get us, I pray. Please please. Come take us home.

Surely Dance has told where we are. Surely surely you know that Mother has gone all funny.

One day, when I come from the beach, full of sand and salt, Mother says, "I have enrolled you in school here."

School? "No! No! I want to go home! I want Lila! I want Daddy, I don't care what he's done!" My breath is coming in squeals. All my plans to be nice, not have a fit, be what she wants, melt away. I shriek.

Her hand is a blur and my cheek stings.

Instantly, she falls on me, hugging me and sobbing. "I'm sorry, I'm so sorry, heartstrings, I shouldn't have hit you."

So this is what it's like to be hit!

"You were having a fit." She shivers.

I pull away. I'm still choking. I breathe—breathe breathe breathe. "I hate you. Lila knows how to treat me when I'm having a fit. I love Lila. I want to go *home*."

Oh! the floor will swallow me up. A roar and a rumble! Run! But I'm not fast enough. Mother is screaming and hitting her own thighs with her fists.

Silence at supper. Miss LeMoine passes our table several times, looking sharply at Mother and then at me. My throat is closed up and I couldn't possibly eat. I chew each bite for a long time, then spit it out on my fork before taking another. My plate has little gray piles.

Miss LeMoine sits next to Mother. "Two Gloomy Gusses if ever I saw. What is the matter?" Miss LeMoine is a cousin, and older than Mother, so she can talk like this.

My mother looks up from her plate. "Willis has broken my heart." Her voice when she says this is cold and clear, not all quavery the way she usually says it. She rakes me with her eyes. "I will have to think of some punishment."

Miss LeMoine snorts. "Oh Anne, your heart is tough as an old boot. I'd go a bit easy, if I were you."

"You know nothing about it."

"Probably best I don't." And Miss LeMoine gets up from the table.

After a moment, Mother gets up, too. She hasn't eaten either, only pushed her food around on the plate. She holds out her hand to me, shakes it impatiently. I put mine, slowly, into hers, like sticking it into a trap. She leads me to our cottage, gently brushes and plaits my hair. She stands over me while I undress for bed.

The next morning, she takes me by the hand again, and we head to the street. "Where are we going?"

No answer.

"Moth-er!" She tightens her grip. We walk, walk, walk silently through the town, past the shops. My feet are falling off!

We stop at a hair-dresser's.

"This is Willis," Mother says. "She has an appointment."

"What for?" I hate hair-dresser shops. They smell bad and the women have turd-curls and long scratchy nails and stained white uniforms.

"A lovely cut, deary!" The ugly woman smirks at Mother.

"But Lila gets my hair cut!" Lila takes me to Daddy's barber, who smells of spice and cuts off a quarter of an inch of my hair every two months. A quarter of an inch, not a bit more. He shows me on a ruler.

I am plunked into the plastic seat, and a crinkly paper and a stinky cloth are wrapped too tight around my throat. My arms are trapped under the cloth. The woman has loosened my plaits and begins brushing.

"Such lovely waves," she says soothingly. I look in the mirror. Yes, Mother's plaits have made beautiful ripples. I look like the picture of the princess in the fairy tale. Daddy will say, "My golden-haired prin-cess."

Suddenly! Whack! The hair—the ripples—on one side all fall away.

I cannot move or speak. Whack, whack. Whack. The shining ropes fall, hit my shoulder, slip out of sight. I dare not look down. My ears show under a stand-out bush of beige. When at last I open my mouth, it is only to gag.

"What's this?" the woman cries. Mother moves quickly toward me, but too late. I throw up on the cloth, the woman, and my golden waves lying dead on the floor.

14

1981

A REAL COUNTRY DO-SE-DO

The first time I came back to visit, before Lila and I had settled in—before our reconciliation or forgiveness had "taken," as Daddy used to say about vaccines—Dr. Brackson took me on a tour of the town.

We cruised the streets in his dark-blue Cadillac with the sofa-seats, slowing for his lecture about the new library, truly new, since there'd never been an old one. The Presbyterian Church moved stick by stone and covered in hideous fake brick. The new bank, the old bank having morphed into an agricultural agency. He wouldn't have driven into Sugar Bottom at all if I hadn't urged him, and as it was, he just bumped along the ruts, passing the old shacks and dirt yards without a word. Shabby barbershop with its broken pole, peeling paint on the churches. Nothing here had changed in years.

Except one thing. When I was little, the Jefferson Davis Café, where Lila and her friends used to dance and drink beer, was tacked onto the front of the Garland Davis Funeral Parlor. The café is still there, called just The Davis now, but the back end is boarded up.

"Where's the funeral parlor?" I asked.

"Oh, old Davis is out of business," Brackson said, "everybody down here now goes to Newman."

I felt so sad. What I remembered of Mr. Garland Davis was that he was two people, the bartender who gave me Cokes, and the spooky undertaker. They even dressed differently, the one in a long white apron, the other in a black suit, bright white shirt, black bow tie.

The whole scene here was something from the old days that had real meaning, which the white churches and the banks, God knows, do not have for me. And it was gone. I remember thinking almost involuntarily—now the dead will never come out and jitterbug.

Well, the morning after the great legal-eagle battle, Lila says, "Honey, drive me over to Garland Davis."

"Garland Davis! Brackson said he's gone. Don't you mean Newman?"

She cuts her eye at me. "Garland Davis *gone?* Ha ha! *Mistah Garland* the *new man!* Built that Newman parlor. Built a new house, too, with fancy siding and a decent roof. No, honey, he's done good for himself. Whatever happens, folks go die."

She laughs a funny new little laugh—born in the last two days. And it's missing something. Joy, certainly. And more.

"Mr. Garland head up our NAACP," Lila says, as we pull up to a neat brick house. "If he *wants* to, I believe he could save the fa'hm."

NAACP in Mattaponi! Dr. Brackson's attitude is now wonderfully clear. He who came here a Yankee. Ah what a dance we dance. A real country do-se-do.

Mr. Davis's house is as neat as Brackson's own, if not as large. Is it that white people here can't adjust to the idea of a black middle class? Or for some reason, they don't want me or any outsider hostile to their thoughts to know about the presence of the NAACP?

Perkinson didn't tell me about Davis either. He had to know, though, being a town lawyer. Was he afraid I'd consult the NAACP? Cause a ruction?

The new Perkinson who says: "You've been up in New Yawk too long."

Lila nudges me, as she presses the doorbell. Now we'll see the Great Man. So I am expecting—something larger than life.

The door opens. "Mistah Garland," Lila says. "It is we."

And there is the NAACP. Staring at our feet! The man is so stooped all I can see is a coffee-colored skull ringed with white fringe. A sturdy cane is planted like a mast before him. He tilts himself back back back to get a good gander. Splotched skin, eyes like veined marbles—not a hint of the Lord of the Dead. He's swallowed in a three-piece tan suit, pink shirt, black knit tie, and he sways on his cane, a fragile Fred Astaire. When he finally gets me in view, he bursts out laughing. "I was expectin' a little curly head!"

Bingo. I never smell the set-ups. One of these days Lila's going to tell me her plans before she tells everybody else, and I'll know we've died and gone to heaven.

The house is clean and airless, the furniture pink velvet and marble. The chairs, though not the couch, which he's prepared for us, are covered in plastic. "My wife is gone these two years," he says, pointing us to the sofa with his cane. He says a hollow ringing "gone," like the one Lila uses for her gramama, Haddy, and Eddie, so I understand that Mrs. Davis has not abandoned him but is dead.

The house has the look of a stage set. The pink, surely, was her choice.

Are undertakers like doctors, not allowed to "do" their own families? What a weird thought.

When we've finished our tale—we? Lila has shut up like a clam and I have to do all the talking, elbow in my rib from time to time to stop a short-cut. When *I've* finished, Mr. Davis, sitting on the edge of a plastic-covered chair, locked hands on the head of his cane, says, "They don't want a black man to have and to pass propitty. They will take it so he can't leave it."

Well, finally it is said, aloud and with simplicity.

"We have a test case in Lunenburg right this minute." He looks at me sharply. Holds himself, with his cane, straight as a stake. Beside me, Lila sighs. Here is a savior worthy of the name. What Mr. Nat Hutchinson and Perk-ups will never be. And probably me, too.

"You know, that is all the organization—the National Association for the Advancement of Colored People—can do." His voice is slow and he enunciates carefully and correctly. "All we can do now, bring cases to court. Most of them fail. The present one we might enjoy some success with."

I wait, but he says no more.

"And Mr. Crowder?" I ask finally. "A case could help him and his family." A test case! Out of the corner of my eye, I see Lila sit up. Lila, part of a law case! Oh, how the ham in her would enjoy that! To be on the witness stand.

Or would she? Would I? Lord. Think of facing the Hutchinsons and Sprawldins on the other side of the table! Well, after the last couple of days, of course I'd get up there and talk. In fact, telling in court the scene at Mr. Falcon Spauldin's might be worth any price. But he, they all, have done far worse to Lila, to Dance, to a whole community.

"We get ourselves and our cases into the papers," Davis goes on. "That is the most important thing. People pay attention. The power of the press. Um-*hmm*."

Lila stirs, again. Chillus's story in the papers. He could be celebrated as he ought to be.

"You know, I have shaken the hand of the President," Mr. Davis says suddenly. "That would be Mr. Johnson, not this present bunch. And I have sat on committee with Senator Byrd. All because I have learned how to use newspapers. Yankee newspapers."

His voice is triumphant, but he is shaking his head, in a strange dual message of advancement and retreat. "There is not a thing we can do for Mr. Crowder."

Lila snatches her purse tight to her belly.

"We have to be careful to publicize those cases we *might* win, or that have a certain dramatic appeal."

"But Chillus Crowder is 101 years old! Surely that's dramatic!"

Davis waves poor Chillus away. "For a celebration. Congratulations! But he is not a destitute mother nor a gentleman cut down in his prime. We need trauma. Heartbreak!"

"*Heartbreak?*" All our hearts are breaking. "I'll give you heartbreak," I say. "Think of this old man set out in the field and left to die, and then picked to pieces by a greedy white lawyer—"

His face closes down.

"Chillus Crowder is history. Honest history."

Shake shake goes his head. Chillus is not the *right* history. "He's old, he's sick, in the hospital. Legitimate expenses, or could be made to seem so. And his own family may be the originators, that is, their treatment called down the County on him."

He knows the story, then. Of course.

Mr. Davis launches into more stories. The Civil Rights March in 1961 when he met Bobby Kennedy. How he saved Sugar Bottom, 1965, with the help of Senator Byrd.

"Harry Byrd fought integration to his last breath," I said.

"Yes, indeed. He was a staunch foe. But this kind of shenanigan was too picayune, it would count against 'im. So he used it to build some bridges. That is my belief. Helped 'im deny malfeasance in the big things. Not ideal, but that's reality. Now and again, we lay down our swords (he says *sodes,* in the old way) and come together." He smiles at me. "And both sides get some good. Here the white folks were all set to bulldoze

Sugar Bottom, the whole end of town, an eyesore, they said. Want to make a shoppin' center. Going to put up housing for the displaced, but you know what that would of been."

It sinks in, finally, that he is not speaking in parables. Someone was really going to bulldoze Sugar Bottom. "Lila's house, too? That part?"

On either side of me, they both nod. Lila's house too.

"Who?"

"Dr. Brackson and the Town Renewal Committee."

Ah, that ride, the whole show.

"But I own my house," Lila says.

"Exactly!" Mr. Davis shouts, as if he's been coaching very slow pupils. " 'And where will these people go?' I asked them, 'if you de-house them for the 'good of the community'? And they filled my ears with talk about this housing, paying the owners for their propitty, etc. Building new houses two miles out of town! 'And how are these poor people going to get to your fancy shopping center?' " His voice trails off, and he sinks exhausted till his torso is almost lying on his knees. The cane wobbles. His suit is getting rumpled—his prop, his armor.

Senator Byrd is dead. King is dead. Both the Kennedys are dead. The NAACP, brave movers and doers, have passed on to bigger venues, far from Mattaponi County. In such small places, the battle was all show, anyhow, a faint blaring of trumpets. And gone. *Gone.*

He is talking still, his voice a croak. Old and tired. A Lila, a Chillus, a Dance in fancy dress. And if we don't leave, he will go on being polite till he collapses.

"About the federally funded park on the outskirts of town. You know 'they' "—somehow his voice puts in the quote marks, he has become self-irony itself—"were going to build a swimmin' pool but restrict it to whites. Until I got the Senator to threaten to take away the federal funds. So they build the pool, the sign is up, big letters: 'State Park Pool. Open to all.' " A tinge of un-ironied triumph creeps back into the old voice. Then a long sigh. "But if you go to the park, you'll see that that pool is filled to the brim with cement." He says "see-ment."

He sighs again, a small sad wind.

"Such is the clever persistence of these people."

See-ment. The word, like the stone it is, drops Mr. Davis into my memory. Mr. Garland. The bartender at the Café, the Jefferson Davis, dressed in a spotless white apron. Mr. Garland, who gave me Cokes. And every time he handed me one, the glass bottle icy and a little wet, carefully wrapped in a white napkin, he'd say, "Your daddy will have my hide! He tells us how Co'cola is so bad for the teeth!" Did Daddy give his Coke and steak demonstration at the *Café*? I'd drink and Lila would nudge me: "Say thank you to Mistah Garland."

Mr. Garland, clapping and smiling as I danced and played the guitar on the table top. And when he was in the back, on the dreary days all funerals seem to take place, he would stand at the black-ribboned door, dressed all in black. And bow to the mourners, as if he were the King of the Dead.

Mr. Garland breaks the silence, as I'm searching for a proper "good-bye." "You and Miss Lila need to find yourselves a buyer, you know. Somebody they will sell to."

Both of us stare at him. And in a moment we are walking silently back to the car. We've been on a victory tour and a defeat, all in an hour. The new world swept so close, too, with its hopes of a reasonable order. And then faded to the old familiar, ugly game. We're too few, too tired. We can't cut the mustard. This is a white man's reel.

What do you do when you feel like this? Like the day of the North Ca'lina paper, I don't want to take Lila home. This time, because home is supposed to be a refuge, and I feel refuge-less. Her house is filled with her beautiful collection of so many pasts. If I went in now, those old things would grow teeth and close on me like a trap.

In the old days, when Lila was in a down mood, she'd call Eddie, "Bring our poles," she'd say. "Willis's and mine." As if she had to specify. Eddie hated fishing. Couldn't sit still, couldn't abide the outdoors, the silence. He'd sit in the car with the radio blaring. Or drive up and down the dirt roads in my daddy's car while Lila and I fished along the river till the bucket was full. (Lila fished. I swished my line.) And when we got home, Lila would make him wash the red dust off the car.

Today—too cold to fish. Too old to fish.

Legally, of course, we could go somewhere together to eat. Even to Leiter's, where I was allowed to sit at the soda fountain in the old days, but she was not. Until I caught on one day, why she was standing stiff behind me and not sitting on a stool. From then on, I took my free Cokes only from Mr. Garland.

Eat. I couldn't put a thing in my mouth. It would turn to dust.

Besides, law or no law, Lila would not be welcome at the counter with me. Even now.

"He a po' old critter. Mistah Garland," Lila says. "Used to be a big stout man."

A pause.

"We all nothin' but po' old critters." That new laugh. "National Association for the Advancement of Po' Critters!"

"Shall we go back to Perkinson? We can at least tell him what's happened." Leaving out the visit to Mr. Davis, of course. At least we've tried both the white route and the black.

Lila shakes her head.

That night, I lie in bed thinking. Dance always says there's something to learn from every defeat—so what have I learned? That I have never before truly understood Lila's weaknesses. Her hesitations, her fears. The dangers to her.

When I was little, that powerhouse in the kitchen, that sly smile, the wisdoms, tolerances, and love. In anything that even smacked of a face-off in my parents' world, they'd wilt. Letting

Daddy ban me from the Café. Letting dreadful old Flea Nose get at me. *Don't tell!* And I didn't. I couldn't have. I *should* have screamed the house down. I should have had a fit when my parents moved us and left Lila. Only I'd caught her fear. And I couldn't do any of those *shoulds*.

Oh yes, they got at her. Early and deep. Fear is a virus. Children catch it so easily. Lila is *brilliant*. Has deep, ocean-deep understanding of peoples' thoughts and motives. And where did this genius take her? Into the kitchens and sickrooms of a small town that used her arts and skills and paid her next to nothing. I can only think she couldn't value herself on some protoplasmic level.

My mother's condescension. Lila knew it for what it was, even chuckled at it sometimes. Fooling the white folks into thinking you're stupid and therefore harmless. My father's contempt. I felt that too, all my life. It burnt my skin off. Lila is black and I'm female. Two exotic species of ape. Old Dr. Brackson. She lets me know she doesn't really trust him, he's the best of a bad lot. He's old and careless of her and probably other old black people as well. In letting me see this, she's allowing me a little bit further into her truth. But do I do something about it?

Oh we've said again and again, Let it go. It's okay. But how could it be? I should take her to another, better doctor. But who? The town is fresh out of good doctors and she won't come to me in New York. Maybe a drive as far as Richmond, one of these days? A day trip. Like Grandmother, an excuse to go to Thalhimers?

So we are learning now to walk in each other's shoes. I'm now in exactly the same situation she was in when I was growing up. She watched me struggle and could do nothing. I'm watching her struggle and try as I might to do right by her, I'm doing exactly the same things she did long ago. I don't have the gumption to scream the house down.

It is plain to me that she did—does—love me. She watched

me being hurt and it wrung her heart. That mysterious love we cannot dictate to has existed between us, always.

Yet we end up leaving one another to fate. She was afraid in the face of three hundred years of overwhelming cruelty. And though she was my lodestar, she had another love—a more vulnerable one. Eddie.

Some children have many warm arms and loving hearts about them, so that they can accept, at an appropriate age, one of the truths we all have to accept at last. That we are not really anyone's one and only except to ourselves. And at the end, we are old and afraid of ineffable things. Illness. Poverty. Death. And weaving among them all, this alone-ness.

15

1947

CONJUHS

I have to start off by saying I did a really bad thing. I ran away from Mother. I took money out of her purse and bought a train ticket home. *How you had the nerve!* Grand-mother said. Daddy didn't say anything, at first, but he had a kind of "weighing" look. How did I *do* it.

When they saw my cut-off hair, Lila's mule mouth went tight. Daddy turned pale. Even Grandmother kept touching my head as if she didn't believe her eyes. "It'll grow back, it'll grow back!"

They're furious at me, of course. Mother wouldn't speak to me on the phone, even to tell me I'd broken her heart again. And Daddy has decided "we are not talking to this young lady!"

But it was too late. Except for Mother, they were all talking at once. Lila whispered, "Honey, you a *mess!*" I know that "mess" for Lila is good, while "nerve" for Grandmother is what mean boys have when they put toothpicks in her doorbell. Or a frog down my shirt.

I was expecting Grandmother and Daddy to grill me right away about my train ride—how did I get the ticket, the *money!* Which I definitely do not want to talk about. Or where I hid.

Because Mother and Miss LeMoine looked everywhere for me, even at the train station. I heard them calling and thought I was going to die. But I hid in a really brilliant place.

Daddy can't get me for fibbing to Mother because I didn't say anything to her. But I fibbed like anything to the conductor on the train, who sold me a ticket and punched it. And he called Daddy when the train got to the station house in Farmville.

Daddy always says you ought to wait to discuss serious things till you're not angry any more. Meanwhile I'm supposed to "think through" what I have done.

This morning, my whole runaway seems like a dream. Except for the throw-up. And the hair-dresser's goo. And the toilets. My hiding place was the Colored Toilet in the train station, the one place my mother would never ever look. And its smell is in my nose forever. Not even breathing Grandmother's violet perfume helps.

Since I got back last night, Lila and I are both staying with Grandmother, who got Dance to put a cot in my room by the big bed. *Lord knows I don't want to have to get up in the middle of the night with the child.* As if I'd cry in the dark like a baby!

So last night I went to sleep in my bed under Grandfather's portrait, which hangs in a big gold frame right over my head. He was frowning more than ever—didn't know me because of my hair probably.

But my baby toys are on the shelves in the room, as always, and the picture of all of us on the dresser. Lila—she's fuzzy and you can barely tell it's her—in the back, Mother holding my hand, Daddy looking serious, Grandmother smiling the way she always does in pictures. She's wearing white gloves and is standing half-sideways with her left foot out a little.

Oh, just to listen to Lila breathe and smell the Lila smell! Chantilly powder, Clorox, cooking. Yum. I wish this could last forever. I don't even care if they're mad me.

Except I mind about my hair. "Lila, do you have some herbs that will grow my hair?"

"Honey hysh!" Finger to her lips.

This morning, here is Precious Eddie, sitting at Grandmother's kitchen table. He's staying at night with mean fat old Haddy.

"What are you doing here? Why aren't you hanging round with your girlfriend!" Which makes Lila mad as hops! "Lila and me are staying with my grandmother."

Eddie is eating gravy and grits and waffles. He puts sugar on his grits and then adds gravy! Triple yuck! And then he stuffs a big piece of waffle in his mouth.

"I bet Laura Keene won't even let you eat in front of her!"

Grandmother taps her eyeglasses on the enamel table top and glares at me. Looks down at Eddie. "Manners are certainly not your long suit, my boy!"

I sit straighter so she will be proud of my manners even if I am in disgrace. She sniffs and sails out of the kitchen.

Grandmother eats breakfast before any of us—toast and cambric tea at dawn. Cambric tea is nothing but hot water, sugar, and milk—in bed! I have to be sick to eat in bed. And then naturally I don't want to eat, so what's the big deal?

In a second she's back. "Miss Anne to speak to you, Lila." My spoon falls in my dish.

"Don't you worry," Lila whispers, "your mama aint studying you this morning." She runs out to take the phone. Grandmother eases after her, to listen in.

"Why your mama cut your hair off?" Eddie asks the minute we're alone.

Oh, I'd forgotten my hair! Hot stuff burns my throat, and tears spurt out of my eyes. I *hate* crying in front of Eddie. I yank on the tufts till some strands come out by the roots.

"Must of did something really bad!"

"Did not!" Why doesn't somebody tell *Eddie* he can't talk to me?

"Ma say your mama run off from your daddy, but now you're home, he aint want her back."

"That's a lie! Daddy did something bad and Mother doesn't *want* to come back."

Eddie raises his eyebrows in his know-all look. "If you tell, I tell you something bring the hair back."

Bring back my hair! But he's smirking. Fibbing, to get me to tell. "You don't know anything. Dance says Laura Keene's boyfriend is going to slice you up like bacon!"

"Ma say you took the train all by yourself. Where you git the money? Bet you stole it."

Oh! How could he know?

"You go git it good, for stealing! How you keep your mama from finding you? She know you on the train, because she call Ma. But she didn't find you and stop you!"

Well! Wheedle all you want! I'm not telling you a thing.

He is eyeing me. "Lawd. You must be sharp—she'd of found me, sure as shoot." Shakes his head admiringly. "Uhm-*hum!* That's something!"

"I found a great place! The Colored Toilet at the train station. I *knew* Mother would never think of there!"

"Colored toilet! Colored toilet!" Eddie doubles up, hooting.

I hope I die before I ever tell Eddie a living thing again.

But now I know why Lila makes me go with her so she can use the White toilets wherever we are. And why she lines even the cleanest-looking seats with paper. Except there wasn't any paper in the Colored toilet at the train station.

"Look, I know all about trouble over stealing. You got any left-over money?"

Don't even look at him! I wish—I wish the Zombies would get Eddie!

"I just ask because that left-over money what get you in the worst kind of trouble. Prove you stole."

"Oh! I have some!"

"Better give it back."

The stolen money—I haven't thought of it all day. Now it weighs on me like pieces of lead. Can't give it to Daddy. He says stealing's worse than cursing. Or Grandmother. She'd have a fit. Thinks anything I do against Mother is worse than murder.

"Maybe give it to Lila?"

Eddie considers, tilting his head. "You give it to Ma, maybe your ma say my ma a sessory. Maybe she even have to go to jail."

Oh! I'd cut off my tongue before I'd get Lila in jail. Eddie knows that.

"Then you better hide it good and wait till your ma come home. Then you got to fess up and give it back to her."

Fessing. Facing Mother and handing her the money. Maybe I won't have to say anything. And if she says, "Oh Willis, you broke my heart!" why I'll scream that my hair is gone forever, not even Lila's yarbs will bring it back. My hair is worth a hundred dollars!

When will Mother be home? Maybe Lila will know after she hangs up the phone.

"Better hide it till then," Eddie says, "so nobody take it and say they found it and maybe you won't go give it back." Eddie's looking as if he knows a hundred people who've done just that.

My biscuits have gone dry and cold. Eddie, who's sopped up his gravy, points his knife at my plate. I shove it over to him and he eats my biscuits quickly, before Lila or Grandmother catches him.

"Mother should go to jail for cutting off my hair."

Eddie grins. "Hair don't count."

Why is it nothing that happens to me ever counts? Flea

Nose—that didn't count, either. *Shh!* Lila said. *Git us both in trouble!*

"Bet you could hide it upstairs," Eddie says when he's done chewing. He slips to the hall door and peeps around it. Motions me to follow him.

Lila's voice on the hall phone, saying um-hm and yess'm. "Lawd, Miss Anne, I can't say to Doc—" And Grandmother whispering to her. Eddie grabs my arm and pulls me up the back stairs. He goes straight to my room.

"How did you know which was mine?"

He raises his eyebrows. "I stay here once, with Mama. I *know* this house."

"You did not!"

"Shh! Did so!"

Lila lived here when she was a little girl. But Eddie couldn't of been with them, my mother and Lila. He couldn't have been. Oh Zombies, dear Zombies, come and get Eddie!

"Don't you have a fit now. Everybody come running, and find you with the money. Where it at?"

"Hide your eyes. Eddie! *Hide 'em!*"

Eddie puts his hands over his eyes, but he's peeping. I turn my back and bend over as if I'm reaching under the bed. But really, the money's still in my shoe. Made a knot under my foot so big I limped all yesterday.

I turn around and hand Eddie the mashed-flat lump.

Slowly he unrolls it. "Lawd! Must be a hundred dollars here!" He licks his thumb and forefinger and peels out the bills. "Eighty-five!" He whistles.

He looks around the room. Chests. Boxes on top of the chifforobe. "Any secret drawers or stuff?"

No.

Under one of the stiff old horsehair chairs?

Finally he comes to Grandfather's picture. I never knew Grandfather, but he has watched me, so stern, from his heavy frame, long as I can remember. *Bad man, bad man!* I'd scream when I was little. And Lila and Grandmother would both croon over me, *Go to sleep. He's a good man. A good man.*

"Your granddaddy was good to me," Lila says. "Talk to him, tell him who you be." And so at night when I sleep here I never forget to say, "Granddaddy, it's Willis here, again. Good-night Granddaddy. Don't fall off the wall and crush me."

In a flash, Eddie's on the bed with his bare feet, tugging at the heavy gold frame. Strings of dust come away with it. Eddie turns him face down on the counterpane. At least Grandfather won't see that he himself is a sessory.

The back of the frame is flat and straight. No place for even one dollar. And in a minute, Grandmother and Lila will surely get off the phone and come looking for us.

"Got any tape?"

I shake my head no. But wait! I have some glue on my toy shelf.

In a second; I've pressed great glops onto the wooden backing, and we spread out the bills, pressing them into the goo. Blowing, whoo, whoof whoof! Oh, hurry hurry. The glue's not drying. It's almost drying, it's drying.

"Enough," Eddie mutters. "These here aint go fall off now." He hops up and hangs Grandfather back in his place.

"It's me, Grandfather," I whisper. "We only took you down —to dust you."

"Don't you lie to the dead," hisses Eddie.

I shudder. "I'll tell you everything tonight, Grandfather, when I get into bed. I promise."

Everything. My hair, stealing the money out of Mother's purse, hiding in the toilet. And men and women both coming in, cursing to see my feet under the door of the only stall.

Eddie snickers. "You bad as Ma! But you can't get no conjuh spell out of a dead white man."

Spell? Conjuh spell? For my hair. Could Grandfather do that?

No! Not hair, stupid. Mother and the *money!*

"Eddie—" He's gone, down the back stairs.

"Will-is!" Grandmother! Coming up the front stairs. There's a huge dust smear on the counterpane, in the exact shape of the frame. Quick—pull it on the floor. Dance dance around; making footmarks, smudges. Now into bathroom. The clothes chute! Whoosh! The air blows my short hair around my ears.

In the mirror —who is that! Ugh! Don't throw up! Swallow the lump!

Go get a new spread from the chifforobe. The bed's a mess, but only as if I'd been playing on it. Grandmother, when she sees the counterpane, will punish me. But not for stealing.

I tiptoe down the back stairs to the kitchen.

"Is Mother coming home for supper?" Oh, say no—say no! Is the spell working? Dear Grandfather, take the money. *Gotta give spirits a present,* Lila says. And don't hurt Mother. But don't let her come home.

Lila looks up from snapping beans. "Thought you was out playing with Eddie."

They're all talking to me again. They can't ever keep up the silent treatment for long. Daddy didn't even lecture yet.

"Eddie went off with his girlfriend."

"Huh!!" Lila sniffs just like Grandmother. "He be sorry, one day!"

"Lila, how do you make a spell?"

Looks at me. "What foolishness you up to?"

"Well, to keep someone away."

"Honey, any spell to keep folks away, I'd use it on that Laura Keene!" Flaps her apron.

"Is Mother coming home?"

Shoots me a great big Awful Look.

After supper, swinging on the cool metal porch swing,

creaky-creak, beside Lila, who is reading the paper with her glasses on the end of her nose. She reads the headlines, slowly, mouthing the words.

"Let me." I snatch the paper, read the whole front page aloud. She nods and clucks at every story.

"When did Eddie live in this house? I'll read you the comics, after you tell me." I don't dare ask about spells again. Grandfather will just have to do.

"I see I have raise me a bargainer. Well, Missy. When Eddie a baby, we move out to Gramama's farm. And look like didn't nothing work out. Eddie daddy—he hate that farm. He a car mechanic, not a farmer. And he have me and Eddie and no job, no place for us to live. Well, he took to drinking some, then he beat me and he make Eddie cry. Eddie cry all the night, and his daddy hate that squalling."

"Eddie's daddy *beat* you?"

"Won't his fault, I reckon. We does by our nature. We just born a certain way." Lila shakes her head. "Eddie daddy never could learn inside manners, couldn't get along with nobody. But he got treated like a dog before he ever acted like one."

"Was that when Eddie's daddy cut you?"

"No, honey. That was later. This when we out on the farm, and one day who come drivin' up, but Dance with your gramama. Dance a young man then, driving for Miz Roberts. So she get out the car, say to me, 'I am not scared of any man, white or black, don't care how mean he be.' She come to the porch—Eddie daddy won't there at that moment—and I was setting on the floor with a black eye and Eddie in my lap. 'Lila, get up and get in my car!' I'm thinking I better take some stuff for Eddie and me, but she say, 'Don't you take a thing but the clothes on your back. Give that good-for-nothing no cause to come to my house and make a fuss over his things.'

"I says, 'Eddie his baby.' She say, 'Then let him act like a proper daddy. I have the law on him he come fooling around me.' So we get in the car and Dance drive to your gramama's house, and she say, "You stay here and work and take care of that baby till all this blow over.' And that's what we did."

"You ran away from Eddie's daddy. And Grandmother *helped* you?"

"Yes ma'am."

"And did Eddie's daddy come here?"

"Eddie daddy went to Jersey and didn't come back for five years."

But Eddie never stayed here that long. Not long enough to know which room was mine.

"Honey, your daddy going now to the Beach and get your mama."

Mother? I'd forgotten Mother! My throat starts to burn again. Eddie was right. Grandfather made a bad spell.

"Tomorrow, next day, they be here. You'll see."

And then Mother'll stare at me and—"Mother will kill me."

"Honey, your mama right thankful for you. On bended knee. You the glue."

Oh, the glue! Every bill left of the stolen money stuck behind Grandfather.

"The glue that stick 'em back together. And then I can go glue *my* place together!"

"You'll go home? With Eddie?" My voice squeaks.

"Yes ma'am. Hallelujah! Git that sorry boy outta trouble, and everything back to normal. Tomorrow, tomorrow everything be back to normal, you'll see."

OUTSIDE IN GRANDMOTHER'S giant yard, the night breathes. The *dead* breathe. Zombies and hants and other things Eddie won't even name, which only come out in the dark. I know perfectly well Eddie made up the Zombies. I was practically a baby and

166

he made up games to scare me when we played in the yard. So Zombies are just a *game*. But when you're it, running and being scared, and it's dark—you can *feel* them.

Lightning bugs are their fire-shooting eyes, blinking in secret code. Daddy says, *Utter rubbish!* and catches some and puts them in a jar. *You can feel there's no fire in them*, he says, making me hold one. *It's Lucy Ferin.* Whoever she might be.

Lucifer be right! Devil bug, Lila mutters. *Born when the lightning strike a tree.*

See how they signal—flash—flash—flashflashflash. Calling the dead.

But they are just a *game*. And I want to be at home, at the little house. Lila and Dance are over there, talking to Daddy about Eddie, who's sick. Really sick. All because of Laura Keene. And a conjuh.

Who's a conjuh? Lila. Who?

Hysh! Lila said. And didn't even notice me snuffling a tear!

Time to tell the doc, Dance said. *Doc can break that spell.*

They'll talk about spells for precious Eddie, but they wouldn't for me. Grandfather's spell didn't work at all, and I've been in the real outs for days—ever since Mother got back. She doesn't want me, the Traitor, in her house!

Lila and Dance went over to my house and wouldn't let me come. Rumpy gets to go. Rump doesn't even pretend to like the rest of us any more, since Mother gave him to Dance. Bounces along like a little black and white ball wherever Dance goes.

I wish I was Lila's Rumpy.

A streetlamp makes a magic circle dividing the dark into two safe spots. Grandmother's yard and my parents' yard. If I run across the street to our house, I can stop in the pool of yellow light and be safe, while the eyes and the breathings go 'round and 'round; waiting for me to step into the bad zone.

The Zombies have Eddie. That's what I think. They have come out of the game, and they have made him very sick. So sick he can't get out of bed; can't eat. A little of Eddie disappears every day. And it's my fault.

He just melting away before my eyes, Lila says over and over.

That the way they do him, Dance says. They! The conjuh and the Zombies.

"Grandmother, go over to my house with me! Please, please!"

Grandmother laughs. "Go if you want."

Oh can't she see how important this is? I jump from foot to foot. Lila has forgotten all about me. I want to see her!

"Too scared to go by yourself? Well, you'll just have to stay here with me then. And keep still!" Like Mother. If I stay around Mother five minutes now, she says, "Please—take the child away! All I ask is a little peace and quiet!" Glares at me and hisses, "Traitor!"

And now Lila saying to me, *Hysh!* Like a dog. Worse than a dog.

I am running. My feet go smack—smack—smacksmack smacksmack on the driveway. Flying!

Safe! In the circle of light. Whuff! Whuff! I hear breathing! I'll have to wait till there's not a single breath. Run! run run! To the house. Touch it!

Safe! "Can't get me now! Can't get *me*." Slip around the back to the pantry porch. We never turn the bulb on unless we want something, or the bugs will come. I can peep in and listen at the little pass-through window, duck under the table, where Lila plucks our dinner chickens, if anyone comes.

In the breakfast nook, my father is in my seat. Lila and Dance sitting in front of him. Rumpy straight and solemn in Dance's lap. Dance stroking him, over and over. Lila's mouth, tight pinchy line! She's really mad.

But not at me! Maybe if I wiggle, she'll look at me, and be sorry she said "hysh!"

But who's that? A stranger. A man, standing with his back to me. Straw hat, white wide pants held up by suspenders. No shirt on! His back is darker than wood and shines like metal. Oh, it has to be the conjuh!

My father rubs his hand all the way over his head. Which he only does when he's thinking very hard. "I've examined Eddie. There is nothing physically wrong with him. What did you do, exactly?"

The stranger shuffles and ducks.

"Take your hat off!" my father snaps. "And next time, put your shirt on when you come to a decent house!" The hat is wiped away. And put back!

"You the one tell me to come—*invite* me," the conjuh says, his voice high and funny. Is he talking in an animal's voice? Lila says conjuhs can take the shape of any animal. When they want to hurt you, they choose something big and fierce or even poisonous. When they want to hide, they can become mice or bugs.

His neck is thick and looks as tight as a bull's. His voice may be teeny as a mouse's, but his arms—even his fingers look thick and fat. All over, his skin is stretched to bursting.

In his other hand, he is holding dark glasses. Dark glasses at night! Hates light! That's a conjuh!

"Who's this person you keep talking about?" My father looks from Lila to Dance to the conjuh himself. "Tell me, or I won't lift a finger!"

Someone mumbles something and my father laughs.

Lila cries to the conjuh, "You can have her! That no count!"

She must mean Laura Keene. Giving Laura Keene as a present to the conjuh!

"My Eddie spend every penny he can scrape on her. And half mine, when he get the chance. He doesn't have a dime, or that slut be sucking after him now!"

Rumpy begins to bark. High and sharp, the way he does when something bad comes into the yard.

"I take her all right," the conjuh shouts, "and y'all be sorry you ever mess with me." He shakes his fist. At my father! Then turns and runs out, so fast there's no time to duck under the table. A smell of sweat and something sharp and sweet—his magic! He stares at me as he goes by. And I know he will never forget me. He won't need a hen's egg to remember me forever.

Slam! He kicks the screen door open. Gone!

Rumpy is jumping up and down in Dance's lap, barking. My father, in the doorway, says, "Come inside, Willis. It's your bedtime." Lila rushes through putting me to bed. Here, not at Grandmother's. Doesn't hug me, doesn't dust me with cool powder.

Oh the conjuh man's staring eyes. Knowing me. And his lashing foot. *Y'all be sorry!*

~

IN THE MORNING, Lila is crying—tears run down her cheeks while she coddles my mother's egg and pats up my father's shad roe cakes. "Let me hug you, Li!" She never never cries in front of anybody. Not even me.

But she shrugs me off. I might as well be a cockaroach! No, she'd at least stamp on a cockaroach. Stomp!

"How's Eddie?"

"Eddie goin' in the Army."

"But he's sick! How can he go into the Army if he's melting more and more every day?"

"Your daddy fix it so they take him, sick and all." Lila barks out the words. " 'Army cure Eddie or kill 'im.' " In my daddy's wag-head voice.

The Army. Then Eddie will go away. Far away. Jersey. The closest Army place is Camp Pickett, but they don't let Colored people go there.

Lila dries her eyes on her apron. "I fix that Laura Keene. See if I don't." Fix her? She gave her to the conjuh, already. I heard her. But it didn't work: *Y'all be sorry you ever mess with me!*

"Can he be an animal, is he like—like a hant?"

Lila stops in surprise. "Who?"

"The man last night. The conjuh man."

"That sorry flesh a conjuh? Ha!" Sniff! "That there Doody Bump—hot for a gal he can't keep."

Not the conjuh? Laura Keene's boyfriend? "He put a curse on us!"

"Let him, all he want."

But it *is* a curse. It's already starting. Eddie's sick and has to go far away to get well. In the Army, he could be killed. And Lila is *crying.* And not noticing me, so I can't even feel anything about Eddie going away. I should be happy. It's what I wanted more than anything. Well, second most thing. But I'm sad.

The next morning, Eddie is in our kitchen. Drooping like a sick cow. How thin he is, great pebbly blue circles under his eyes. Rests his head on his hand as if his neck can't hold it up. And doesn't even eat. He is wearing a good shirt and tie, and polished shoes. An old cardboard suitcase—Lila's suitcase she takes to the Beach with us—at his feet.

My father sticks his head in at the door. "Robert will be here in ten minutes. Then you're off."

Eddie opens his eyes. All red and dull. Don't even see you. This's how you are when the Zombies have you. But the Army's very strong. It can beat anything. The Army will get Eddie back.

It's my fault. I *wished* the Zombies would get Eddie! I wished that Eddie would vanish. "I didn't mean it! I didn't mean it!" Oh, the conjuh will get us all. Eddie, Lila, Dance, and me.

"What you didn't mean? "Lila looks at me sharply.

What can I do? How can I make up for my wish? The conjuh's eyes bore into mine.

I know I have to give something, something important.

Oh! Run. Run out of the kitchen. Maybe there's time. Ten

minutes is forever. Ten minutes is almost an hour. Out of the house, over to Grandmother's, pound pound up the stairs.

"What's this? A herd of wild horses?"

Pound pound into my room. "Grandfather, your spell didn't work. But the conjuh's did!" Oh I'm glad I didn't sic the bad things on Mother. Truly. I am.

Wobbling on the bed. The portrait is too heavy! What to do?

Slip your hand between the wall and—there they are! Pull, slowly, slow-ly. Two of the bills come loose. Riiiippp! One has a big hole where the glue stuck too tight. Throw it away. Now a ten and a twenty, another twenty. Another ten. Can't reach any more. Grandmother's footsteps, coming up the back stairs.

Pound pound down the front stairs, out, through the yard where last night I was so scared. Through the bare ground where the safe pool of light was. *Oh I'm sorry, Eddie! I promised God I wouldn't be mean to you, and then I wished evil on you—I'm sorry sorry sorry! But you can take this money to the conjuh and get him to make the spell go away.*

Eddie is alone in the kitchen.

"Here! From where we hid 'em." I shake the bills in his face. No answer. I touch his arm. "Here! Quick! Give 'em to you-know-who."

He opens his eyes. Stares at the money, then at me. A little smile. An almost Eddie-grin. He takes the money and folds it up small.

Footsteps—I put my finger to my lips. "It's to make you get well." The door swings open. Eddie puts his finger to his lips too.

"Robert's here," my father says. "I told Lila she could go with you as far as the Army hospital in Washington. No, not you, Missy!" Shaking his head at me before I can even open my mouth. "They'll be gone two days."

Two days! Never mind. I'll have Lila all to myself when she

comes back. And I'll forgive her for saying *hysh* to me. I'll think good thoughts. Even about Mother.

Eddie gets up. He picks up the suitcase. He's still smiling. It's working.

My father shakes Eddie's hand. "Don't get into any more foolishness, now," he says. "Come back a man."

Lila, sniffing and wiping her eyes, follows him out the back door. They get into my father's big car. Robert is wearing his chauffeur's uniform. Eddie is leaving in style.

So—every night Lila can stay here. I'll be so good. I'll make it up to her that Eddie's gone. I'll be her Rumpy. Follow her like a shadow so she'll never be lonely. Make her sit down and rest her tired legs while I clear the table. Read the paper to her and rub her headache away. And things too numerous to mention.

The conjuh will be gone and something good will happen.

The car backs slowly up, the engine revs, *brruddnnn*. They're turning out of the drive—

A great scream fills the air. A high whining yelp, like a hant. *Ayyeeee!* I duck my head and put my fingers in my ears.

"Oh my god!" My father flings open the door and runs out. And Dance, Dance is wailing, "Ohhh ohhhohhhohhh!" The hant scream dies, and Dance's voice, too, as if someone had cut them off. "Dance!" They have Dance. They have my Lila!

"Stay here, Willis." Mother, ill-looking in her bathrobe, in front of the door, barring my way.

"No, no! I want Lila. I want *Lila!*"

"It's Rumpelstiltskin," Mother says. "He must have gotten loose. Robert has run over Rumpy."

16

1981

TWISTED

The phone rings. It's Dance. Dance has never called me before, and my heart pounds. I yell into the mouthpiece, "Dance, is it *Lila?*"

He clears his throat. "Miss Lila's fine. I talk to Mistah Davis and he say to tell you to talk to that Mistah Lutz."

"What? Has Lila been, has Lila got a problem?"

"Nothing wrong with Miss Lila. Mistah Davis say that Mistah Lutz, who put in the 'lectric grid to the farms—Mistah Davis want you to get down here, go see 'im."

"Go see who?"

"Mistah *Davis* say for *you* to go see Mistah *Lutz*. Soon's you can." He's speaking very slowly, as to a slow child. Well, that's me, sure enough.

I know Mistah Lutz—Lila calls him Mistah Lush, and he's certainly rich enough for the name. But why should I talk to him? "Dance, what is going on? Are you calling from Lila's?"

Wheeze—more of a sigh than a laugh, this time. "No'm, the pay phone behind the drug store. Aint want to git Miss Lila's hopes up. Mistah Davis say Mistah Lutz buy the fa'hm. If you ask him to. Mistah Davis say we all got to co-operate these days, get anything done." The operator cuts in, "Twenty-five cents please."

"So you come down, go see 'im. I got to hang up now." The line goes dead.

Well. But what the hell—I can't just call up somebody I haven't spoken to or thought of in 20 years.

∾

PERKINSON SITS, hands folded, eyes lowered. After Dance's call, I drove down from New York as soon as I could to find out what was going on. I haven't mentioned Mr. Davis or Mr. Lutz. In fact, I can't ask anything outright.

Today, Perkinson is wearing a bow tie—like the redoubtable Mr. Nat. "Miss Willis," he warbles—the "Miss" is new too. "What you went through the othah day is shameful. However I don't b'lieve the forced (fo'ced) sale is mal-fee-sance. There is a pro-pri-ety in these things. They were not done right. You made a legitimate offer (awfa) to pay the hospital, requested a copy of the will. And the Commit-tee's fee is outrageous. That," he is half-smiling, "I can get reduced. By half."

"How on earth?"

"First, because Mr. Nat says so. Second, your (yo-ah), shall we say, 'altercation' with Spauldin was right on the street. A witness has stated what he saw and heard—you approach the awfice, Spauldin comes out, cussin', assaults you physically. He lay a hand on you?"

Now Perkinson slips, slick as spit, out of Mistah Nat's ol' Va-gin-ya cadences, and back to plain talk.

"So," I said, "if I say yes, do we have a winning hand in this game?"

"Not quite. But the witness signed an affidavit."

"Did he tell you Spauldin (I almost say Sprawldin) was pig drunk?"

His pen weaves through his fingers, back and forth. "All in our fave-ah."

"So." I'm mesmerized by the flashing pen and the wavering of facts and am not thinking straight. "What now? Can we get the farm back?"

He laughs indulgently. Sets the pen down. "Well, Miss Willis. We law-yas may seem, to the outsider, like a bunch of greedy individ-jules, but we can't go *too* far out o' bounds, in any *di*-rection."

Bounds, again! "Please. What's happened and what do I do?"

He sighs. "You might look around, see can you find some-body to act for you. In addition to me."

I'm almost back at Lila's when it hits me. Perkinson is repeating what Davis said to Lila and me and apparently to Dance. A white buyer. *His* white buyer. And Perkinson is saying that, while nobody is going to step out in front of the speeding truck, he and the "good" big-bellies in their bow ties will work with us, minimally, behind the scenes, so I won't go to Yankee newspapers and slop all over their "bounds."

Lila is still at the kitchen table.

"Perkinson says he's getting Chillus's legal bills cut in half. And Sprawldin's attack on us—someone recorded it."

She doesn't look up.

"*Li*-la!"

"I been setting here thinking and thinking, honey." She groans. "You know I don't want a mess. These folks—you rile 'em up, they liable do anything. But, whew! it *hurt*, losing that fa'hm. One more thing gone. But I got my house—maybe that have to do me."

Relief? Am I off the hook?

"But, honey, one hundred-some years? My gramama earn that fa'hm, earn it with her *soul*. So I say—go ahead on, do what you got to do." Voice so calm. But her face twists in Chillus's rage. Goose bumps crawl up my arms. Has Dance talked to her?

"*Do* it, honey."

"But—" A waver! What I thought or hoped was that the whole thing was melting away. "Lila, I'm not the right one for this."

"You the one we *got*."

"What does Hard say?"

Her face twists again. "Huh! That gal want the money she get if the fa'hm's sold. I told her, *That be about fifty cent.* She say, More like fifty dollars and that's more than she got now. Say she go get outta this here hellhole—honey, this here hellhole's my *home.*"

I say, "So Mr. Davis and Perkinson say we should find a white person to help us buy the farm. That would take a miracle."

Oh, that little laugh. I get a sudden picture of Lila driving a car (probably never so much as sat in a driver's seat), slamming it, with that laugh, straight into Mistah Sprawldin. Jesus, I'm bloodthirsty!

"No miracle, honey. Good old-fashion knight in armor. White *knight* to do it *right*." She's nodding deeply. "And you know the one. If he want to. Leastways he has got the *know* and has did the *how*."

So Dance *has* talked to her.

"Friend of your daddy, the Bilk-co man, we call 'im. *Light unto darkness.* Lit himself up with a million dollars while he was doing it, too."

Mr. Lutz.

And I'm the one has to go to him because he was a poker pal of Daddy's.

Drinker, Jester. Great White Knight? Everybody calls him "Pops."

∼

I'M JUST LIFTING my hand to the bell when the door swings open. A man in an electric wheelchair, cowboy hat pushed back on his head, looks up at me. Eyes watering, liver-spots dotting his hands. "I been 'specting you." So, who's been talking? The Sugar Bottom Telegraph—often called something worse.

He spins his chair into the living room. I sit where he points —another chair with a plastic cover—and his features and voice slowly meld into Pops, the man who came to town with his huge machinery. Mattaponi Lighting Company, what Lila calls "Bilk-co" because all her folks have to pay a lot more for power, while the whites don't. A Town Father sleight of hand called "up-grading delivery apparatus."

When I was little, this was all beginning, and Pops went around glad-handing, giving out maps and cigars. *"Prove I'm legal down to the ground!"* He hired black men for his crews, Said he wanted people who *chose* this work rather than falling into it *'cause they aint got the brains for anything else.* The white people wouldn't apply for his jobs because he had "darkies" on the crews. But he said, "I pay anybody who'll do the work and do it right." He got away with it because he didn't pay the "darkies" quite what he would a white crew. And he made those tricky Town Fathers a bundle of money.

I keep my mouth shut for once.

He motors over to a sideboard, pours a snort in a short glass, picks ice cubes out of a silver bucket with silver tongs. In my memory, he's a stick figure. Tall, cave-chested, buck-toothed, always wearing that ten-gallon hat to hide his bald head. And spurs, though he rode a four-wheeled not a four-legged bronco. When I was little, he'd wink at me, light a cigar, and slip me a piece of chocolate wrapped like a gold coin.

"I miss yo-ah daddy, gal, I sho'ly do." His voice is hearty and folksy, but his eyes are keen and sad. "Now. Let's see if I got this right. You want to buy a run-down propitty on the old

Mattaponi, and your legal-eagle cousins in County won't sell to you. Whoo-hah!" Winks at me. "Coupla nice old fellas, Mr. Nat and old man Davis, they told me all about it. Got any money?"

"I could probably get a loan on my house in New York."

He wheels his chair around on the carpet. "I purely *(pyo'ly)* love this place, know why? Grew up in a trailer park. Now I got a double-wide living room. Never tire *(ti-yah)* of it."

The crackery doesn't hide eyes as sharp as Chillus's. He's piercing me to the bone. "I know you just go give that land to Miz Neal. Honey, she's using you."

"So? I spent my childhood using her."

He laughs. "So, so!" He sobers. "No loans, honey, you can't go to a bank. Money talk travels. We need to twist this thing a little bit." He rattles the ice in his glass. "I'm in the O and A Club, old and ailing. Looking at W and D, worthless and done for. But stick with me, you got *options.*"

He rolls back to the sideboard and rings a hand bell. A tall black woman steps in, whispery dark uniform complete with little white cap. "Julia, open that bottle o' bubbly in the Frigidaire, please, bring Miss Willis a glass. Tall skinny one. We celebrating a success here. Thank you, Julia." He adds ice to his glass, pours more bourbon. "Good woman, Julia. Old Davis's daughter. Coulda been as big a deal as her daddy if she'd a been a boy and white. You know I lost my right leg to di-ah-beet-ees? Your daddy could o' saved it, but not these new-fangled butchers. Sometimes my old leg hurts so bad I could cry. Not the stump, the ghost o' my gone one. You heard 'bout that? Julia, she comes, night or day, presses down against the bed where that leg used to be. Full weight. Ten minutes, that pain is *gone.*"

Julia, silent as breath, is back at my elbow with a frosty long-stemmed glass. There's nothing of her father that I can see, neither the fragile Mr. Davis of today nor the jolly barman/King of the Dead of yore. I can't get over the picture of her on Pops's bed, pressing down on a ghost leg.

"Chin-chin," Pops says. "Where most o' my food and drink goes these days." He mops himself, takes another gulp. "Now, we can't do a thing till the old man dies and the order to sell goes th'oo. But then I'll buy that land under one o' my bidness names. You aint dark my door in twenty years, so Spauldin won't suspect a thing. Mr. Nat, he'll probly figger it out, him and Davis know everything. But they're my backmen. Mr. Nat keeps me in good with the law, Davis is the one got me my whole crew, back when. Trick is, buy cheap and cross palms with silver. There's a complaint, aint there? Physical attemp' on you?"

I nod. The champagne has fuzzed my tongue.

"I want you to sue. Git attention off that land. I'll hire you a big D.C. lawya—can't slap around the old doc's daughter on the street here, waltz off scot-free."

"Well, he didn't exactly—"

"We talkin *law* here, honey. Not *exactly* anything. I want you to go for big. Just leave 'im 'is feet! I can tell 'im—cripple's just one hair *(hay-ah)* better than death!"

My sip of champagne pours out of my nose. Pops hands me his napkin, then spins his chair, the motor whining. "So—Imo buy that land, cut down half the black walnut trees the old lady planted—won't no flies on that old lady, Davis'll tell you. She weaseled Old Crowder into deeding her that farm, then put in those trees. Worth a fawtune."

"Walnut trees?"

"Over a hundred years old, what's left of 'em. I'm trading you for one-half. I could take 'em all, but I'm one-half a decent man."

I shake the head that's fast sinking beneath the waves.

"This's sneaky, gal. Long's the old man is 'live, those woo'ves could cut those trees and jack up the legal fees again—Young

180

Perkinson jewed 'em down, you know. So go careful." He turns in his chair again. "Imo put the deed in a cawrprit name with 51% shares to you. The rest to Davis. You do with it whatever you want. My advice—lemme cut all the trees, then everybody'll have some cash. But it's up to you." He waits and when I say nothing, he sighs. "I'm doing this for your daddy, gal, he woulda got a good chuckle. And because, when I look in the mirror on my last day, I want to see a *man*."

At sundown, I follow Lila past the garden, on up the ridge. And there they are. A regiment of dark scored trunks and branches, new leaves making dancing fingers on our faces. The ground underneath is bare dirt. *"Nothing* grow under a walnut," Lila says, putting her hand on a deeply scored trunk. Must be over five feet around. "Poison drip off 'em. Devil trees. Nut meat burn your mouth, too, you eat too many."

Don't I know it. The hulls burned my face but good that time when I'd have sold my soul to be the daughter of her flesh. She laughs. Probably thinking of the same scene.

Then she sighs. She's looking around. "One time, Gramama brung me here, told me, look up at *the green gold! Baby, look up!* I was 'bout five-years-old. Only gold I see was in her mouth, band round one of her front teeth."

"This is what you want, Lila, right?"

She's looking down at the river. The slanting sun makes orange-and-black ripples on the water. On the far side, the flat fields are unplowed and slovenly. No ridge, no trees, no house, no garden. "All the white Crowders dead now," she says. "Not a one left. Land gone to waste. My other gramama have it right— Inyun, from down the river. I told you 'bout her. Used to say don't nobody own nothing, just the breath in your lungs, the dirt on your hands."

Dirt. Mud and loggers' slash. This place will be torn to bits.

A meadowlark begins his sunset song—long, sharp whistle, clear and true. I used to pretend they were wild Indians. Not like Lila's grandmother, but storybook Indians hiding in the woods, getting ready to whoop down with their tomahawks. I'd run run run, down the garden to the house. Safe! At night it was owls, owls became the enemy, with their secret signals. All so black-and-white, what we dream up in ignorance. How innocent we are, how evil the foe.

"Wish I could tell Uncle." Lila's hand lies flat on her heart, not digging now. "Told 'im you and Mistah Davis working for us—him and me and Hard. But he don't know us now."

17

1949

THE YEARLING

"I'll give Lila some money, and you two can go to the picture show," my mother says.

The picture show! Usually I'm not allowed. Just once in a blue moon with Daddy, to see a Western. And for Mother to suggest it? She must be sick again. She's in her nightgown, still, in the middle of the day. And she won't look at me—that's another sign. But she doesn't smell funny.

The picture show! The picture show! Please God—don't let her change her mind.

"Lila, what's playing?" I ask. Haddy—fat Haddy, laziest human being on earth, Grandmother says—goes to all the shows. "Squandering money instead of feeding her children!" Grandmother snorts. Haddy tells Lila the movie stories in every tiny detail. Then Lila and me go up stand at the Mecca, looking at the billboards and studying the scenes to see if we can pick out what happens to all the stars.

"Yearling," Lila mumbles around the hatpin in her mouth. Already she is putting on her red hat—tucking her hair under the brim.

"Oh lord," Mother says, throwing up her hands, "not

another deer story. Then you can't go, Willis, you simply cannot."

Lila freezes, hatpin half in place.

"Not go! Why not! Moth-er! You just promised! You *promised!*"

Mother's lips purse. "You may've forgotten *Bambi*. But *I* haven't!"

"I was *four*. Now I'm eleven!"

"Ten and a half." She flushes. "You crawled under the seats, Missy, screaming and bumping into people's legs. I have never been so mortified in my life."

"But they killed her—they killed Bambi's mother!"

I even cried in the book, when Bambi's mother was killed. In the movie, his father, the King of the Deer, appears and says *"Come!"*

"You'll get completely hysterical. My god! Poor Mr. Morris had to shut down the picture."

He didn't. Not even for five minutes. But this is how Mother always tells the story.

Aach! Stick out my tongue. With my back turned, of course! Cross my arms, tap my foot. Then breathe heavy, heavier—gasping. Dizzy. Shoulders begin to shake, head spinning. I'm *making* a fit. I am good at fits, but not at pretending them. Lila is frowning at me. She says it's a lie to pretend to have a fit and one day I'll freeze like this.

"Sweet Jesus!" Mother's voice is half-exasperated, half-softening. She wants to get rid of me. Why?

Pooh! Who cares?

"Can we go, then?"

"Well. But if I hear one word—"

Mother gives Lila the money.

"Why can't I take the money?"

Silence. Stares from both Lila and Mother. Mother's never trusted me with a penny since you-know-when. But now she stops, her purse still in her hand. Fishes out a bill and holds it up. A whole dollar!

"Treat Lila, now. That's enough for an entire barrel of popcorn."

Snatch it quick, before she can change her mind, and dash for the door! Lila now has her hat firmly on and her gloves. And we are—gone!

The movies movies movies movies movies! Toe in, toe out —shimmy to the left, shimmy to the right!

The Mecca is uptown right across from the Armory. The old cannons, all painted with spots, have their snouts up in the air, aimed right at the marquee. Every Fourth of July, the Veterans march up and salute and fire off the guns and blow out all the snot. When the war ended, you'd have thought they'd smash the movie house to bits. Va-voom!

The Mecca did actually burn down a while back, though it had nothing to do with the war or the Armory. It happened in the middle of the night. Afterwards, everybody said a little colored boy was sleeping in the loft where the Nigras have to sit—I guess his mother forgot him. And he's supposed to have burned up. Daddy says that's nonsense, he was called out that night, and no one was injured. But Haddy swears it's true.

Oh! There's a line. All the good seats will be taken—the ones right in front where Daddy won't sit. "You'll ruin your eyes," he says, and goes so far back you can't get into the story at all. Once, when the movie was crowded, it was a Western, natch, we couldn't get seats together, so he let me go close. I was sucked right up into the picture. That makes you all dizzy when you get out. Delicious!

At the ticket office, Lila unrolls Mother's money and we step inside. "Y'all can sit in the back," Mr. Morris whispers, looking over his shoulder. He's wearing his dirty old movie uniform with the fake gold epaulets. "Just keep quiet." I wonder if Mr.

Morris remembers my Bambi scene, and if he too was mortified.

But I know, really, it's because of Lila. He's not supposed to let any colored person into the downstairs unless she's nursing a white child. And I'm so big now, I'm not officially a "child" any more.

"I want to sit up front."

Mr. Morris clears his throat and glances around again. "Ackshully, you better go down here and let Lila go on upstairs. I told your mama you could come in with Lila, but the thee-ater's mighty crowded."

Not sit with Lila?

Lila pulls me along. "Let's sit upstairs, we can go next to the balcony rail."

Right. Hateful old Morris.

The balcony is dim and smells of smoke. Maybe from the fire. Ugh! Bet they used the old smoky seats up here instead of buying new ones when they rebuilt the theater.

The balcony is almost full, too, but we find seats at the rail where we can lean over. "We could spit on the people down there!"

Lila laughs, "Honey, *hysh!*" But it's the good "hysh!" The one that's like being a *mess.*

"I bet Eddie did it when he came here. I'd like to spit on Mr. Morris. But I'd never get to see another movie my whole life."

Lila sits upright in her seat, clutching her purse to her stomach so nobody will snatch it, and laughs at Woody Woodpecker. He isn't as funny as Tom and Jerry, but I like his crazy laugh and practice it when I'm by myself A-A-A *A!* A! When Daddy and I came during the war there weren't any cartoons, just planes flying over and bombs dropping. It didn't look real. The picture was full of jumps and speckles and lines. But Daddy said it was real, and I was to forget it. If somebody says you have to forget something, you remember it forever.

Oh! Music! Writing on the screen. *"The Yearling,"* I read the words to Lila, in a whisper. "Starring Gregory Peck—look, there's the Florida jungle! Remember when we went to Florida? Didn't it look just like this?"

A deer raised by a boy! The little deer is so beautiful, I start to cry immediately, before anything has happened at all. But then a lot happens and I'm crying for real, trying not to sob aloud so Lila won't be mortified.

I hate the parents for killing the deer. *Hate* them so much I feel like I'm exploding. Just because it ate in their old garden. Of course it ate. It was hungry. And it was a *deer*. If I was that boy, I'd never speak to them again as long as I lived. So what if they were my parents.

Oh, the lonely hollow sound of the boat horn goes through and through and through me.

"Why did they shoot the deer, Lila? Why?"

"Shhh, honey. Ast me later."

Grown-ups are so dumb—except for Lila. Dance knew things, too. When Rumpy died, Dance left our house. Left town. "Can't stand it here no more, Missy, 'thout old Rump." Lila says he lives in Jersey now. Mother can't understand that. "How he can leave everything he has known and cared for all his life?"

But I understand. His heart was broken. Truly broken, not pretend. And Mother forgets that he lived in Jersey during the War and worked in a factory.

And Eddie left. He had to take the bus because Dance was so upset he couldn't drive. Eddie is in New Jersey, too, at an Army fort.

When we come out of the theater, out to a whole 'nother world where everything, even the time of day, is different, it makes you feel sad and dis-com-bob-u-lated. Are we really still here and it's broad daylight? My head is stuffed from crying, and my eyes are dry and aching.

"Let's go on cross the fields," Lila says. "Too early to go home. Sides, your mama see you been crying." So we head into the field of broom straw behind the Mecca, and on up to the old cemetery.

Oh good—we'll sit where we used to when I was little and maybe she'll make acorn and stick dolls. I used to think of what it would feel like if Lila wasn't there in the cemetery beside me. Scared I reckon! Oh I was such a baby! Rustle! Rustle! *Lila, what's that?* And my heart would go like a frog in a jar! Hants and Zombies. Eddie was scared too, but he pretended he wasn't.

"Lila, know something? I don't believe in hants and Zombies now, the way I did when I was little. I know Eddie and me made 'em up."

"You a big girl, hunh!" Lila sits on a footstone. No one we know is buried in this particular spot. We wouldn't sit on anyone we know. She crumples some rabbit tobacco in her hands. Then fishes a little piece of white paper from her purse. Rabbit tobacco smells like crushed daisies and spicy herbs. Her fingers move slow, slow—the way they do when—

A knot comes into my stomach. When she brings me out and we smoke rabbit tobacco, when Lila slows way way way down to hardly moving, a storm is coming.

She slo-owly rolls the paper tight. Each roll makes my stomach twist, like the cigarette. Licks her lips, licks the paper, seals it.

"Lila, why did the boy go back. They shot his deer! How could he stand it?"

Dance couldn't. Lila says Dance isn't coming back. Probably ever.

Lila lights up, takes a puff, and sighs. The smell is sharp and sweet and pricks my nose. She's not looking at me.

"I reckon he see they didn't have a choice. They was his folks. He was a people, like them. Not a deer."

"He'd have been better off a deer." I'd be a deer, not a person, if I could. Lila and me.

Another puff. "Got to face life, honey, one time or 'nother."

Uh oh, here it comes. A big one. *Tell Willis, Lila, so she won't have a fit.*

Long pause.

"Everybody got to face life. Sad and bad and mad and glad."

I reach out for the cigarette.

"If your mama could see you." But she let me take it. It's lumpy—bits and twigs leaking out of the ends. Sparks dribble into the dirt.

"Watch yourse'f. You don't want to burn up this cemetery and put holes in your shirt." That makes me almost laugh. Burning the cemetery and then getting little holes in my shirt.

Puff—don't suck in—Eddie taught me that. And blow out fast as fast. But it burns! And the smoke stings my eyes. How does Lila do it without choking to death? And my parents, with their Lucky Strikes?

"Nasty!" She says, taking the cigarette away from me. "Nasty stuff!" As if it were medicine—

Suddenly I can't stand it! "What is it? Lila, what what what? Mother, letting me go to the deer movie. Giving me money. Oh! I forgot our treat! I was so excited about the movie I forgot the money Mother gave me."

"We stop at Mr. Perk's, get us some ice cream on the way home."

"Maybe a chocolate popsicle."

She nods. Knows I'm not allowed. But I never get pimples.

She puffs, puffs. Then scrubs out the cigarette in the dirt with her shoe. Stretches her legs out. Sighs. Stretches again. Crosses her hands in her lap. Looks at me for the hundredth time out of the side of her eye.

It's coming.

"Honey, you know your daddy been away for a long time."

I do know. Of course I know. "He's in Durham at Duke Hospital, studying more doctoring. I've heard all the arguing, too, when he comes home. Mother crying, 'You're going around with those floozies!'"

"Shhh, now. Don't take on. When your daddy come back next month, for good, you know he want to work at the hawsepital."

"The hospital is in Farmville." Farmville is a million miles away—at least an hour.

Oh! I sit bolt upright. "Is Daddy going to move there?" So much talk, about Daddy and Mother, and whether they will live together.

"Well, honey. Y'all *all* go move there."

Move! *All*? Suddenly—the movie—the mother, coming to the door with the gun...

This is Mother's doing!

"Your mama and daddy want to go off to a new place, good place, start over. Good school there for you, too."

"No! She can't! Leave here? She couldn't even understand about Dance leaving. And where will *you* live? Lila, where will you be?"

"Honey!" She laughs, but it is not a sweet Lila laugh. It's a bullet going through me!

"Where?"

"I stay with some folks down the road from your new house."

Ah! "Then that's all right. I can go anywhere as long as you're there. But Lila, what about your house here? And Eddie, when he comes to visit—"

Lila sighs. "Well, I promise your mama I help get y'all moved."

"Moved! That'll take a week. Then what!"

"Well. Honey, after y'all get settled, reckon I have come on back here and see to my stuff. Keep things right for Eddie when he come back from the Army. And you need a place 'sides your gramama's to visit."

Visit. My throat closes. "You'll leave me?"

"Don't cry, honey." The red hat bobs from side to side, but Lila isn't really looking at me. She reaches for my hand. I snatch it away.

"You promised. When I was a baby, just born, you promised you'd stay with me forever." The world swarms up in my stomach, bees in my mouth!

I jump up.

"Honey! I promise I stay till you thirteen. Thirteen near 'bout a grown-up woman." She looks tiny, sitting there on the grave, at my feet. Her eyes round and funny.

"You never said thirteen. Besides, I'm ten!"

She looks down at the ground, shaking her head.

Mother! This is all *Mother's* doing. She's wanted to smash things—forever.

"I'll stay. I stay longs I can, I promise you that. Come what may. I stay if they lets me. Till you thirteen. If they let me. For now."

For now. For now.

My legs itch, I burn all over. I'm standing up. I dance up and down.

"I hate you!" But she just shakes her head. "I don't, oh Li, I don't! But I hate *Mother*. I hate Daddy. And don't you dare tell me not to!"

Running. Running. Dodging headstones. Out the iron gates. Waving broomstraw—blurs—switching my legs and catching my feet. In the movie now, with the boy running. I am the boy. I am the deer, with its sad round eyes looking up. Then the mother came out with the gun. It knew. Bang bang.

Pounding down the hill. Rail-road track at the bottom. Hope I die. Yes! God—let all of us just die and blow away.

"Will—lee!" No! I won't stop. Never stop! Run run run till I fall, fall, fall. When I do, she catches up with me, panting.

I lie still, my head buried in my arms. "We'll stay here. You and me. I'll stay with Grandmother and you'll come to me every day, like always."

Silence. I roll over and she rubs at my skinned knees, all green with grass stain, a little bloody. Her eyes say everything.

"I'm your girl, aren't I?" Choking. The words squeak. "You wrote my name on the black hen's egg—to bind me to you forever."

Dark hollows in her cheeks. Beautiful hairs on her lip, soft twitchy mule's lip. "Honey, you my girl all right. *Nothing* change that. You my girl for *ever.*"

Takes my hand, mine lying limp in hers.

Our hands are dead.

When you're dead, you're—nothing.

She said "Forever."

That "forever" sounds just like "nothing."

18

1983

GONE

"Uncle gone," Lila says as I step in the door. Voice hollow—that old *gone* gong. And at the same time, she sounds rushed, as if she's in a hurry, and we have to fly to do something.

"Now? Yesterday?" I spoke to her just two days ago.

"Last month."

"Why didn't you tell me?"

What with some jobs and responsibilities in New York, I haven't been down here in a little more than two months. Perkinson wrote me about her grandmother's will, a month ago. He'd finally run it down. Now that I think of it, Chillus must have already been dead and those devils didn't need the will anymore. Perkinson didn't mention Chillus. And I didn't ask. Happy and secure in the Pops deal.

And Lila and I talk twice a week. She never said a word about Chillus.

Oh! It hits me. She went to the funeral? Of course she did. And who took her? Hard? Of course Hard.

God, that sounds jealous. Okay. Yes. Almost the way I was with Eddie.

Now I have a thousand questions. Well, swallow them. Unpack, give her my presents, some odds and ends and a new flowered dress for Easter. Last year she actually wore the dress I brought her. We went to the town pageant. A white Protestant playing Jesus lugged a real wooden cross over the high-school football field at dawn.

Usually when I bring her things, clothes or special foods with Zabar labels, they go on display. She likes to show her friends the presents I bring her from New York.

MORNING. By the time I'm dressed, she's in the kitchen, sausages and eggs on my plate. Coffee laced with chicory the way Daddy used to like it. And she herself, waiting, sun hat on, plastic cooler by the door. Plans are made, destinations set.

"Let's go see if the fa'hm still there," she says as I gobble my eggs.

I stop cold. God. The fa'hm. *Sold*. Perkinson told me when I called him yesterday. Sold for expenses, like Hard's paper said. Sold as raw land to one of Mr. Lutz's corporations. Why wasn't I told?

Naïve idiot.

Well, there goes the half a man. Half the Bilko man. A flush of anger and fear and—who knows what—sweeps across my scalp. This damn place is slipperier than a bucket of eels. According to Perkinson, Lila is listed among those to get something from what's left after expenses.

Sprawldin, he told me, had collapsed. Apoplexy. When a lawyer tells you that, it's probably not a figure of speech, but an honest-to-god stroke. I tried not to gloat. Actually there's nothing to gloat over. I never even heard from Pops' fancy lawyer about that lawsuit he was so keen on.

I haven't told Lila any of this. And now she wants to go to the fa'hm.

And there're these things she's not telling me, too.

Driving, neither of us saying a word. I creep along on the old dirt road, getting us nearer and nearer. What if the place has been razed and scraped bare, and a road to the river put in by Sprawldin, to "increase the land value?" The barn bulldozed? That barn, with its adz-cut logs, its clay-and-wattle, probably 200 years old. Surely everything will be changed.

Here's the last curve.

And here's the old chimney, sloe vines waving! No changes. Nothing. No Sold sign. Way over to the left, there's a logging road—you can always tell by the mess, ruts so deep it looks like a meteor crashed and rolled. One great slash. Up to Pops's trees.

Did he cut them all?

Beside me, finger pressed into her chest, she swivels her head, takes it all in. Silently.

And it hits me. She knows. Knows it all. The Sugar Bottom Telegraph.

We get out as usual in the weedy drive. She straightens her hat, pushes it firmly onto her head. Reaches into the back seat and takes out a walking stick and two bamboo poles. Fishing rods! And a coffee can for worms—just as like old times. But the way down to the river is grown up in weeds. Hell, saplings the size of my arm and a poison ivy hell.

I'm following. If this's what she wants, I'll slog through anything.

We walk slowly, still without a word, up to the falling-in porch. She leans the poles against what's left of steps and threads her way across the holes, to the door, and into the skeleton of the old back room where Eddie was born. Even the roof is gone. Nothing but two walls with slats, the wind whistling through.

I sit on the stump where Eddie always sat and look up into

the poplar trees. Bees drum. A smell—clean, green smell that isn't quite sweet, isn't quite spicy—the poplar trees are blooming, tulip trees, they call them. My grandfather's favorites, so tall and straight. A hundred feet up in the air. He called them his "stalwarts." The blossoms come out green, with yellow and orange centers. Tulips from Mars.

I can't think of Chillus dead. He was, in his way, eternal. Earth. Stone. Lila's right. Not dead, but *gone*.

Her footsteps, creaking over whatever's left of floor. I hope to hell she doesn't fall in.

Silence. The whole place is not only a ruin, but has that sad, strange aura that comes when something once yours is now someone else's. Has Lila been here since we were here last? Hard wouldn't bring her.

What is she thinking and feeling? Lila's reactions to such things as ownership and belonging aren't like mine. She takes in the abandoned, saves and cherishes.

She comes up to stand behind me. "Let's go."

I take the rods and the worm can. She walks in front of me swinging her stick through the weeds. Swish! Swack! *Git on, Mr. Snake!* Must be effective because I've never seen a snake when Lila's around. Copperheads and water moccasins live at the river. Kill you in a minute, she used to say. Swish! Swack! They know better than to show their noses.

We don't turn at the overgrown path to the ridge where the walnuts were or are. I'm relieved. I feel so bad just thinking about them. I thought we'd won. Bilko.

She sidesteps onto a narrow trail that leads back along the road, the spot where the old Mercy Seat, her gramama's church, once stood. Not even rotting sticks left. Her hat bobs on in front of me, down a two-track road through the grass and weeds. "Huh! Git along! Huh!"

The river is further off with every step and here I am

lugging the rods, which keep snagging low-hanging limbs. Well, I can toss the worm can. Nope. Better not.

Finally she stops, and we're in a dim clearing under tall old oaks. More trees. Trees really are history, I guess. If we don't cut them down, they outlast generations of puny humans.

These trunks are mossy and gray. Here and there lichen-spotted stones jag up through the leaves. She points her stick even further in, at a tall stone, an obelisk. "This here the old-time graveyard. For the slaves. You standing on my gramama, I believe."

God! I leap off the rock I'd stepped on. What is that won't let us stand on a grave?

It's a shapeless garden rock. Two, actually, side by side. "One of these is her. One of 'em is Mama." I look more carefully and see that these two rocks—her mother and her grandmother—lie in a crowd of others, circling around. I count eleven. Each about two feet wide, tops slightly flattened as if someone with dull tools had tried to make a square. No place for a name, no outline of a grave. Only the tall obelisk looks as if a human had placed it here.

Going back to earth. Not dust to dust, but leaf mold to leaf mold.

Lila pushes her hat off to hang on its string down her back. "My gramama was born a slave. Three years old when she was freed." She's in her storytelling style. "And Mama asked to be buried next to her. Say she want her mama's earth.' "

Earth, where you're nobody's or everybody's. Nothing to show you ever lived. Nothing to keep you from blending and mingling with everyone and everything. An earth soup. Nourishment. I never knew Lila's mother, and I know they were not close. Yet here we are . . .

"That there," pointing with her stick to the tall stone, "the new old graveyard." A new raw road cuts through the trees to it, on the other side of the grove.

Why didn't I ever know about any of this? The feeling of left-out-ness burns in my throat. Hard knew about this place. Eddie too. They must have come here dozens of times. "Why didn't you tell me before?"

Little laugh. "Honey, you never ask."

She walks around muttering over the old stones, while I absorb as much as I can of the things I've never asked her.

Silence grows long. Grows horns, as our discomforts will do. Then she beckons and heads to the big stone. It is about six feet tall, rough-hewn. "This where I want my old bones to rest. Church folks tells us we gotta be buried in town, now, but don't matter what they say. This where we all are."

We.

I feel a long sigh building, and I lean the fishing rods and worm can against an oak tree and stand straight. There, on the other side of the obelisk, a new grave, red earth cracked and sunken in. Plastic white flowers marking the head. Lila leans over, brushing a bright plaque with her handkerchief.

CHILLUS ULYSSES CROWDER 1880—1983
TILLER OF SOIL

Ulysses? For Grant, surely. Not the wily tiller of the seas. This Ulysses lived for a hundred aught three years within a mile of where he was born.

"Clifford brought this stone in here. On a mule wagon, before they cut in that new road."

"Clifford? Eddie's daddy?"

Then, oh! it hits me! There, on the other side of the stone is another plaque, the first and oldest, greened with time:

Pvt EDWARD NEAL DOGGETT
EIGHTH ARMY 7TH INFANTRY KOREA
1932 — 1957

Eddie. *We.*

He was 25.

Oh Eddie, I can't be jealous of you now.

We played. We fought—like brother and sister. And I have had her to myself, all this time. All the time, that is, that I allowed myself. The *gone* years twist in my heart.

Lila roots around in her purse and fishes out a flower, a ceramic rose the color of wine with a livid fringe at the tips of the petals. Leans down to push the metal stem into the earth just under Eddie's name. There are others, three four five—an earth-spattered, stiff little garden. Picks them out one by one; polishes them with her handkerchief; puts them back. Not one for every year. Just one for every time she got a ride out here. I was her official driver, yet I never knew!

Precious Eddie. A soldier, a Pvt. A boy in trouble sent off to be cured by the Army. On his first leave, he'd married Laura Keene. On money I'd given him—did he tell Lila about that? She attended the ceremony, she says, sitting in the back of the church. Disapproving but loving him.

Then, *gone!* Off to Korea. And a bullet, she told me when I first came back to visit. A bullet in the kidney poisoned him, whatever that means, taking two years to kill him, up in a New Jersey VA hospital. And nobody, not the Army, certainly not Daddy, could save him.

I was far away, in school. And she'd left me. We weren't together when her Eddie was dying. I only half-took in the fact of his death. How could I have been so unthinking?

But mad and hurt as I was, and she too, we went on. I still am the one who didn't die, who came back. Who loves her every day in my heart.

How can you be *dead*, Eddie?

I wipe my eyes with my knuckles.

Am I to blame for you, Eddie? Haddy said Lila threw you away, because of me. Had no time for you. But God knows that's not so. Lila yearned for you, Eddie, even when she had to leave you with Haddy till she could come home, from me to you. Yearned for you when all she had was me. What—who—would we all have been if you'd come home to her?

When he was little, Eddie used to come to our house, sometimes, drink Cokes, dance in the kitchen to be-bop, sit with Lila and me in the cemetery—the white cemetery where all *my* people are buried. And Lila would make him soldiers out of acorns and sticks while she made me animals. *Tchew-tchew-eheheheheh!* He'd aim the stick guns at me.

Once he stood next to my grandfather's grave, under its marble spire that says BELOVED PHYSICIAN. Touched the letters. Pitiful gnawed little fingers. He said: "*I want me a statue, too.*"

"I want to be here."

What?

"Haddy promise me. But Haddy gone."

Yes, Haddy is at the new cemetery, in town. Can you picture fat Haddy struggling though these woods?

"Clifford promise. He gone too."

So. Eddie's unmentionable father, the bugbear of our childhood and Lila's young womanhood, had softened enough with time to bury his son and promise to bury his wife.

"Think I can ask Hard Rock?" Lila seldom calls Liz-beth Hard Rock! "You should of heard her when we bring Uncle here! 'Me, sashay th'oo them woods, snakes all over the place?' " Hard's little squeaky voice.

"Lila!" Without thinking, I grab her and hold her. She stiffens. "No ma'am, you will hold still for this hug!" Crinkly starch of her dress and apron. Warm flesh and ironed cloth smell. Tickly cheek. Now wheezing sounds. Laughing? Crying?

"Lila! I'm *sorry*.

Sorry for not asking. Sorry for being part of the things that hurt her. For being unforgiving and hard in my heart.

Sorry for time. Lost time.

"*You* bring me here." Against my ear, she wheezes again and coughs, as if it's as hard for her to say as it is for me to hear. "We don't got that on our paper. But *promise.*"

I straighten up, let her go. She promised my mother. Holding me in her arms—promised things unimaginable and unkeepable. We have promises, broken and kept, between us. Ah, I won't cry! I won't!

She hands me the cloth she used to clean Eddie's roses. I wipe my eyes with the dirt from his grave.

"Lila." This one should be easy. Easy to make, with my mouth. Just means telling people to do such and such and making sure they do it. Not like our paper, which means I'll have to do hard, maybe long things and make unbearable decisions. But this, this easy one, is the one that will turn me to stone. I know it. If I, a white woman, try to bury Lila, an old black woman, in a non-official, no doubt illegal cemetery— trouble on a stick. I choke and then almost laugh at my old baby saying.

"Li-lulie," old baby name for her.

I wish for us: a time to really go fishing, a thousand fishings, a thousand dinners. And christenings, and weddings. Time to sit and listen to eons of storms come up and roll away. Time to go to other people's funerals. Dozens of them. Bury everyone we know six feet under.

"I promise I will *try.*"

She doesn't say a word, just nods. She knows: promises— the best we can do.

19

1983

WE

The rain whips the bus windows. Head lights shimmer across the yellow line on the slick road. The world feels slippery, we—the bus—moving through it uncertainly.

The call, the one that always comes at 2 or 3 AM, wasn't from Brackson or even Perkinson. Our notorious North Ca'lina Paper seems to have made no official difference at all.

It was Dance.

"Willis?"

And I knew. You *know*. It was her heart, in spite of all those trips to Brackson, those sessions with the stethoscope. Her worrying finger, probing that spot on her chest. I—we—knew.

Dance called the ambulance, Brackson. Hard. Me.

"She say you better come if you want to see her."

The shabby bus station in Henderson is dark. Empty. Midnight. How many times have I come here? The closest stop to Lila on the long route that goes from New York to Florida. And Lila in a cab. Or just a cab driver bobbing up, sent to meet me. The few times I didn't drive down.

No cab tonight. I have to walk to the hospital.

In the five minutes that takes, I'm wet, my duffle is soaking. I stumble inside. I have our paper out, ready to show our connection. Not her blood kin, but kin by this paper.

No one stops me. I swing through the dingy hall—the silence of a small-town hospital after midnight, unquestioned, lugging my bag. The sticky sound of wet shoes on the linoleum floor. Intensive Care. A circle of curtains around the hub of a nurses' station.

Bright lights. Draped carts in the corridor. Empty stretchers. Stink of acetone and disinfectant. The hiss-click of oxygen.

I don't even have to identify myself, the nurse in charge comes up to me, smiling. "Here's Lila's medicine!" she sings out. Other nurses appear, smiling and nodding as if I am long awaited.

"How bad?" I mouth, clutching the nurse's sleeve to turn her as she leads me toward a curtain. On the phone, when I called in from New York, she wouldn't tell me anything.

She searches my face. Eyes blue and sharp, but not unkind. "Myocardial infarction."

She studies me to see if I know what that means. I do.

But I am thinking, Lila's not old—70? That's not *old*. A first heart attack. Hearts heal. Sort of. Sometimes.

The curtain parts. The nurse's voice goes high, as nurses' voices always do, and too loud as if calling the sick from miles away.

"Here's your medicine, Miss Lila. Here's the one you been asking for. Didn't I tell you she was on her way?"

Lila. Oh god, so much smaller than you can imagine. Surrounded by machinery and tubes and wires, swaddled like an infant in white flannel sheets and drapes. Diminished, without her teeth. She's never let me see her without her teeth. Eyes flying open, sunken and wild.

She's frightened. Holds out her arms. No tubes in her nose. A good sign. The soft skin, the same. The fuzz, the same. From her mouth comes a smell—not bad, that is, not foul. But different. Thick. Dark.

My grandfather used to diagnose by smell. He knew diseases by their traces in the very air coming from the sick. Suddenly I see, in this smell, Lila's heart, with its wounds. "A hole in the back of her heart the size of a quarter," Dance said. A quarter had seemed so small, when he said it. But it's huge. I wonder, suddenly where he got the image.

"Honey, it *hurt*. Um-*hmmm*." Lila is whispering to me, holding my hand very tight. "I know it won't an ordinary thing. I make Dance call the am'lance."

"Quiet. Don't talk. I'll sit." I keep her hand in mine.

"Peed in this here bed, wet all over myself. Half dozen times, I reckon."

"Doesn't matter. It's okay."

Eyes shut.

"What happens to a person who dies, Lila?"

"Honey, you listen to that Dance, he tell you dead folks love to jitterbug."

"Li-la."

"Don't nobody know, honey. Nobody. I see my gramama times I feelin' bad, but she don't tell me a thing."

Click: eyes open again—smiles! Gestures with her free hand to the monitor above her head. "Always did want to be on the television!" Little laugh. Little Lila laugh!

And suddenly she's asleep.

"She was waiting for you," the nurse whispers. "Wouldn't sleep hardly. Drove us crazy. I kept telling her, 'Honey, it takes hours to get here from New York.' "

Train to the airport. Plane to Richmond. Bus from Richmond. Hours. Twenty-two hours since Dance called. I feel my own head nodding with fatigue, and from the heat of this little piece of purgatory.

She sleeps. I have memorized every dot and wrinkle of her

face. So still. Peaceful. Breathing as always, in and out, without a sound. The monitor blips away smoothly.

"Folks says, 'Rest and peace.' But honey, when my time come, I don't want to rest. I want to get up and go!"

The times we talked about death. Nothing really about Daddy and Mother. Nothing about Eddie. Never anything about her.

Don't die. Oh, Lila, please don't die—

Brackson arrives. There's nothing to say. He just missed it, that's all. A hole in her heart the size of a quarter. If she were white, he'd have found it—

I'm the one who missed it. All my love, and I missed it. That finger—Lila's finger, boring into her sternum.

Ub-swish, said her heart, its leaky valve. *Here, here,* said the finger. Plain as day.

I STAY IN HER HOUSE. The next day, I rent a car from the old garage on Persimmon Street. The owner knows who I am. Knows Lila. Says he is sorry to hear of her problems. "Don't usually let out a car, less I'm working on one and you aint got a ride. But I let you have this one for a day or two. I thank him, pay for two days, and take off. It is old, and it smells like motor oil and cheap hamburgers. But the engine purrs along. At the hospital, I find Braxton by her bed.

"Well," he says, "she's old."

"No older than you."

"Ah!" Shakes his head. "We two have both lived beyond our time! She's had a hard life. The body gets tired, you know. I knew somebody'd call you." Voice drifts down into silence.

"What's—what can we expect?"

He looks away. "This was the first. She's pretty strong. She'll have another one someday. Could be tomorrow. Next month. A year."

A year . . .

"Longer rather than shorter, is my bet. She's got that strength." He says *stren-th.*

"Isn't there anything you can *do?*"

Head shakes and goes on shaking. His tremor. "No surgery to fix this."

When he's gone, she wakes up. On cue. "Child, got to tell you something."

"Rest."

Shake shake shake goes the head. "Got to talk, honey. You know our paper."

Of course I know our paper. And my promise. No nursing homes. Don't even think of my other promises. "Let *me* talk. I'll get you to New York." I hold her hand—don't want to rub it, when you're sick, your skin gets so tender. "You'll stay with me till you're stronger. Or if you'd rather, we'll find somebody to stay with you in your house. Dance."

Shake shake.

"Bessie?" Mr. Perkinson's Bessie had offered to look after his little girl.

"Honey, Bessie *dead*." Whisper like a rasp.

"Dead!" Bessie, white head nodding over her tale of her one and only, rocking on her porch? "Starve to death."

"Lila. Hush." No one starves to death in this day and age.

"Got poorly on her feet and wouldn't call nobody. Nobody check on her for a while." Sigh. "Then the preacher went 'round. And find Bessie gone!"

That part sounds plausible enough. Maybe Bessie had a heart attack too. But to die, alone—with Perkinson in town? *"I had a Lila . . ."*

Holding her hand. Anchoring her here.

Just two weeks ago, at the old cemetery—all the things I've

never asked. All the things I don't know. Stuff I know about people who mean far less to me.

"You'll come to New York. I'll drive down and get you." Even if I have to rent a decent car. My brain is whirling in plans, how to keep my promise. How to make her happy.

"And then I'll come back with you when you're ready, we'll spend the summer in your house. The two of us." The plan sounds suddenly like a paradise. As if we have a chance now, at last, to have what we always wanted.

She squeezes my hand. Eyes tight shut. Mouth is moving, but I can't hear. Lean down—Sleeping. Smiling, grip like iron.

The nurse says, "I couldn't help but overhear. That's what she needs. *You*. She kept saying, 'My baby comin' to get me.'"

"Can she—can she?" Can't even get the words out. I am paralyzed with fear.

"Love can do a lot," the nurse says. "Love is the only miracle." Her face is wan and pale. A good face. And one that won't lie. *A lot* is a possibility. Not a promise.

"About Bessie—Bessie Roberts. Did you hear that part?"

"Bessie Roberts. She did die. Yes."

"Starved?"

"Well. They brought her here, still alive. Poor old thing. No reason that we could see, no illness. Just skin and bones. She'd given up, is my guess. She had a phone, you know. Yet apparently she didn't call anybody."

Waiting for somebody to call her. Died of loneliness. Starved.

AWAKE. Eyes like green marbles. Clear and bright.

"Went to that Perkinson," she says, even her voice is stronger now. But she says Perkinson, not Perk-ups, so I can't miss how serious she is. "Last week. Made me a will."

"Please!" I can't bear it. "I'll—have a fit."

She snorts. "You listen to me now. You aint go like this, but I left everything to you."

"Li-la!"

"Want you to have my house. The fa'hm is gone, the house is still here."

The blasted house.

"Your mama give me that house. And you go have it from me. That's all. The fa'hm, we work for that place, whew! And it's gone."

Swallow. Be calm. No arguments.

Her face goes all keen and sharp. And suddenly she's laughing!

"Don't you look at me with them owl eyes! Listen here. I got to leave that Laura Keene and her son somethin', or the will's no good. That what Mr. Perk-ups say. 'Leave 'em something, they can't contest." Ah, Perk-ups!

But wait. Laura Keene's son? That would be Eddie's child! "Your grandson?"

All at once, like a shower of burning stones, I'm learning everything.

"Name Ed. No good. Dope fiend. Only good thing he ever did was give my Eddie some blood. Tried to give him a kidney, but it won't a right one."

A hero. A child—how old was he? Giving blood? Offering his father a *kidney*?

"Mine won't right for 'im, neither. Grown man now. Mean as a snake. I knows."

What do we know? How do we know anything?

"Now I want you to member this here, 'cause you got to take care of it for me. I left him my TV—got two, you know. He kin have either one he want. He can see with one or hear with the other!" Her eyes spark. "And for that stuck-up Miz Keene, I left her my rockin' chair."

Pause. I'm supposed to nod agreement. I nod.

"You see she get it. And take that cushion out! Don't forget that."

"Get the rocking chair to Laura Keene and take the cushion out."

She sinks back onto the pillow, laughing again. "Hope I be a fly on the wall, see her face when she set down, too. Got a crack in it to pinch her ass!" The laugh rings out.

My god! She's having *fun*.

What on earth do you suppose poor Perk-ups made of all this? The busted TVs and the pinch-ass chair?

And then, suddenly, she's asleep.

AND I CAN'T STAND it. Can't *stand* it! Hollowed out. By fear and dread. Something stuck inside me keeps me from breathing, swallowing. When she's awake, I live each second like a jewel. But when she's asleep . . .

I look at that still face. So calm. But in sleep, so – thin, so tired. Jesus . . .

I tiptoe out, get in the rented car, and drive. Just drive. Not crying, hardly breathing. When I look up, I'm on the old river road, not far from the fa'hm. The fa'hm. There's a little off-shoot, just tire tracks, and I pull into them. Get out and walk down to the Mattaponi. It purls and curls right next my feet. Lights play on it, like dancing diamonds. I don't know how long I stand there.

Suddenly, there's a scream, from the woods. Loud, and high. I drop to my knees, cover my head with my arms. After a moment, I sit up. What a fool. It wasn't a person. Must have been some kind of bird. Late afternoon, the sun is sinking. Must have been an owl. I get to my feet, shaking. And make my way slowly back to the hospital. She wakes up as I walk into the room.

~

SHE'S BETTER. Sits up like a little queen, orders food, then makes a face. "Sturff!"

I sneak her some orange juice from the cafeteria and a piece of cornbread. The nurse knows, and turns her back, smiling. When patients fool around, they're better. Thinking about life.

The Public Health Nurse comes to fill out papers. Sits with a metal clipboard on her lap and asks questions. All very necessary for Lila's welfare after she leaves the hospital.

"Where was she born?" The woman looks at me.

I look at Lila.

"Born in Mattapon' County."

Nurse scribbles, mouth a tight stingy line.

Lila looks at me. "Down the railroad track, near where Dance live at. In a shack with holes in the wall."

"I thought you were born at your grandmother's, like Ed.

"Wishes aint hawses."

"Date of birth?"

"Something of August 19 and 10. Least that what my gramama say. That what she put on the black hen's egg."

The poor woman stares from one of us to the other.

"Make it June 31," Lila says, shrugging.

"June has 30 days." Stingy Mouth pinches her lips even tighter with dismay. She reminds me of my father's ramrod nurse, Miss Fleurnoy. Flea Nose.

"August 31st. Can't be July. Haddy born in July." I'm swamped. But I do remember celebrating her birthday sometime in August.

She's enjoying herself. The questions go on and on: Mother's maiden name: Cora Crowder. Died 1945. Father: Edward

Neal Senior He died in—I don't hear the year. Husband: Clifford Doggett. Dead 1971. Only child: Eddie Neal Doggett. Born 1932, died 1957.

Not even the gone ones bother her today. And I'm getting her statistics.

But statistics are not what was missing. What we missed swirls round us, whispering promises into the air.

Tomorrow she's to be moved out of Intensive Care and into a private room, and I'm getting ready to leave tonight. I'll be back in a week, to prepare her house. She won't be able to come to New York—too much of a trip. Dance will help me get things ready. And then we'll take her home. I'll borrow money, rent out my house. Fix things so I can stay with her for two months. Three.

She sleeps, eats, sleeps, looks at me, smiles, sleeps. The afternoon passes. Reading by her bed, a medical book lent me by Brackson, all about myocardial infarction.

When she's awake, she wants to know, at her house, can we go out on drives? Will Dance put in a garden for us? Yes and yes.

And I: Will she teach me to cook some of the things we like? We! Corn cakes, those little sweet breakfast cakes with crisp lace edges?

For a day, we are living it, a glorious summer. Living it in our hearts.

Then all at once, I fall into a pit of sorrow. Empty. Cold. All the days, weeks, lifetimes long ago. When I lived with her in our make-believe house. When we had left and I didn't even have make believe. What you live in your heart, can you ever have for real?

Time for my bus. The nurse tells her the Browns are coming to see her as soon as she's in her room and ready for visitors. And Dance. "You'll get to tell them all your wonderful plans," the nurse smiles at us both.

"You tell Dance about the garden we want." I make my stiff lips smile. I'm so scared. I'm so *scared*. "Love you, Li-lulie."

"Love *you*, honey."

There will be another phone call. Some night. Somewhere. "Five days. I'll be back in five days. I'll call every day."

"I'll stay for now. For now."

At the curtain, looking back at her. At the waltz of her heart on the monitor. At her eyes, fixed on mine, not smiling, but steady. She puts her hands to her mouth and away, and I do the same. I blow my kiss at her the way I used to when I was the frightened child I am again right this minute.

What a short time, a lifetime. My duffle is still damp from the rain.

20

1983

AFTER

L ila died before I got home that night. I believe we both knew. If we'd had our summer—we!—the new Lila and Willis—I believe we would have accepted our gift of borrowed time with love and gratitude.

Instead I got lost in an awful nightmare. "She was set up in her new room," the nurse told me. "She had her folks in to visit, telling them all about the plans you two had made, and laughing. When they left, she—just . . ."

I went first to Dance. But he wouldn't come to her house with me. Shook his head and looked away. He couldn't. Dance left town for 30 years after Rumpy died.

Liz-beth helped me. Hard. So kind. We picked a dress, one with long sleeves though it was summer. "Dead folks' skin is not like livin' folks' skin," Mr. Garland Davis said, leaning on his cane. He let his new wife choose a hair style and all the other funeral details I knew nothing about. I hadn't been responsible for any of this when my parents died. Or Grandmother. I would have found it easier with them.

Liz-Beth wouldn't go into the funeral parlor with me, so, guided by the new Mrs. Garland's light touch, I picked a coffin.

Sturdy but not too grand. She calculated Lila's social position to a T, added to it my love, and eased me into the right decisions. "Now I know her friends would like to see—"

"Yes, she 'preciated her good Sunday meetin' clothes, you know it!"

On the other hand, "She won't one for puttin' on airs."

I didn't know this woman, but clearly she knew Lila. And her hand on my arm, marking each decision, was surprisingly comforting. Lila had something called a funeral policy. She'd been paying little amounts on it for years. We used it down to the last cent.

When I asked about the old cemetery, both Mr. Garland and his wife looked at me and then away as though I hadn't spoken. I didn't bother to ask Perkinson. I was already contending with a black community enjoying the scandal of a white woman in charge of a black woman's death rites. One of Lila's cousins was suing me for elder abuse. Perkinson sent everyone copies of our "paper" and a note about the "proper and legal will."

Lila's young pastor, who "took" her church one Sunday a month now, was kind and sensible. "Pay gossips no mind," he said. "The good folks here know what you and Miss Lila were to one another, whatever they choose to say in public now."

The service at the church was brief. I was the only white person present. Dance wouldn't come, which didn't surprise me. But Hard stood beside me and held my arm throughout, even though, to my horror, I sobbed. My mouth made little sputtering sounds. I was having a fit!

Because the new cemetery is as far out of town in one direction as the old slave cemetery is in the other, there were no graveside ceremonies. Several people came back to Lila's house for refreshments. And again on the Davises' recommendation, I served a lunch spread from the one restaurant in town. The little crowd stayed to hear the will, which Liz-beth told me was the custom.

She remained a rock of strength, even in the face of trouble. In fact, she probably enjoyed it. The cousin who'd found out earlier about the North Ca'lina paper and the will, handed me the letter of complaint right then and there, and I opened it and read it aloud to the entire group.

When I was done, the pastor shook his head, and Hard said, "Don't you pay her no mind. She aint have the money sue a fly."

I made a little speech. "I've arranged with the stone carver for a simple stone for her grave," I said. "Anyone who thinks she'd have wanted a fancier one can get it, and put mine at the foot. The estate consists of her house and its contents. The house, she left to me," I was looking at the will, not the people, "and I give it now to Liz-beth. Lila never told me anything any other family members or friends did for her and none are listed in her will. Liz-beth knows you all and if there's a problem, she can see the right thing is done." She was looking at me with her mouth open. "I hope you remember Dance," I said. Now they all stared at me. "She mentions TV sets for her grandson, a chair for her daughter-in-law. I've written them out as she said them. I ask Liz-beth to take care of those things for me." She was still staring. After a moment, she nodded.

Then people left. In a minute all but the pastor had walked silently away. Even Liz-beth.

After a while, he, too, began making his move to leave. I gave him a check for the church, a donation, since he hadn't charged for the service.

"Do you think—believe—there's something afterwards?" I asked suddenly, not even meaning to.

He cleared his throat. "I do. Probably something we are not prepared for." He held out his hand to shake mine. "She chose well."

I laughed. "You mean because they all hate me now, instead of each other!"

I wanted to ask: Did my re-entering her life with my love create good or bad for her? But reassurance after the fact is worth exactly the breath it takes to speak it. Lila probably did plan this all pretty much the way it happened, for good and for ill. The general on the battlefield. The Gazelle of Perfect Deflection.

21

1986

POSTSCRIPT

E arly evening. Rain is coming, you can smell it in the air, a delicious clean smell, something fresh and new. I'm driving on the old Henderson Road. Stopping, as always, on the green metal bridge over our Mattaponi, unchanged even to the rust on its struts. It still straddles the divide, the neat, scattered white farm houses and tamed woods on the town side of the water, and the wild, black lands on the other. Some things take many lifetimes to change.

The water swirls along beneath me, singing its way to the ocean. I hope someday it will wash us all clean to the bone.

At the fa'hm, there's nothing. Weeds. Whoever bought it has let it go. I almost hoped to see a neat new road past solid, handsome sheds. Pigs in pens. No decay. But really, I knew better. What had Dance said? *Some folks want cause other folks got.*

The tulip trees and the skeleton of the house are gone. Are any of the old walnut trees left? I'm not going up the ridge to see.

It's Sunday, and peaceful. No one is around except the meadowlark, fluting his love and sorrow. The blood-root and buttoneggs are gone. The beautiful old chimney is now just a pile of rubble, covered in wisteria.

I won't come back again. I keep looking for Dance in New Jersey. Maybe I'll find him one day. For both of us, this place is unbearable without her. We know the dead will never come out to jitterbug.

Here's a good stone in the heap, damp and smelling of rain and earth. Tucking it under my arm, I head down the weedy path to the grove. The old oaks, smelling sharp from the rain, bruised with the light of a stormy sunset, are time itself. Shadows.

I put my stone down just under Eddie's plaque. Her bones are not here, but she is. I clear my throat, as if she could hear me—but I can't speak. Her spirits were her history, forming for her and her family a line of connection, like a string of islands. From Africa to this place. I wanted to ask her if she would come, like her gramama, sit on the end of my bed, a presence as comforting as the little red cinnamon hearts she hid under it—promises, when I was four and she left me for the night.

Once she said you don't get any real "good" from the dead, which I now take to mean, no practical advice. Only love and comfort. We are what we are and any crossing over must be in our own skins.

She has not come to me.

I take a ceramic rose out of my purse. Like Eddie's, except white. Kneeling to shine them all with Kleenex, seven now—then pressing them into the earth, one by one.

Hers in the middle, like a ray of light.

AUTHOR'S NOTE

. . . to witness something like that implicates you, it allows that reality to go on living inside you, growing darker, more impenetrable, unless you accept the challenge of living with it and trying to make it clearer instead of ever darker . . .

—Francisco Goldman, writing
about the brutalities in Guatemala

In the 1940s and 50s, when I was growing up in Virginia, my White family lied with every breath. They claimed "purity"— pure blood, pure motives, pure hearts: *The slaves were happy. We saved them from a godless life in Africa. They weren't ready for freedom.*

Even at six, I saw how deeply this was wrong. The Black people I knew, who'd lived for generations with their mixed and dangerous history, taught me the truth. They taught me that cruelty and fear touch everyone, just as Goldman says— the doers as well as the done-to. All our lives are skewed. For their safety, they invented a powerful language that disguises truth as joke. No one is funnier than the old crone who sees the world falling on her and turns to you and says, "Honey, can I borrow your hard head?" Or the harassed man, in the grip of "the law," who refers to Sheriff Hodgkiss as Hawgkiss.

When I published the first edition of this book in 2012, readers said how interesting it was to see the way "it used to be." But my indicator arrow on the Jim Crow meter shows that it's the way "it *is*." What we're seeing today, in 2023—this raging fear and hatred of "others" that threatens to overwhelm us all— gets its power from Jim Crow, plus the white reaction against the Civil Rights Movement, plus the violent blowback to President Obama. These are all closer to us in time than slavery, and their ugliness hasn't yet been universally acknowledged and repudiated.

In this light, I see what an incipient racist I am. And this second journey inside, clawing at my blinders, has been harder than the first nostalgic love story of a hungry child and the woman who gave her sustenance. I have looked again and again at the subtle lessons in every encounter with Lila Doggett throughout our forty years together. And at the ensuing shifts in my attitudes, particularly toward the end as I saw and heard the quiet under-messages I was giving this woman, to whom I owed my life and my humanity, an old, brown-skinned woman living in a poor and "primitive" area. The under-messages suggesting that she was less than she was, and that I in some way knew "better" what was good for her.

Today's attitudes go further, claiming that "others" are taking for themselves something that rightly should go to whites alone. This is the spawn of the South's big lie that still infects everything. We feed it in our shadows. And today we are giving it dangerous new twists:

"You (fill in the blank) will not replace us."
"*Woke* is a greedy Black lie."

"*We've* done nothing wrong. *They* mustn't teach our children to feel ashamed."

So by closing our ears, our hearts, our minds, we allow brutal intolerance and sly "alternate facts" to trickle into our corners, and we don't see how they've stained us until we try telling ourselves they didn't.

It's work, scrubbing yourself.

And heartbreaking to recognize that you may never really get clean.

ACKNOWLEDGMENTS

I want to thank Deborah Garner, wonderful novelist, who has steered me through the labyrinth of self-publishing. And thanks, too, to the lively Rowdy Writers of Georgetown, for their support and wild spirits. My love to my husband, writer, artist, car mechanic, all-round genius and loving companion. And my gratitude to Jamelle Bouie, Imani Perry, Isabel Wilkerson, from whose books and essays I am learning the true history of our era.

But most of all, again and ever, to Lila Neal Doggett, for the history of our hearts. For every minute, every second, that we shared.